Bowl of Berries Book Club

A Sweet Sisterhood Novel

Author Speaker Life Coach
LAURA LOVEBERRY

Silent Witness, LLM Publications
Printed in the U.S.A.

Bowl of Berries Book Club

Excerpts from Invite Delight book glean from a collection of *Life is the Berries* articles from *Simply Hers, Everything Men*, and *Simply Seniors* magazines published by *Chestney Publishing.* (www.simplyhersmagazine.net) Marlanea McGraw of *Chestney Publishing* and author Laura Loveberry of the *Invite Delight* book, have an agreement for Laura Loveberry to modify, compile, arrange, and publish within this book *Life is the Berries* articles. www.lauraloveberry.com

Cover Design and Format: Laura Loveberry, Patrick Cook and Lisa Cook of www.joyousjourneyphoto.com
Editor: Rosalie Currier
Proofreader: Michelle Patrick & Lisa Wood
Illustrator: Laura Loveberry

ISBN # 979-8-9886500-4-1

Publisher: *Silent Witness,* LLM
Printer: *PRINTED IN THE U.S.A.*

Wilma Lou Kyle
DEDICATION

A voracious reader describes my mom. I asked her to look at my novel outline and give me advice. For 30 days in a row, she studied my updated outline and helped me. Every time, MOM forgot I asked her the day before.

Mom's short-term memory lacks. It's Alzheimer's.

When she napped, I worked diligently, correcting the outline. When I showed her the adjusted outline, it was all new to her each time. Genius describes her input. For 30 days, I repeatedly surprised her about writing my first novel. She made wise suggestions daily. Only on the last day of my one-month stay she did NOT give me suggestions. The conversation went something like the following.

"Mom, I'm writing a novel outline. Do you want to look at it and make suggestions?" I asked again.

"Oh, you're writing a novel?! Wow! Sure, I would love to help," Mom said.

After she looked at it, Mom said, "Laura, this is remarkable. How did you come up with this?"

I explained she helped me tweak it for the last 30 days, giving me amazing help and finding my plot errors. She did not recall. The last day of my visit, she said no changes needed.

Mom is a generous soul despite her Alzheimer's challenges. I am blessed. What a wonderful reason to dedicate my first novel, *Bowl of Berries Book Club*, to my always supportive momma, Wilma Lou Kyle!

My love for Mom will not fade. Ever.

"I loved Laura's newest novel *Bowl of Berries Book Club*. Such a sweet, quirky, fun book. Delight in the twists and turns of each character as you get swept away in the storyline of their antics and adventure. This book ends with all the makings of a Hallmark movie and will not disappoint."

Robyn Dykstra, *National Christian Speaker & Best-Selling Author*

"Oy Vey! *Bowl of Berries Book Club* packs with hope in hardship and tops with a cherry!"

Gerrie Mills, *Inspirational Speaker and Author*

"I loved every part of this book! It is unique, funny, and suspenseful with drama, keeping me on the edge of my seat. I could not put it down."

Jodie Johnson, Surrender the Secret Facilitator & Spokeswoman for Life

"What a hoot! The sisterhood, secrets, and surprising plot twists grabbed me. It's the perfect giftbook to inspire deeper friendship. I'm buying bunches to give away."

Regina Mae, Singer, Songwriter, Nashville Recording Artist

Dear readers,

Who would think a jewelry artist, a bank vice-president, a poverty-stricken alcoholic, a self-conscious singer, and an inspirational speaker would end up in a book club together?

I certainly wouldn't. Never in a million years. Who would ever plant this variety of women together along with a tattooed dude? No one. But an unexpected book club sprouts out of a botched bank robbery, a bowl of berries, and a brand-new book. Who knew? Their bond grows deeper than anyone expected. As their lives intertwine, will their deep-rooted secrets, shocking twists, and crazy adventures prune them beyond what they can bear? Will they cultivate fruitful lives after digging deep into the darkest season of their past? What would you find if you unlocked the vault of your soul?

Five complete strangers are about to find out.

Can the unexpected, but possible, occur?

Will the improbable, immeasurably more than we ask or imagine, actually happen?

In our time together, I hope we will laugh out loud, love the characters we meet, and learn to lean into the LIGHT in our hard seasons. My desire for us is to taste and see the sweetness of LIFE while enjoying this book like a strawberry dipped in chocolate!

Thanks for joining with me and my first novel. I wrote it with you in mind.

Laura Loveberry

Caroline Forbes-Radshaw
Bank Vice-President

Rashida Jackson
African Jewelry Artist

Sherry Kay Strawberry
Inspirational Speaker

Carrie Rae Hunklenuckle
Shy Singer Girl

Cash Jones
Tattooed Dude

CHAPTER 1

Dear friends, don't be surprised at the fiery trials
you are going though, as if something strange
were happening to you.
1 Peter 12:1 NLT

I'm a hot mess. Who isn't? A drop of sweat rolls down my back as I tap my foot repeatedly. But in our mess, we're called to bless, right? "Love God. Love people." Oh, why do I run late for my speaking events? I puff a stray hair out of my face, standing in line at the bank. I need a life coach. Wait. I am one.

It's a good thing Kyle called, reminding me to pick up change for my book table. I adjust, holding my purse and my duffle bag overstuffed with bags of strawberries, signage for my product table, and copies of my new book. Bringing in the chocolate-covered berries prevents melting in the car.

I sigh, tap my toes, and glance at the clock.

Evidently, I'm not the only one glad the pandemic faded out and the lobby doors open again. It's busy, but the drive-thru line stretches even longer. It meets the road. I couldn't even pull in the car line if I wanted.

I sweep over the unique mixture of people in line. A woman of color with an African scarf wrapped around her head catches my eye. A macho man flexes his muscles while admiring his tattoos standing behind her. In front slouches a Native-American girl peering out from behind her hair. A blonde business woman in a power suit click-clacks in stilettos to assist a transaction. And what's up with the twitching dude with the black hoodie pulled up over his head? His beard looks fake.

Aren't hoods banned in banks? Whatever.

All this diversity would be the great variety of readers I need to review my new book. What an assortment! I smirk, imagining these complete strangers together in a book club. Could God do exceedingly abundantly above all we ask or think with this group? God could. But it would not happen with us. Not in a million years. Our lives hold nothing in common—not a thread. Nope.

Puffing my cheeks, I shift in my place in line and billow out a long, calming breath. I pray silently for the weekend to go as God plans for my book launch and speaking retreat. I smile. God's got this. No need to fret.

Bang! Bang! Bang!

Gun shots! Chaos erupts around me. Screaming bank patrons scatter in every direction.

"Don't push the panic button or you're DEAD," a voice bellows behind me.

Pandemonium ensues.

Above the high-pitched screams and mayhem, a roaring voice commands, "Get down on the ground!"

No way! Not me.

Screams build volume, piercing my ears. I slap my hands over them. Think. Think. Think. I jump into survival mode as customers drop to the floor on all sides. I hurdle over a body in the fetal position. Sprinting around the corner, bolting down the hallway, I follow the bouncing head of the African-clad woman. We blast at top speed. My hair whips behind me. I hear only my breathing.

Everything rolls into slow motion.

As our line of frantic customers race toward the rear exit sign, a husky man in black wearing a mask blocks the way to the exit. His looming silhouette holds what looks to be an . . . AK-47.

Someone cries out in terror. My mind darts like a ping-pong game in action. My head swirls while my legs and arms pump rapidly.

The leader of our fleeting pack skids to a sudden halt. We collide with her backside. Grabbing the sleeve of her African gown, I yank her into a doorway on the side. The breathless customers trailing us stumble into our escape room.

It's a vault.

We hear the gunman's feet marching toward us.

Bang! Ping.

Gunshot? He shot at us! I can't believe this.

"Shut the door! Shut the door! SHUT THE DOOR!" I yell.

Laura Loveberry

CHAPTER 2

. . . a heart that devises wicked plans . . .
Proverbs 6:18a NIV

Are we all screaming at once?

The last person tumbles in through the doorway. It's the business lady in a skinny suit-skirt combo. That pint-sized blonde slams the huge door, shutting us in safely from the approaching footsteps.

"He shot at us," the dark-skinned woman states. "He shot at us!"

She builds in volume, reiterating the phrase, eyes narrowing, nostrils flaring. Her brow furrows, jabbing her hands on her hips. Between each statement, she sucks in air, heaving as anger oozes.

"How DARE he shoot at us!" she states one last defiant time.

The yelling morphs into our recovery panting.

I hold trembling hands to my chest, attempting to catch my breath.

My enlarging eyeballs dart around the confined space. We smash tightly against the walls.

No one speaks a word. The vault is sound proof. The sealed door isolates us from any outside commotion.

"Quick, call 911," I whisper with exaggerated emphasis, breaking the hush. We whip out our phones, punching the emergency number repeatedly.

No connection.

In a flurry, we dial our loved ones.

No bars!

I hear the young woman with the long black hair gasp erratically, panting for air, shifting from side to side.

We're isolated and trapped.

Between winded breaths, the business suit lady explains our predicament. We're locked in a vault with no way of accessing the outside world. She paces in a two-step pattern back and forth.

The hyperventilating gal with black hair and Native American features asks sheepishly if there is enough air in here for everyone. She leans forward with her hands on her knees for support as she catches her breath.

Really? Faces turn quickly to eyeball each other in panic.

Our eyes open wider, then dart around, searching frantically for a vent.

With a deep voice, Manly Man, points to a metal grate, thundering out, "We'll be fine." Our eyes focus on the small register near the ceiling. He crosses his buff arms confidently.

Whew!

We huddle, safe from the gunman momentarily, and it appears we will not suffocate. My heart and breathing race, but at least ventilation exists.

I smack my forehead. My speaking event! My book launch!

I'm never going to be on time now.

"Hey . . . *gasp* . . . do we need a plan to defend ourselves . . . *gasp* . . . if the gunmen open this door? . . . *gasp* . . . There is no way to hide to hit him on the head when he enters . . . *gasp* . . . How do we defend ourselves?" the dark-skinned lady asks our befuddled group.

She jams one hand on her hip with a questioning expression.

Blank stares.

We glance around at each other, still breathing hard with shirts untucked and tousled hair.

The young girl shudders. Manly Man remains silent, merely shrugging.

The petite Miss Business blonde, who slammed the massive door, speaks up with both arms crossed.

"We just stay calm and cooperate. This is our best odds for survival. We will be just fine." She tucks in a stray strand of hair, continuing, "I am the vice-president of this banking facility. The protocol states to cooperate, release any money demanded, and allow the police officers to handle the situation."

She stretches out her hand to us.

"My name is Caroline Forbes-Radshaw. I am at your service."

Caroline attempts a smile. Her top lip quivers a tad.

Petite and dainty describe her features. Her pointy-toed stilettos match female news broadcasters. She reminds me of a TV reporter with her French-cut nails, perfect makeup, and polished look. As she speaks, she tucks in her shirttail and professionally shakes each of our hands. Her powder-blue suit matches her powder-blue shoes, complementing her powder-blue clutch, pairing with her sparkly, you guessed it, powder-blue ring.

Caroline appears as one put-together chick despite her twitch lip action.

I puff my cheeks with air. I fall apart. My tousled hair hangs straggly, and I sweat profusely, creating wet armpit splotches.

There's another thing I forgot. I wanted my nails painted with white French tips like Miss Professional, Caroline Forbes-Radshaw.

Who cares about their nails right now?! My hands tremble even when I press them against my churning stomach. I don't know if we will get out of here alive, let alone if I'll ever speak at an event again. Ever.

I'll hide behind the muscle guy. That's my survival plan. He will be an effective human shield. It's a good thing he spotted ventilation because, as big as he is, he'd hog up most of our precious air in this vault.

Just saying.

As my mind bounces between random irrational thoughts, the big guy barks out, "I got yo back, ladies."

He flexes his bulked-up chest.

"I'll be standing guard at the door protecting y'all. I'll take a bullet for ya. The name is Cash. Cash Jones."

"I doubt that," the African woman mutters under her breath with a not-so-subtle shake of her head.

He leans against the massive vault door with cranks and levers. Without the high style, he's a "wanna-be" James Bond. He's gruff. Standing with his legs spread, he rolls up his t-shirt sleeve, showing us ladies his tattoo.

"Cash is King," he proclaims as he flexes his biceps three times and fist pounds his *Cash-is-King* tattoo two times. He then points at each one of us squarely between our eyes.

I strain to keep a serious face.

He's a character straight from a "Rocky" movie.

Don't giggle. Do not giggle, Sherry. Stay composed, I demand of myself.

His dollar-sign tattoo resembles a superman "S." He wears jeans, a plain black t-shirt, and biker boots. The tat "C-A-S-H" spells across his knuckles, too. He's the lone man in our misfit pile of people.

Isn't this something?

I am trapped in a vault, with complete strangers, and one of them bears the name Cash.

How ironic? Kyle and I need actual cash after spending our savings printing my self-published book, and I am missing the biggest selling event tonight, too. No way I'm making it. At least I have a dramatic excuse for being late.

And, I've got a hot topic for my next book project. Trapped in a bank vault makes a gripping first chapter. I pull my hand to my chest. My pounding heart shakes me back to reality.

Why do I fret about my speaking event? We could all die! Shy Girl rocks and snivels. African-motif Scarf Lady clenches her teeth and rubs Shy Girl's back. Cash looks down and flexes his biceps out of fake boredom. He's got to be inwardly trembling in terror like the rest of us outwardly. Miss Banking Lady, Caroline Forbes-Radshaw, paces in her stilettos as her eye blinking adds to the twitching lip.

Our lives are in peril trapped in this vault while I worry about my speaking event. What's wrong with me? I must be in shock. I squeeze my strawberry-shaped earrings, reminding me of my hubster. Kyle Strawberry would know what to do, but he's not here. I puff out my cheeks, wrapping my arms around myself in a tight hug.

CHAPTER 3

For I was hungry and you gave me food,
I was thirsty and you gave me drink,
I was a stranger and you welcomed me,
Matthew 25:35 ESV

Frantic minutes morph into a slow hour.

Shy Girl twirls her hair in her fingers and continues rocking back and forth. She's losing it. I hear subtle whimpering. Maybe conversations with others will calm her down? At least it will take her mind off our panic? From the girls, I notice twitching, feet rubbing, sighs, twiddling hands, and other non-stop fidgeting. Business-suit Caroline paces. We can use conversation to distract from our confinement.

"Cash, you from around here?" I inquire.

"Yeah, I just moved to Villa from Chicago wit my girl, Dani. Everyone thinks we be married, but we just have the same last name. Jones. Ain't that a hoot. Why get married? She wants to, but we ain't yet."

He stands with feet spread slightly and arms crossed like a tattooed Emmy statue.

"I had two bros, but one died in a gang fight. The other lives in da Big House in Jackson. I ain't never met my dad and my mom died. That about covers it."

"What is the Big House, may I ask?" Caroline Forbes-Radshaw, the suit lady, inquires.

"You ain't never heard of da Big House?"

Cash cusses lightheartedly, slapping his leg, informing her she lives a sheltered life.

"It's Jackson Prison. He's a lifer," Cash says, smirking.

Caroline flushes red blotches.

She pushes her cat-eyed glasses back in place. Caroline's eyes twitch. She apologies profusely for asking, while Cash shrugs his shoulders.

"No biggy," Cash replies nonchalantly.

Shy Girl keeps rocking. The African-robed lady rubs Shy Girl's shoulder, attempting to calm her nerves. The flinch tells me it's still not working.

I move the topic back to Caroline, inquiring about her family.

"Sterling and I have no children," Caroline states matter-of-factly. She continues pacing in two-step intervals.

She presents herself as proper and together. It's hard to picture her with a burbling, messy-diapered baby in her arms.

My gut jolts in sudden pain. My stomach flinches with the usual cramping I experience with intense situations. There's no bathroom. Why didn't I use the restroom before I left?

Bad choice.

I cringe to suppress the cramping. I need mind over matter. My eyes dart around the room, distracting me from my intestinal issue.

"Lord, please, not now."

The room is a metal container. Antique lockboxes line the walls. A single ceiling light illuminates our confined space. We all stand as if we are in a crowded elevator, avoiding eye contact.

Awkward.

"My legs still shake. Does anyone else need to sit?" I ask.

I set my overstuffed bag in the center of the room and slide down the wall. I am wearing my blingy flip-flops. My dress heels poke out of my bag. I won't be needing those. Wearing my spandex shorts under my skirt was a good choice.

My cramping subsides for now. I puff out my air in relief.

The girls follow suit, gliding their backs down the wall, lowering gently. The dude plops down on the tile floor. We form a circle facing inward with my bag in the center. It's like a campfire with friends and my big bag being the "firepit."

Except, we are not friends. We are complete strangers.

My bag is not a firepit.

The only thing burning here is our disheveled bodies because the temperature rises. Our faces shine with sweat.

We are one hot mess.

Shy Girl keeps rocking while her hair sweeps over her face. Her chin remains down. Miss Professional no longer paces but she taps, taps, taps her French tips non-stop. Big Guy's odor situation floods the space. I notice the banker lady dabbing perfume under her nose. Good idea. The African-dressed gal straightens and re-straightens the row of colorful bracelets dancing down both her arms. Her fiddling keeps her mind occupied off of our predicament.

We sit bewildered in our own allotted space. I lean my head back and stare at the ceiling. I can't judge the length of time, but my constant rubbing of my feet together may drive others crazy.

How long before our release?

I break the awkwardness of the hour with a question.

"Let's get our minds off the rising temp and our troubles. How about we share our names, where we are from, and tell a little more about ourselves? I can start. I am Sherry Strawberry . . .."

"Who?" the African-dressed gal interrupts, "Sherry Strawberry? I know that name. You write for *Simply Hers* magazine. I cracked up reading your last article about how you peed yourself at a speaking event."

Giggles pop up.

"Giiiiiirl, I could not believe you confessed to peeing yourself for the town to read. You made me spit out my coffee when you wrote how your pee flow sprayed out like a lawn sprinkler off your fancy stilettos," she said. "Yeah, we know who you are."

"Well, then you know I have to go when I have to go," I reply, grinning feebly. "This could be a problem without a restroom."

I reach in my bag and hold up the famous sparkly shoes.

"Here are the same stilettos I doused and wrote about in my article."

Laughter blurts. Shy Girl slows down her rocking. The bank lady's tense shoulders drop slightly. I take a deep breath.

I anticipate my potty problem will surface soon. As the group giggles, I squeeze my internal muscles, holding back the flow again. If they only knew.

Oh me! Oh my!

"Okay, back to introductions. I am Sherry Strawberry, and I am 'BERRY' happily married to my hubster, Kyle StrawBERRY." Cracking a slight smile, I tap my strawberry earring.

My attempt at humor makes Big Guy roll his eyes and curse, so I drop the "berry" business joking and continue introducing my family.

"We adopted one child. He's an adult, now, and on the autism spectrum. Drew's attempting to live life on his own. This increases our prayer life. You could call us the 'BERRY' bunch."

My eyes dart to Big Guy. He shakes his head in disapproval of my not "berry" funny joking.

"Wait a minute," pipes up the only male in our group. "Ain't you the lady on the sign as ya come into Villa? 'Home of Mrs. Michigan, Sherry Strawberry,' it says. I'm a gonna tell my girlfriend I met you. She'll think it's cool I met someone famous."

"Well, thank you, Cash. But I am just like everyone else here. I represented Michigan back in 2007, but that was years ago. My looks wrinkled up since then."

I smile and wink.

"I take advantage of the Mrs. Michigan title to market my speaking ministry," I admit.

Grinning, I say, "This brings me back to finish my intro. I'm an author, speaker, and life-coach. I encourage women to sprout through their hard seasons and grow upward to the LIGHT."

Reaching into my bag, I pull out and hold up my new book, *Invite Delight*.

"So, y'all are my official book launch audience now. You're a CAPTIVE audience."

Giggles float around our vault as I do my Vanna-White impression. I pose with the book up to my face, smiling as a more wrinkled supermodel. Cash jumps up and imitates my model walk with exaggerated hip swinging. His mocking me brings giggles.

"I'd love to read your book," the beautiful African-clad woman comments.

I place my hand on my heart, smiling, then dart a glare at Cash, continuing his awkward runway strut.

"I'll introduce myself next. I rock the name Rashida Jackson. I am a single mom of two beautiful twin daughters, Jona and Jamila. These seniors earn straight A's at Villa High. We moved here from Chicago seventeen years ago. I'm a momma bear."

Rashida flashes her pearly whites.

She dresses as boldly as her bright smile. Her African robe and scarf must be hot because she unwraps a layer of her garment, folding it neatly beside her. I marvel at how beautiful her dark skin looks against her brightly colored outfit.

Rashida states, "I am a fine-art artist of creative jewelry."

Caroline compliments her dramatic accessories. "You made this?" she asks with a bit of awe.

Rashida nods "yes" as we girls touch her jewelry, raving over her craftsmanship and skills. Cash rolls his eyes to the ceiling, cussing and muttering something about girl talk.

The stunning, bold artist raises up her hands, rattling the many colorful bracelets stacked up her arms as she continues, undaunted. She bats her long false eyelashes, enhancing her dramatic looks.

"I do art shows, record a video blog called a vlog, sell these hand-dyed African print scarves, and draw caricatures on Facebook Live every 'Wacky Wednesday.' I set up a nonprofit for families of victims of serious crimes. A percentage of my profits goes directly to families affected by these violent crimes. I am the only one I know with a nonreligious nonprofit."

She pauses, looking directly at me.

"I am an atheist," she states.

I cringe inwardly, attempting to control my outward expression.

"You'll never get me to step one foot in the door of a church . . . ever."

The others glance toward me, waiting with raised eyebrows.

I simply smile softly. What's up with her adamant attitude against church?

Breaking the awkward moment, I say, "And the pretty lady beside you is next. What is your name?"

We all turn to the beautiful woman with dark, thick hair framing her face.

She hides behind her hair like a baby chick, sheltering under the wing of a mother hen. Her greenish eyes peek out of blinking eyelashes. Her baggy sweatshirt displays a forest of trees on the front. She has on a pair of faded blue jeans, worn moccasins with leather fringe, and no make-up.

Clearing her throat, this natural beauty peers out behind her thick hair. She quietly whispers, "I'm Carrie Rae, raised on an Indian reservation. My dad was a white missionary who married my Cherokee momma. Everyone says I look like my mom. I have two brothers, and I'm the quiet one."

Carrie Rae looks down sheepishly at her moccasins, signaling she finished.

I guess her age is around twenty-one. She's strikingly beautiful and doesn't know it.

"Thanks for sharing, Carrie Rae. Do you have a last name?" I ask.

Carrie Rae twitches.

After a long pause, Carrie rolls her eyes, admitting reluctantly, "Hucklenuckle."

We girls burst out in a gaggle of giggling.

Cash doesn't giggle. Cash roars.

Using cuss words in a comical-only-to-himself manner, Cash asks about the unusual name.

"What kind of name is that? Ain't you an Indian? That's one crazy Pocahontas name."

He curls over, thundering into deep laughter, cursing up a storm describing the name.

Carrie Rae predicts the laughter response, but her beautiful Indian skin turns four shades of crimson, nevertheless. I feel for her, but I burst into laughter with the group, too.

Shame on me.

With a feeble attempt to suppress my giggles, I try to rescue Carrie Rae from embarrassment by addressing our gang.

"Okay, Carrie Rae has lived with this name for a while. Let's give Hucklenuckle a break."

Cash pounds his fist on his thigh, spewing profanity and laughter. Louder laughter spurts out of everyone with the repeating of her exclusive name. Carrie Rae commences her rocking motion.

I continue to speak, squeezing my internal muscles to prevent myself from peeing.

"Let's change the subject. If I laugh anymore, I'll pee. And there's no place to go. I am as serious as the Nile River. Let's stop the laughter."

Leaning over laughing, Rashida slaps her hand on the floor repeatedly.

She mumbles about needing to make a makeshift restroom.

"The birth of my twins destroyed this body of bladder control. I just don't announce my predicament to the town as some people do," she says.

She gazes at me, moving her hand in a wand motion, snapping her finger three times and flashing her contagious smile.

"Some secrets are meant to be kept."

We hoot it up loudly. I leak a smidgen.

Cash Jones jokes about the nightmare of his manly testosterone trapped with this feminine girl talk.

"It's worse than prison," he says, pulling his hair with both hands, mockingly.

Does he know about prison firsthand?

I don't dare ask.

We small talk for a couple more hours, attempting to calm our wadded-up nerves.

Rashida delivers a pep talk. "We can't change what's happening outside this vault. We can make the best of what's happening inside."

What is going on outside of this vault?

Our fidgeting increases. Carrie Rae oscillates her rocking motion. Caroline taps. My mind races. Rashida plays with her dangling bracelets. Maybe talking will sidetrack our worry. Fretting does not help. It grows our anxiety with the girls.

Cash flexes his pecks back and forth alternately. He's the only one appearing not anxious. He yawns, and I witness spray float out of his mouth, splatting on Caroline's jacket.

She looks down at her speckled sleeve and her eyes widen two sizes bigger. Her head starts to quiver. She scowls up at Cash Jones. He's oblivious to Caroline's appalled glare.

I jump in quickly, "Since I am definitely missing my retreat weekend, we might as well eat up these strawberries."

I hear lip smacking as I open the clear Ziploc bag, emptying the chocolate-covered strawberries into my prettier bowl.

"I planned to display these strawberries at my event table in this fancy bowl. Strawberries are part of my branding. They draw customers over to my Sherry Strawberry book table."

Delightful moaning proceeds from our circle of misfits as each one grabs a strawberry.

Apparently, we worked up an appetite, and these chocolate-covered morsels hit the spot. Cash shares amusing stories about strawberries. Caroline adds a picture-perfect memory from her childhood. Rashida shares a comical story of her twins with chocolate-smeared faces, denying they ate the chocolate treat. We laugh, beginning to bond over our makeshift meal.

Are we avoiding our reality of being trapped in a vault? Yes, we distract ourselves from being locked-up. It works.

It's like a bonfire with S'mores as we sit in our tight ring, so we sing campfire songs. Is a spark of comradery kindling? Since it feels like a church camp outing, hymns and praise songs follow. I raise an eyebrow when Rashida sings along, knowing every word.

She's an atheist?

After today, nothing surprises me, not even a hymn-singing atheist in African garb.

I do my sign-language drama for each song. I don't dare sing loud. The others don't need to hear how off tune I can be. I sign to songs much better than I sing vocally.

Carrie Rae sings a tad louder than when she started. Her lovely vocals stand out. When I mention the beauty of her voice, she looks down, singing softer, deflecting any attention.

We are opposites.

I love to sing and lead large audiences with my sign-language drama set to music, but I can't vocally sing a lick. I screech like a Siamese cat in heat. Carrie Rae's voice is golden, and yet, she sings shyly behind her flowing hair. She turns red if we hear a peep, even with her melodious voice. Our names, Carrie Rae and Sherry Kay, go together well, but our personalities differ like salt and pepper.

Suddenly, my cramping jolts me. I press my gut.

Oh no!

CHAPTER 4

Saul went in to relieve himself.
David and his men
were far back in the cave.
I Samuel 24: 3b NIV

My eyes cross. I cannot hold back the inevitable.

I dart a narrow glance left and right. How will I relieve myself? Where will I go?

"Um . . . we have a stinky situation here. When I get in intense situations, I cramp. We all know where this will lead. We've sat in here for hours, and I am trying, but something's got to flow," I confess with flushing cheeks.

I roll my bulging eyes in a circle.

The group peers around, catching each other's glances.

"I'm going to dump the rest of these strawberries into my large bowl. This empty Ziploc bag will become my portable toilet. Thank heavens I brought these into the bank."

"Hallelujah, there's an air-tight seal!" shouts Cash in laughter. "I see more plastic bags of strawberries sticking out your bag, so we can eat up, then use the empty bags as toilets for the rest of us."

Cash takes the liberty to open another one of my bags of chocolate strawberries. Helping himself to a big berry, he smiles, munching away, oblivious to my humiliation.

He acts like he's sitting at the movies . . . eating popcorn . . . only they're my strawberries . . . and I tremble at the thought of the upcoming horror show.

"No thank you, for the plastic bag idea," proper Caroline Forbes-Radshaw states. "I can hold it for days before I . . . well . . . you know."

"I cannot hold it anymore." My voice quivers, "So let me take this plastic bag. I cannot believe I am doing this. I apologize in advance."

Snatching up the quart-size Ziploc, I stand while scanning our confined space.

They do not train us for this in ministry.

How in the world do I attempt this? I am a bold inspirational speaker. I embarrass rarely, but my face burns four shades of pink to burning red. Laughing this off isn't working. I will never write about this in a book . . . ever.

Authors omit this detail from hostage novels for a reason.

Thankfully, Cash turns to face the wall. I half smile at the girls. Whew. I have business to do.

Caroline holds up a little Kleenex pack she dug out of her blue purse, matching her blue shoes. Of course, vice-president of this bank, Caroline Forbes-Radshaw, remembered to grab her purse while fleeing a gunman, and it holds perfectly folded Kleenex. I'm surprised they're not blue.

Little Miss Proper prepares for every possibility.

Caroline scrunches her face, handing me a single tissue. I cannot even fathom her doing what I am about to do. Neither can she.

But I must do what I must do.

Rashida jumps up with her Africa scarf in both hands, exclaiming, "I will make a scarf door."

She holds the cloth between her two spread-out arms to block the view from Cash. He nibbles on the strawberries nonchalantly. At least his back is to me.

Thank goodness for the makeshift door.

Who's eating at a stinking moment like this? Cash. Cash Jones. And he munches away. The rest of the girls give me sympathetic glances, knowing they might be next.

"Hold the curtain tight, Rashida," I say. "Am I in a bad dream?"

Pinch.

Nope. I am not.

Caroline whispers to Carrie Rae, "We will never speak of this again, ever."

"I heard that Caroline," I bemoan from behind the temporary curtain.

"Life is the berries. When I gotta go, I gotta go. Sorry, everyone."

Soon, Cash spouts curses describing the potency of the floating odor.

"That reeks! How can such stench come out of sweet Mrs. Michigan?"

He moans on the floor, shouting more profanities and pounding his boots repeatedly. He plugs his nose, swearing he can taste the stench.

I gag, too.

"We can throw that bag full of crap at the gunman when he opens the door. It's toxic. He will die on the spot," Cash declares.

Rashida raises her eyebrows like it's an intuitive plan. Cash bellows extra curses, rolling into the fetal position, laughing at his own joke. My face flushes a deeper red. Carrie Rae waves her hand subtly in front of her nose, then ducks behind her hair.

The seal fails to contain the stench.

The odor wafts to all. Cringes, nose plugging and gagging ensue.

Caroline Forbes-Radshaw comes to my rescue again. Pulling a mini-lotion bottle out from her purse, she suggests we all put a dab of scented lotion under our nose to "freshen up" our intake aroma.

It works. The lotion deflects the rancid scent, but Cash gives me a high five for my being so powerful with the pew bomb. I laugh him off and leave him hanging, giving him my stink-eye glare.

My humiliation fades, but the aroma does not. Will I live this down? Scene one horrifies.

"Did you just hear that? Caroline, is that the sound of the combination?" Rashida asks.

You might snicker rereading the Bible verse in this heading. I did.

CHAPTER 5

*May the LORD watch between you and me
when we are absent one from the other.*
Genesis 31:49b NASB

We listen intently. Nothing.

Abruptly breaking the silence, Rashida jumps up, pounding her fists on the vault door, screaming, "Get us out of here! Get us out!"

Caroline, eye twitching, says, "Trust the police to handle this, Rashida."

"No way! Are you kidding me?" bellows Rashida with piercing eyes. "Police cannot figure out crimes. We need to take matters into our own hands."

Spewing spit through clenched teeth, she glares at each of us with tiger intensity.

Carrie Rae, hair swaying, rocks faster than a woodpecker in motion. Sitting cross-legged, clutching her moccasins, her rocking intensifies. As Rashida's ear-piercing shouts reverberate through the space, Carrie Rae slaps her hands over her ears.

My eyes open wide and my eyebrows lift. Perhaps I should reason with raging Rashida.

"Will this pounding even be heard on the other side? If they hear it, will the bad guys take drastic measures against us?" I ask.

Rashida flails her arms with increasing intensity, adding the rolling action of her head to her non-stop pounding. My words do not faze her. She thrashes more. Is she going mad?

31

Cash calmly stands, moving his back against the other half of the massive vault door. His arms cross with one eyebrow raised. Cash watches nonchalantly as Rashida spazzes out. Cash simply waits. He continues staring, unfazed by her furious attack on the door.

After several intense minutes, Rashida slows the pounding, taking deep breaths with o-shaped lips.

"Are you done yet?" asks Cash, poised like a calm cloud, talking to a fading hurricane.

Rashida darts a penetrating glare at Cash, turns her back to him and drops to the floor. Her arms cross against her chest as she breathes rapidly.

The storm dissipates.

Carrie Rae's rapid rocking slows to a subtle sweeping motion. Cash lowers to the ground with legs outstretch and ankles crossed. He looks down at his pecs, admiring himself. He brushes imaginary dust off his shoulder.

The tension fog slowly lifts.

Rashida's breathing returns to normal as her muscles relax. Caroline smooths out a wrinkle in her skirt and closes her eyes. Carrie Rae ceases to rock, falling asleep behind her curtain of black hair. Cash folds his arms, tilts his head, and fades to sleep with a smirk.

Eventually, the five of us nod off.

****

I stretch my arms high, waking up from the night with little sleep. It is morning, right?

Yawning, I gaze around the vault at this variety of new friends. Cash snores slumping against the vault door, arms crossing against his chest. The *Cash-Is-King* tattoo peeps below his sleeve. The right side of his mouth dangles a drool, jiggling with each snore.

Hmm. I guess he's our best protection and the first line of defense from the gunman.

We got trouble.

Caroline sits up tall with her knees together politely, even when sleeping. This formal vice-president of the bank doses with proper posture. Caroline Forbes-Radshaw demonstrates perfection in every way. Even her makeup doesn't smear. She can do no wrong.

Carrie Rae Hucklenuckle slumbers crisscross style. Looking at her causes me a gentle smile, like thinking of her last name. I did not know Indigenous Americans actually sit crisscross-applesauce. She does. Her hands rest on her moccasins, and she hides behind her veil of beautiful hair.

Rashida Jackson, the colorful African momma of our group, cuddles close to Carrie Rae. Last night, Rashida acted ballistic, but now she sleeps with one arm over Carrie Rae's shoulder like a protective mother hen.

I hum in my head the songs from last night and grin.

Great day, Carrie Rae sings angelically. Too bad she shies away from sharing her gift with others.

Pinch. Pinch.

Yesterday's bank robbery is not a bad dream. And what takes so long outside the vault?

Sigh.

I study our ring of strangers, new friends, each identified by a distinct style of shoes circling around the half-eaten bowl of strawberries. There's Caroline's powder-blue stilettos with the pointy toes and all business. Next to her, the chunky leather boots of Cash Jones, necessary as he clunks his way through life.

The soft moccasins of Carrie Rae Huccklenuckle represent her. *Giggle.* Her fringe leather moccasins walk quietly, like Carrie Rae herself trying to live unnoticed even when she sings.

Rashida's flashy sandals match her artsy jewelry, bold personality, and African wardrobe.

My black flip-flops fit me with the crystal gems blinging along the straps. Comfort and bling-bling describe me to a twinkling tee. I endeavor to shimmer, shine, and sparkle for Jesus with every comfortable step I take.

Oh, my! Look at my toes!

I am unfinished. I need to shave my hairy toes. How embarrassing. Caroline Forbes-Radshaw would never leave her house looking like me. She probably waxes her toe hairs. She's perfection personified from head to toe. I need her professionalism if I expect to grow the inspirational speaking ministry.

How can I fret over silly insignificance at a time like this?

We could die. They shot at us! Am I that shallow? Studying the variety of shoes and souls in the room, I determine to pray for each unique person. How wrong to focus on missing my book launch outside when I should attend to the people inside. Am I self-centered or what? Am I driven with selfish ambition or God-guided?

"Okay, God. Please lead me with your Holy Spirit today while locked in this bank cell. Open my companions' hearts to hear about Jesus. Open doors for us to talk about Jesus. God, open my mouth to share Jesus. Oh yeah . . . and God, please, please, please, open this massive vault door."

"Lord, are we trapped together for a reason?"

"God, will YOU do immeasurably more than we ask or imagine, adding purpose to our predicament?"

This will make a great message outline for me to speak about someday . . . if we ever get out of here. My heart races and my forehead beads with sweat again. God works all things for our good for those called according to God's purposes, right? I want to live my life for God in all places . . . even locked in a vault. I wipe the sweat from my upper lip.

My apprehension gushes in sweaty waves.

Will we ever walk out of here . . . alive?

I should write to Kyle and Drew in case we don't make it out with our lives. Death looms. My hands tremble. My eyes tear up. I pull my shirt away from my sweaty back. I pray we all survive, but I'm writing a letter to my guys just in case. Will my sweaty fingers be able to grasp the pen?

I remember my notepad for signing up emails at my product table. I reach quietly into my duffle bag for the notebook, disturbing none of the sleepers.

Flipping to a blank page, I pop a strawberry in my mouth, savoring the taste. I half grin. These strawberries relieve our hunger. Who knew berries would be our lunch, dinner, and breakfast?

Tapping my strawberry earrings while praying for God to inspire me, I start penning a farewell letter to my forever love.

 CHAPTER 6

Husbands,
love your wives,
just as Christ loved the church . . .
Ephesians 5:25a NIV

"Dear Kyle,
You're the best hubster ever.
You love God, who guides you daily. This first attracted me to
you. I loved meeting you right after I became a believer. I prayed
about finding a person of faith . . . and I met you. God's timing rings
perfect.
I remember our first kiss. What's up with me crawling right
through your car window??? You touched my face at the same time
our lips touched. That caused one doozy of a crawl-through-the-
window first kiss. You melted me.
You still fire me up today.
You spoil me, treating me like royalty. Your kiss on my forehead
with your "it's-good-to-be-home-my-Queen" greeting keeps me
smiling daily. I love doing life with you. I wish we were back playing
ping-pong, euchre, or enjoying kayaking right now.
Inside your hug is my happy place.
You loved me through our years of infertility treatments and
my barren hard seasons. When we adopted Drew, we experienced
such joy. As Drew became more challenging and diagnosed on the
spectrum, you continued to be the rock in our shaking family. As

Drew slammed into puberty, our lives broke a bit. Drew's meltdowns overwhelmed me.

I lost my mind . . . nearly.

I'm so grateful we found help for Drew and weaned him off meds. His breakdowns settled. We climbed a mountain. With God's help and your steady hand, we pulled out of the despair valley. Your wisdom prevailed. You were a rock when I needed one.

Can you believe Drew lives in his own apartment? It's not perfect, but it's progress.

Life with you and Drew blesses.

Sorry for the times I got bossy. I apologize. You were right. There, I admit it. Your patience and kindness triumph through our trials. God blessed and disciplined you into a man of God's Word.

In marriage, we opposites attract . . . then attack. Ha. But we work it out. We identified you as a departmentalized waffle and me as sprawling spaghetti. We process differently. The goals to love and respect improved our marriage.

Bossy, demanding, defensive, and moody qualities, we worked hard on decreasing. Yah! Loving, respecting, kind-speaking, empathetic, and compassionate traits we worked on increasing. Oh yeah! You and I developed resolute staying-power. We persevered with your arthritic chronic pain, Drew's autism, and my barrenness. We hiked emotional foothills together, making us stronger mountain climbers.

Team Strawberry!

I love how you pray over me daily and give me God's perspective. The Bible is our plumb line to vertical living. When I fail as a wife or a mom, you encourage me back to healthy Biblical thinking. You support my inspirational speaking, writing and life-coaching ministry.

God knew what he was doing when he put us together.

Whatever happens with this bank robbery fiasco, you gave me a beautiful life. Kyle, my hero hubster, I love you to the end of the earth . . . and beyond. If I don't make it out, you know I ran into Jesus' arms. I love you forever. If I earthly die, it's not goodbye. It's see ya later.

You're my Knight in Shining Armor forever!

Your Queen Sherry Strawberry

P.S. If I die, nobody cares if you leave your hunting gear all over the living room. You won't be persuaded to watch another "chick flick" or HGTV show again. Enjoy controlling the TV remote! Bonuses!

P.S.S. I give you my blessing to remarry. Pick someone who can cook better and loves our unique Drew.

P.S.S.S. Give Remi extra dog treats from me.

P.S.S.S.S. Tears splat as I scribble this down. Last night, I longed for your cuddles, sniffling myself to sleep quietly. I pray you never see this farewell letter, and instead, we can snuggle together. I want to come home . . . to us."

I breathe in deep, massaging my hands. I finish Kyle's letter, or should I say book? It's lengthy. Tears flow.

How cathartic. Kissing the letter, I appreciate Kyle more with my reminiscing.

Interlocking my fingers, I stretch my hands out in front of me. I take a robust breath, wiping my eyes. I touch my blingy strawberry earrings, turning up a soft smile.

Now for Drew's letter.

I pray Drew will grasp this letter through the autism. It may ease his transition to life on earth without his momma. Lord, give me wisdom for this note writing. I swipe a slow rolling tear, determining to begin.

"Dear Drew,

I thank God for you.

You are the answer to years of prayers. You bring laughter. You know techy stuff better than me. And you give hardy hugs!

I love how you work at not over-reacting. You don't like change, but you learn to adjust. You are generous and giving. I just don't like it when people steal from you. You trust too much sometimes. Be wise with friend choosing, Drew.

I am proud of you for keeping a job. Life is hard, but you stay at it.

You love family well.

It's a miracle you're off all meds. You're best without them. You melt down less. I thank God for this every day. The group home helped you learn life skills and learn more about God.

Drew, you can do this life without me.

Keep Christian friends around you, keep reading your Bible every morning, and keep Jesus close. Church is a good place for you. Remember your faith in Jesus. Jesus never leaves you. Stay tight with God to be happy.

Listen to Dad. Thank you for working hard to calm, to breathe, to think through your choices. Warrior onward.

Sometimes the answer must be "NO" in life. You can accept "NO" responsibly.

You learned to drive and passed your driver's test. This surprised us and improves our prayer life. Boom! You sure love cars and made us proud when you saved money to buy your own. Be careful driving and remember the unprotected left-hand turn. Drive safe. Never use your cell in the car. No one else drives your car. Let no one smoke inside it.

I love you forever. I would not be the person I am today without you teaching me I can do hard things, too. You grew me as a mom, speaker, and life coach. Thank you for the training grounds.

You and Dad should keep enjoying Joni and Friends Camp every year. It's the best!

Be strong and courageous, like God told Joshua when Moses died.

I love you forever. Be good. Keep adjusting to changes. You got this. Listen to Dad. I'll see you again . . . in heaven.

I Love YOU,

Mom

Whoa!

I rub my face, puffing out air. Tears stream. My letter peppers with teardrop splats. Just breathe. I tap my pencil to my lip, pondering if any others may want to write letters. Rashida, Caroline, and Carrie Rae will, but I doubt if Cash will hassle with a letter. I should offer them my paper. I raise an eyebrow. This could be interesting if Cash writes his letter. Can he spell all those cuss words?

CHAPTER 7

These things write I unto thee,
hoping to come unto thee shortly
1 Timothy 3:14 KJV

I'm surprised nobody woke up yet.

Cash starts to stir.

"Good morning, Security Guard," I whisper to Cash, stretching his arms and yawning. Thank goodness, he wipes the wobbling drool off his face.

"Yeah, yeah, yeah. Are we still in this stink box? What's happening outside of this vault?" Cash answers a bit too loudly, waking up the others. He rubs both hands over his face.

He manages to add profanity, declaring, "Now I need my plastic-bag toilet."

"Good morning," I whisper to the others, opening their eyes.

Cash goes digging for a plastic freezer bag, dumps more strawberries into the bowl, and clutches the empty bag.

Hoping to get this over quickly, we face away from Cash with his back turned to us.

"I'm done," Cash states.

We turn back around. Caroline shakes her head in disgust at Cash Jones. He grins with his chest puffed out, holding his plastic bag in the air like a prized fish.

He poses, smiling broadly . . . and accidentally drops his half-filled bag of morning pee!

The flow of yellow liquid splats out, floating toward us!

"Get back!" Cash hollers.

We scram!

Instantly, the gals jolt up, jumping back on our tiptoes, pressing against the walls. Cash whips off his shirt, dropping on all fours, soaking up the man-made lake before it reaches us. We scurry away just in time.

Whew!

We crunch our noses, making scrunch faces with gagging gestures.

Cash raises up pompously, the sopping t-shirt dripping liquid down his arm. He's a gruff version of the Statue of Liberty, holding up a drenched shirt instead of the torch. He balls up this urine-soaked T as it releases more fluid down his hands. Stuffing the wadded shirt into the plastic bag that once held strawberries, he smiles a grin of accomplishment. He seals his bag as more liquid oozes on him. Nonchalantly, he tosses his bag near my "toilet" Ziploc bag into the corner.

Without wiping his dripping hands, Cash reaches over, grabbing the other open bag of strawberries and pops one in his mouth.

We girls glare in disbelief.

"What? What's wrong?" Cash asks us as we scowl with frozen faces.

The cross-eyed expression on Caroline's mortified face lingers with the odor.

Cash couldn't care less about dripping urine, handwashing, or hygiene. Three clean bags of strawberries remain. Rashida declares Cash can keep for himself the bag he holds dripping with urine.

"What were you writing in your notebook, Mrs. Michigan?" Cash asks, unfazed by our horrified expressions.

He licks the strawberry chocolate off his urine-coated fingers with a lip smack.

Gross.

Chocolate and urine. I gag.

"Not to discourage anyone, but I wrote a farewell letter to my husband and my son, just in case . . . um . . . things don't end well," I reply hesitantly.

In eerie silence, they exchange glances around the room, jolted by my answer.

Carrie Rae whimpers again. Caroline's proper posture slouches. Cash mumbles profanities under his breath. Rashida glares, dropping her head in her hands.

Suddenly, Rashida pops her head up.

"Ya know what? That's important. May I have a couple sheets of paper to write my twins?" Rashida asks me, searching her purse for a pen. "I don't have a will. This is crucial if . . . if this does not go as I want. You never know. Unexpected outcomes crush our lives. Trust me. We should all do this."

She points directly at each one of us with two raised eyebrows.

Assertively, she reaches her hand for my notebook. Everyone agrees they want to pen letters. I offer to tear off the papers when Cash grabs for the notebook with his unwashed hands. The girls wince as I snatch the notebook back away from his nasty hands.

We gals laugh. Nobody wants to share Cash's germs.

It takes a couple hours to complete their letters with lots of pen tapping, staring off into space, and deliberating.

When Carrie Rae searches in her backpack for a sharper pencil, she whips out a water bottle three-quarters full. She grins ear to ear.

We cheer, applauding the discovery, and agree to pour out only one capful each. We will attempt to go as long as we can without drinking. Caroline requests no lips to the bottle or the cap. We agree to pour a capful in our mouth with our heads tipped back.

We all thirst and enjoy our first capful with smiles and satisfied moans.

I narrow my eyes, tilt my head. This won't last long.

Tightening the cap on the bottle, Carrie slips it back in her backpack. She's the gatekeeper for our thirst.

Lunch is chocolate-covered strawberries. Surprise. *Ha.* Nobody accidentally grabs from Cash's bag of berries either.

We discuss the length of our confinement. What kind of chaos must be happening on the other side of this vault door? I hear whimpers from Hucklenuckle again.

We imagine how upset our families must be.

Caroline taps her fancy fingertips, informing us the Waco standoff lasted 51 days, Iran standoff went 444 days, and Wounded

Knee lasted 71 days. Carrie Rae rocks, but peeks one eye through her hair with the mention of the Indian standoff. No one can believe how long we've been trapped . . . and how satiable these strawberries taste even after a day of eating nothing but the berries. The juice of the strawberries quenches our thirst. Cash smiles contently. He's unfazed by anything.

After a few hours, everyone uses their portable potty bags.

Even Caroline.

Afterward, she develops a twitch in her head, matching her lip twitch. I'm pretty sure I see tears. Her fair skin turns redder than the strawberries, too. Poor Caroline. Rashida's scarf is a godsend.

With her hand over her mouth, Caroline stutters about understanding why novels leave out these restroom issues when trapped. Her propriety churns over this ordeal. With customary profanity, Cash says he would leave in every detail. I shake my head, listening to the dichotomy between them.

As we deliberate the details of the bank heist, I wonder what everyone wrote to their families. If we get bored enough, maybe we will read them aloud. Rashida's been quiet since she started her letter. She wrote while breathing hard, with her arm up, blocking the view of her writing. At one point, she scribbled furiously with a deep scowl.

Caroline taps her finger on her lip, staring at Rashida with an inquisitive eyebrow raise.

I glanced at Caroline's letter earlier, and her handwriting flows with perfection. Of course. She does everything correctly. So proper. So private. She won't share her letter.

Cash's letter will be a hoot for his girl Dani to read, for sure. Again, I doubt he can spell his cuss words correctly. I shake my head with my inward thoughts.

When I peeked at Carrie Rae's letter earlier, her handwriting was extremely light, just like her whispering voice. I'm nosy, but it was too faint for me to read, peeking over her shoulder. Will I ever know what they wrote in these letters? Do our lives have anything in common?

My eyebrows arch high.

Cash stands up and announces, "Who wants to hear what's in

my letter?"

Carrie Rae sits up taller. Caroline leans in. I rub my hands together in anticipation. What in the world did Cash write?

Laura Loveberry

CHAPTER 8

Pure and genuine religion
in the sight of God the Father
means caring for orphans and widows in their distress . . .
James 1:27a NLT

Cash repeats himself, belting out, "Well, who wants to know what I wrote?"

He stands tall, planting his feet at shoulder width. As he unfolds his crinkled note, he informs us, "I ain't no rule follower, so my letter gots a different message than yours. You ladies may get heated when ya hear from me . . . Mr. Romance."

Cash rubs his tattooed knuckles across his bare chest a few times and flexes his pecs twice. He raises one eyebrow, smirks, and kisses the air like he's Mr. Macho.

I roll my eyes. Rashida shakes her head. Caroline and Carrie Rae crack a subtle smile.

Cash shows off his shirtless, tattooed self with a Tarzan double *boom-boom* fist pound on his chest.

"To my Dani girl," Cash reads, flexing his pecs, holding out his masterpiece. *"You got one hot biker body. You a brick house. Your curves melt my heart. Even with a couple of yo teeth missing, I love kissing yo mouth."*

I can't help but giggle. The girls grin.

Cash stops reading, asking, "What? Is this too romantic for ya ladies? What can I say? I got game. And it gets better."

He flexes his shirtless pecs three more times.

I scrunch my face, and we groan simultaneously.

Disregarding our giggles, Cash continues reading proudly, *"I love smooching the gaps between your teeth."*

Caroline coughs suddenly, nearly spitting out her strawberry.

Erupting with laughter, we roll on the floor, grasping our sides. Even Caroline laughs uncontrolled after her choking fit.

Who writes this in a letter, shares it aloud, and is proud?

Undaunted, Cash reads louder to be heard over the giggles, warning us the best part is coming with his added poem. *"Roses be red. Violets are blue. You wear biker boots. I do, too. So, jump on my motorcycle, and we'll hitch. Yea, I'll marry you. . .."*

Cash continues reading, adding profanity after profanity, peppering in more impropriety. Carrie Rae raises her eyebrows, covering her ears with both hands. In a stop motion, Caroline thrusts a palm-out hand at Cash. She interrupts before he finishes the remainder of his cuss-filled poetry.

"Cash, please refrain from using offensive language in this fine banking institution." Caroline speaks, cracking a smile, then giggling uncontrollably, shoulders shaking.

I cover my wide-open mouth, widening my eyes in disbelief. Did Cash just write a wedding proposal filled with inappropriate words? It's taboo to laugh at such wordage, but proper Caroline loses it. The rest of us bend over, gasping for air.

I can't breathe.

Is it funnier because Cash reads proud as a male peacock, strutting with his chest out? He's clueless to the impropriety of it all. Or is it more humorous because proper Caroline can't hold it together, laughing at the unfathomable wedding proposal? Or are we all stir-crazy?

I should not find his uncouth poetry amusing.

"I'm sorry, LORD," I pray swiftly.

I'm losing my Christian testimony for laughing at it all. Oh my. Perhaps the sweat, stench, and anxiety affect my reasoning. Secretly, Cash's poem with his steady rhythm and rhyme impresses me.

We try to gain composure as Cash concludes with an added rap beat, *"Let's marry when I get out of here. We be driving to the sunset, while drinking a beer."*

Cash pauses, sipping from a pretend beer can.

He looks directly at us, raising on his toes, informing us we will love this next part. He smiles broadly.

"With your stubby nails and blue tipped hair, we're gonna have a steamy affair. Be my biker queen, and wear my ring. You got the best, 'cuz Cash is KING! Yeah, CASH . . . IS . . . KING!"

Cash raises his hands yelling, "BOOM! Now that's romance, ladies."

He drops his letter in a mic-drop moment.

Cash struts around our confined space doing a dance resembling a turkey gyrating.

Puckering his lips, he says, "We may be poor, but we both be rich in love."

He kisses the air, posing Wrestle-Mania style, tightening his fists and bulging his muscles.

As we settle down, Rashida asks, "Who wants to read theirs next, ladies?"

"It will be impossible to beat Cash's wedding proposal, I know," I say. "Maybe I'll read next to calm us down."

As I read my letter, the girls and Cash whoop it up at our first kiss when I climbed in the car window. They discuss my letters and ask questions afterwards. Caroline surprises me with all her questions about my barrenness, adoption, and Drew's autism. I openly answer each one. Why is private Caroline so intrigued with my personal details of infertility?

Now, it is someone else's turn.

Rashida Jackson volunteers to go next. Clearing her throat, she stands with her weight on one hip. She starts by complimenting her twin girls on their character and accomplishments. Rashida shares her aspirations for them to reach lofty career goals. She raises her bangle-bracelet hand high and waves with click-clanking echoes.

Apparently, the girls overachieve and accomplish much. Proud Rashida asserts dramatically of the girls' fortitude.

Rashida describes the twin's father, her husband, as a man who devoted his life to the teachings of Jesus, reading his Bible night and day. He was an elder in the church. She described him as handsome, strong, and a person who followed the Bible rules.

We perk up and look around. Didn't Rashida tell us she's an atheist?

I turn my head discreetly, looking at the others with my mouth hanging open. Caroline's eyebrows raise. Carrie Rae loops her hair behind an ear.

Rashida reads on about how well her husband treated her. Obviously, she still loves her deceased husband deeply. Her voice quivers as she describes him fondly.

I get the hint she carries disdain for the church. Her words convey love for her godly husband, but not for God. Rashida lived happily married to a remarkable husband, but her heart remains broken and not healed from his loss. She pauses, gaining control. Her eyes fill.

Next, she describes their two sons and the amazing potential the boys possessed before their deaths. Tears flows. The letter shakes in her trembling hands. She confides she experiences night terrors yet today. Rashida exhales. Her nose runs as she reads on with determination.

She just wishes their father could have held his twin daughters.

What?! He died before their birth. My mouth drops open again.

I hear a gasp from Carrie Rae.

According to Rashida, he would have been the best father to Jona and Jamila, the now fatherless twin girls.

How awful! How tragic! No wonder Rashida overprotects her twins.

Carrie Rae and I flow tears, feeling her pain with every quivering word she chokes out. Caroline dabs the corner of her eye with her tissue. Cash stares straight ahead at nothing.

How did Rashida's husband and two other children die?

It had to be seventeen years ago, because the twins are seventeen. Rashida wipes her cheeks and running nose with her African scarf. No one makes a sound or moves an inch. How devastating. We sit stunned.

She reads on how she loves her girls and apologizes for being overprotective. She closes by encouraging them to be strong on their own power, remembering life brings unexpected tragedy.

Her last line reminds them to find their strength within themselves. No one speaks as she folds her letter.

Then silence fills the vault and stays.

Breaking the long hush, Caroline whispers gently, "Were they killed in a car accident, Rashida?"

Carrie Rae's head twist abruptly facing Rashida.

Rashida looks down, wiping her nose and shaking her head "no" without speaking.

Cash throws around some foul language, demanding to know what happened. He's deep into the letter.

Carrie Rae air slaps at him, and I give him piercing looks that could kill for using obscenity when asking.

Whispering, I confess, "We shouldn't have asked you the details, Rashida. We apologize and feel your pain. We just don't know what to say."

I scoot closer, wrapping my arms around Rashida, who now wails loudly. Soon Caroline and Carrie Rae join in the emotional group hug. Rashida's shaking shoulders tense up.

Cash, over by the vault door, throws his hands in the air and ponders the ceiling.

"What part of Chicago are you from?" Cash inquires, avoiding her eye contact.

I turn to Cash, catching the corner of his eye and mouth. "Stop."

Rashida cries out her years of sadness and crushed dreams bottled up inside her as we girls embrace. Her whole body shakes. Leaning on each other with puffy eyes and messy hair, we sit in silence as she trembles in our embrace.

"Naperville. I am from Naperville," Rashida whispers.

Another long pause floats in the vault air.

Cash, staring at Rashida's face with squinty eyes, replies, "I've been to that part of town, but it was a long time ago—seventeen years ago."

Maybe Cash knows more about Rashida than he lets on. Cash stares at Rashida's face intently. Does he recognize her from his past?

No way?!

To everyone's surprise, Caroline whispers to Rashida, "If you can share your broken heart, I can share mine."

Caught up in the emotion, she opens her petite purse and unfolds her neatly pleated letter.

Caroline Forbes-Radshaw takes a deep breath. "I can't believe I'm sharing this . . ."

CHAPTER 9

When I kept silent,
my bones wasted away
through my groaning all day long.
Psalm 32: 3 NIV

I peer around the room with raised eyebrows. I sit up tall in shock. Caroline will read her personal letter?! Who would believe this?

She takes another deep breath, keeping her proper posture as she stands with both feet straight and legs together.

Rashida trembles, pulling up her knees in a fetal ball.

My interest piques, but it will probably be boring and unemotional, especially compared to the trauma retold by Rashida.

Everything about Caroline appears picture-perfect, not anything like Rashida's heartbreak.

Caroline stands as tall as her petite body allows. She reads her letter straight through, without a stop, like a Map-Quest Garmin giving directions in a woman's voice.

"To my darling, Sterling . . ."

She married a gentleman. And, of course, his name is Sterling. Figures. This fits her silver-spoon life. Cash rolls his eyes. Carrie Rae and I smile, tilt our heads, and listen. Cash stares at the ceiling.

Caroline continues, *"I am writing this letter as a farewell to you from the bank vault. If I ever said this job kills me, it came to fruition now. If you are reading this letter, I did not make it out alive from the heist. There are no guarantees when dealing with criminals, and this*

51

is taking longer than expected."

Cash nods his head in agreement.

"Sterling, you are an amazing partner in marriage. I love reading books in the evening together and love our deep discussions about the highlights of our studying. I hoped to reach our combined goal of reading four books a week for the year, but if I am deceased, you'll need to double your reading to accomplish this. I love how you challenge me to grow intellectually. There is so much to learn in the world, and we hold books at our fingertips."

Now Cash shakes his head in disbelief. Did Cash ever read a single book in his life? I doubt it.

"You have been remarkable with our retirement, investments, stocks, and our 401K. If you're reading this, it's ironic because we worked hard and won't even get to enjoy purchasing the yacht together like we planned for retirement. You have been a solid provider and a husband who does right. I like our current boat, but you deserve the yacht."

Cash turns his nose in the air. He holds an imaginary tea cup with his pinky out, mocking the fancy statement. He makes a prude expression, wobbling his head like a church lady. I crack a smile.

"I enjoyed our dinners out, sailing clubs, playing doubles tennis, and golfing tournaments. You supported my success in the banking world.

As you know, I think you would make an amazing father. It is my deepest regret that I cannot give you a child to keep your name and legacy. I am truly sorry. After our countless infertility treatments and failed adoptions, we just could not bear it anymore.

Our nursery set up for eight years was too difficult for me to take. I will always remember your sadness when we donated all our nursery items to the crisis pregnancy center."

I place my hands on my heart and lean closer. My heart stings as she reads.

"It was the saddest day of our marriage and the end of our baby dreams. Remember the young pregnant girl who delighted when she saw our gorgeous crib we donated? That helped and hurt our hearts at the same time.

Life is tough."

I cover my face with both hands and tear up. Noticing, Carrie Rae scoots close, rubbing my shoulder gently.

"Honey, you have helped me through the infertility as no other man could do.

For this, I am thankful.

I am not the perfect angel you think I am, though. For years, I have held an unfathomable secret from you. Truthfully, I am not worthy of your love. I failed you deeply and there is no hope for my soul.

I love you, but I am a broken woman with a dark secret.

No, I would never be unfaithful to you with another man. What I have done is far worse. I am a selfish woman, and I deserve my punishment. You do not deserve my punishment, and that's the hardest part."

Carrie Rae, Cash, and I lean in, listening more intently. Rashida breathes out a quiet breath and relaxes as she focuses on Caroline's words, too.

"If we get out of here, I promise to tell you my darkest secret, because the weight of my guilt is too much to carry if I keep living. This is something I have done. There is no recourse—no freedom from my guilt."

Rashida's eyes open wide. She sits up as Caroline reads on like a robot. I gulp. My eyebrows scrunch. Something from the past tortures Caroline. She is not perfect?! Who knew? Nobody flinches.

"I love you.

I am sorry you live with a damaged wife. My desire to control everything probably comes from my culpability of guilt.

I secretly live in the darkest night of the soul. I experience no freedom from my guilt and agony deeper than the depths of life.

I suffer silently.

My consequences haunt me. My perfectionist ways are my striving for relief. Who understands the psychology of my mind's battle? I just know I failed you. I failed myself. I failed God. My pain runs to the depths of my heart and deeper still.

I have no relief, nor do I deserve it.

My punishment is my destiny. I am broken in this vault with time to ponder. If they free us, I will remain locked in my personal vault of an unforgiven state. I know my introspective nature disentangles my secret truth.

I love you deeper than my torment haunts me.

Thank you for loving me more than I deserve. I am a flawed woman, and your desire for children will haunt me to my grave. I don't deserve to escape.

I am held captive in my mind, but so in love with you, Caroline Forbes Radshaw"

We sit in stillness, staring forward. No one moves.

Who knew she battled inwardly? I sit frozen with a blank outward expression.

I saw only her perfection.

Rashida shakes her head slowly back and forth.

No one speaks in this most awkward of silence.

Something haunts Caroline, and I know what it is. Private Caroline just opened the deepest part of her soul.

Who saw this coming?

No one.

Who am I to comment? Who am I to address her? I am not a trained therapist. I am a life coach. We deal with simple goals. I am not in any place to even consider advising her deep turmoil. Do I feel God prompting me? Maybe I do.

My heart pounds almost loud enough to pierce the silence. It thuds as my mouth dries.

I pray silently, "Lord, if you want me to be a vessel for you to speak through, please give me my next words, Lord. Amen."

As gently as my dry lips can whisper, I say meekly, "Caroline, I think I know what happened."

I gently place both hands on my heart.

"I know how women can find the peace they desperately seek. Do you want me to keep talking?"

Caroling stares straight ahead.

She speaks to the air without making eye contact. "You are a barren woman, Sherry, by no choice of your own. I caused my barrenness and deserve my punishment. I am a selfish woman deserving my pain. I could have allowed my baby to be adopted by parents like you. I did not. I had a plan. I had a work promotion and career goals to reach."

She sounded like a soft robot speaking while in a deep stare, "The abortion-planning business people told me it would be quick, simple, and no worries. They said they would scrape tissue out. I would return to life as if nothing even happened. They said it would be a painless procedure. After I signed the papers, everything was supposed to be fine."

After a nightmare long pause, she shakes her head. "It's a lie."

A single tear rolls down her cheek, splattering on her folded hands.

Caroline opens her clutch and gently wipes her tear, continuing. "They lied. I never recovered physically... or mentally. Later, when I thought the timing was right for Sterling and I to start a family, we could not."

Caroline takes a deep breath.

"I made my OBGYN doctor promise not to tell my husband about my decision to abort our first child. Sterling never knew of my pregnancy with his baby. That was seventeen years ago."

Pulsating silence.

"I could have given my baby to parents like you. I could have kept my baby. We would have a teenager right now. Instead, I believed the lies of the abortion business about a simple fix."

Caroline's face fades to white.

Her decision haunts.

Caroline sighs a drawn-out breath, saying, "Whatever happens here in this vault, I'm in hell either way. If I live or if I die, I am in hell."

We wait. The emotions—thick.

I wrestle inward. Should I speak? I talk too much. Should I talk right now? I plead for God to open the words of my mouth or shut it.

"Caroline, do you know who wrote the book of Psalms in the Bible?" I ask softly as she stares forward, folding her Kleenex neatly.

"David wrote many of the Psalms," I say.

I continue talking after a silent prayer for wisdom, "David, known as a man after God's own heart, wrote many of our encouraging Psalms. David made a devastating choice like you. He was not serving as he should when kings go to war. He was not thinking godly. David was thinking of himself."

I hear Rashida mumble under her breath that I am a Bible-thumping church lady. She glares at me. Really? Doesn't Rashida want Caroline to find peace? I need to block Rashida out and focus on Caroline's tender heart.

I continue, "King David conspired to kill a man in an attempt to hide his adultery when his mistress, Bathsheba, became pregnant with an unplanned baby. David connived to hide his sexual sin. He devised a quick fix. He planned the death of Bathsheba's husband. David thought the murder of Uriah, Bathsheba's husband, would hide his sexual sin, fixing everything. It did not."

I continue, "The prophet Nathan pointed out this crime to David. When confronted, David repented of his massive wrong. He wrote Psalm 51 about being washed clean. He broke. King David found relief from his haunting sin and rotting bones. David flew free of his guilt, but he suffered consequences. He lost his child with Bathsheba to death after the baby's birth. David agonized with heartbreak over his sin, but he found freedom from guilt and peace with God when he repented with a contrite heart. He turned from his sin, bowing to God for forgiveness."

"Caroline, are you broken like David?" I ask her gently.

CHAPTER 10

And you will know the truth,
and the truth will set you free.
John 8:32 NLT

Caroline nods her head to confirm her brokenness without making eye contract. She stares straight forward into her personal abyss. More tears splatter on her pristine blazer.

"Do you want to know forgiveness?" I inquire earnestly. I long for her to know the tranquility found in God's forgiveness.

Rashida fidgets and starts tapping her foot. It distracts me. I pray to God to help me focus. Cash belches. Then he murmurs with profanity for me to back off.

"I am not worthy. I deserve this pain," Caroline responds.

"The Bible says this about our failures, 'For all sinned and fall short of the glory of God.' We all sin, Caroline. Everyone in here sins, including me," I inform her.

"I got a bigger hidden sin than all of yous," pipes up Cash as he breaks the mood and goes on a cussing rant.

I pull the conversation back to Caroline, ignoring Cash, who, by bragging about his sin, disrupts purposefully.

"Caroline, the Bible deals with death, too. You speak right about death. 'For the wages of sin is death, but the free gift of God is eternal life in Christ Jesus our Lord.' I found this in the book of Romans. It explains you cannot be good enough to earn your way to heaven. Heaven with Jesus is a FREE gift. In Ephesians, it says, 'For by grace you've been saved through faith; and not of yourselves, it is a gift of God.'"

Finally, Caroline turns her head, and our gazes meet.

She squints, appearing to focus on my words.

"Thank you, God, for helping me remember verses."

I spot Rashida out of the corner of my eye. Rashida mocks me, shaking her head. Her bottom lip protrudes, and her arms cross in defiance of my words.

Sheesh!

Turning back, I say to Caroline, "There's more to the verse in Ephesians, if I can recall it. It's Ephesians 2:8-9. It says, 'For by grace you have been saved through faith; and that not of yourselves, it is a gift of God, not as a result of works, so that no one may boast.' This means you definitely cannot be good enough for heaven. Nobody can earn heaven, Caroline. But God has a plan."

Rashida quips, "He snatches some people too soon."

Really Rashida? Why stifle our discussion with interruptions?

Ignoring Rashida, I explain, "God sent Jesus to come to earth to die for our sins, so we can be forgiven. Then Jesus rose from the dead because he paid for our sins. Now we can have heaven with Jesus. There is one more verse I want to tell you about. It is John 3:16."

Cash interrupts again. "Hey, I saw those numbers written on Tim Tebow's black strips under his eyes at one of the football games."

Not again!

I wish Cash and Rashida would stop interrupting here. I want to finish talking to Caroline about finding forgiveness.

"Let's eat, guys. Sherry Strawberry lays it down too thick. It be way too churchy in here. Lighten up, Miss Sherry Preachin' Berry. What are you anyway? The church lady? Do you go door to door with a white shirt and black tie like those dudes with the black books? They cram the Bible down your throat just like Sherry," Cash says.

What in the world, Cash? Why bash this conversation? Obviously, Caroline needs hope. Lord, guide me.

Rashida chimes in, "I'm with Cash. Let's eat. Life is hard, so let's eat chocolate-covered strawberries. That helps everything."

Cash laughs as Rashida mocks, "This Bible talk is blah, blah,

blah. We cannot wave a magic wand for our pain."

I scoot between Cash and Caroline and whisper to Caroline, "Do you want to know what John 3:16 says?"

Cash grabs his bag of strawberries and starts munching.

Rashida grabs the other bag, offering Caroline and Carrie Rae the strawberries. Caroline mouths a no-thanks with her lips. Carrie Rae quietly tells Rashida she wants to hear what I have to say.

Good.

At least Carrie Rae has my back.

Rashida snaps her head back in surprise when Carrie Rae quotes John 3:16 loudly. "'For God so loved the world, that He gave His only begotten Son, that whoever believes in Him shall not perish, but have eternal life.'"

All eyes turn toward Carrie Rae.

She can talk loudly, but now she goes back to her soft voice. "Mrs. Strawberry, will you please keep sharing with Caroline? She needs to know God loves her and can forgive all this."

Carrie Rae reaches for Caroline's hand, whispering, "Caroline, Jesus loves you."

I turn to Caroline, who nods her head as another teardrop splatters.

Grabbing my notebook, I draw a stick man on one side of a valley and a cloud with the word GOD in capitals letters on the other side. Then I sketch a bridge in the shape of a cross between the two hills and over the valley. I label the cross-shaped bridge as "forgiveness."

I explain how God so loves Caroline, quoting the verse again and putting her name in the verse. I ask Caroline what side of the valley she stands. She pointed to the "man" side of my drawing and not the "God" side. I ask her if she wants to cross over to the "God" side as I point to the crossbridge marked "forgiveness" on my paper.

Tears flow as she nods vigorously.

I inquire if she believes God sent Jesus to die for her sin so she can be forgiven.

Caroline nods "yes" again.

More tears stream down her face.

I ask if she believes Jesus rose from the dead so she can know she has heaven. She nods in agreement. I explain she can be with her aborted baby and with Jesus when she dies.

At this point Caroline all but shouts, "Yes. I believe. I am definitely a sinner, and I need Jesus to forgive me."

"Is your faith and trust in Jesus Christ right now?" I ask with my own tears flowing.

"Yes! I ask Jesus to take this sin away from me."

Caroline, looking upward with tears streaming and hands raising, prays wholeheartedly, "God, I am so sorry for my wretched, wretched sin. I am like David. I am the worst of sinners. If you can forgive me and wash this pain away, I will be forever thankful. I beg you to forgive me. I beg you to take away my sin."

My eyes open wide. What an earnest prayer!

"Do you believe in Jesus Christ and believe he died and rose from the dead for you, Caroline?" I ask as a prayer.

"Yes, I believe! Thank you for loving me, Jesus. Thank you for dying for me, Jesus. I am sorry for my sin. Please forgive me."

She collapses against me. "I needed this for so long."

Raising her eyes upward, Caroline said, "You heard my prayers, Lord. Last night, I prayed for you to show me the way out of my prison. I feared death. I grieved about my abortion decision. You're giving me new hope. Oh God, thank you."

Now the once-so-proper Caroline stands to her feet, lifting her hand in the air.

Her tears continue spotting her blue blazer, and she sways left and right, repeating, "Thank you, Jesus. Thank you, Jesus. Thank you, Jesus."

"What is going on?" Cash gripes, shaking his head back and forth cursing.

No one predicted Caroline would let her hair down and raise her hands to the sky. Rashida murmurs something about church emotionalism and not real life.

Rashida holds onto unforgiveness. A deep bitterness oozes from her.

Caroline startles herself and lowers down meekly to sit back in the circle. She smiles a content smile. Tranquility surrounds Caroline.

I pull a card out from my purse, slipping it to Caroline, saying, "Here is a business card for a ministry counseling service I refer women to. There's a phone number to call for post-abortion counselling. I trust them."

I explain, "As a barren woman, I am amazed how God brings women to me. Some made decisions about the baby in their womb they regret deeply. I am honored to pray with them, sharing how Christ can set them free of guilt and give them a new life. Because of your newfound faith in Jesus, you will reunite with your baby in heaven."

Caroline glows. Her arms wrap around herself like a hug from Jesus. She beams.

I witness her deep transformation, but the tension remains thick in the vault.

Rashida scowls.

She snatches another strawberry, shoving it in her mouth. Obviously perturbed, a cloud of stress hovers over Rashida. She mumbles something about there not being a God. A loving God would not let people die.

"God is dead," she states.

The dichotomy between Caroline's peaceful face and Rashida's bitterness emerges.

Carrie Rae closes her eyes, sitting cross-legged on the floor. She sings softly, *"Two people on the road of life. They've both been hurt so much on the inside. They both have a choice to forgive. One path is the wrong way, the other lets you live."*

I rise to stand behind Carrie Rae and use my sign-language drama to sign, forming a duet. Cash pulls out his cell phone, turning on the conserved power, and starts recording Carrie Rae singing and my dramatic sign language to her lyrics.

Caroline beams with her newfound inner peace, rocking gently side to side as Carrie Rae sings.

Rashida grimaces and huffs an indignant breath, but watches, nonetheless.

Carrie Rae's breathtaking voice fills the vault as she sings the chorus, *"Break free from these stone-cold walls. Set your heart free, let it go. Choose love, choose life, chose the way that you know. Let forgiveness flow oh, oh . . . forgiveness."*

Rashida squirms.

Cash keeps filming our duet of signing and singing.

Caroline closes her eyes, soaking in the lyrics. Her face reflects her newfound forgiveness with Jesus.

And it's clear Caroline forgave herself at long last.

Driven with purpose, Carrie Rae sings stronger, *"This one can't let go of the pain. Shackled to a hurt that still remains. Looking out from behind these prison walls. The door is open, but she won't heed the call. Break free from these stone-cold walls. Set your heart free, let it go. Choose life. Choose love. Choose the way that you know. Let forgiveness flow."*

Rashida cocks her head around, squinting her eyes narrowly, listening to the lyrics.

Carrie Rae opens her eyes, singing with a glowing smile on the next verse.

"This one walks the road Jesus traveled before. No chains, no locks to hold him down anymore."

Caroline jumps up, raising her hands toward the ceiling. Swaying to the music, she mouths "Praise Jesus" again and again.

Carrie smiles radiantly at Caroline and belts out her tune, *"Following the cross in the road. She holds the key that opens the door. Break free . . ."*

With perfect tone, Carrie Rae blasts out the final chorus as powerful as a church gospel choir singing in the Spirit. As Carrie Rae ends the last commanding note, we tumble on top of her, laughing and praising her for her beautiful singing pipes.

Even Rashida shouts, "Giiiiirl, you can saaaaang. I never heard anything so big and beautiful come out of a shy sparrow!"

Rashida piles on our group hug as the tension dissipates completely.

We're all in this together.

Cash continues to film our joyous laughter. He ends the video recording by turning the camera on himself and raising one eyebrow.

"I've just been to church," comments Cash as he looks into the phone camera, and now records himself. He lowers the camera on his chest, flexing each pec individually before stopping the recording.

"Rashida," Cash laughs, "You done stepped your atheist-self into a church service of sorts."

We tumble back into another group hug, only this time Cash piles on top.

"Get off us, Cash."

"You're too heavy."

"You're too stinky."

"You got no shirt, bro. EEK! You reek!"

We shove, pushing Cash off our group hug.

"You know you love it," Cash quips, staring down at his pec muscles, flexing them back and forth. I give a long, continuous groan, covering my eyes and shaking my head.

"I don't know what today is, but we just had church in the vault," I say.

"Let's have chocolate strawberries for communion," Cash says.

Oh my. That sounds sacrilegious. Only Cash would be so disrespectful. I roll my gaze heavenward.

God answered my morning prayer.

I prayed to open a suitable time to speak about God. God blew open the doors of opportunity . . . blew open my mouth . . . blew open Carries Rae's singing voice . . . and blew open our minds to the transforming power of God.

I smile at Caroline, who returns a tender smile.

Who knew Caroline bore such a burden? Before our eyes, she confessed, repented, and found peace. She's free. As Caroline thanks Carrie Rae and I profusely, we direct her praise back to God. We're mere vessels. God saves.

Then I turn toward Carrie Rae. "Would you want to share your letter?" Her Christian perspective might be an encouragement to Caroline.

A visual sweep of eyes moves onto Carrie Rae . . .

If you know someone needing help with forgiveness like Caroline found from her past, Focus on the Family Counseling Department is a ministry counseling service available at 1-855-771-HELP (4357)

CHAPTER 11

Do not let any unwholesome talk come out of your mouths,
but only what is helpful for building others up according to their
needs, that it may benefit those who listen.

Ephesians 4:29 NIV

After our lunch of . . . *surprise* . . . strawberries, we ask Carrie Rae if she wants to share her letter with the group. Quietly, she declines, fading back into herself. She reverts to hiding behind her hair and subtle rocking.

What makes a person so quiet?

"Can we have Sherry read her book to us? I really enjoy her articles. I will probably recognize some of them. Do you all want to listen to pass the time?" Rashida asks picking up my book, modeling it with melodramatic flair, twirling in her flowing robe to the clickity clack of her bangles.

I giggle.

Everyone nods in agreement, except Cash.

He grunts, mumbling again about needing more testosterone in here. Rashida presents my book back to me theatrically, and our book club officially starts.

Turning to chapter one, I remind everyone to pay attention because I include life-coach questions every few chapters. I explain we can hold group discussions. Deciding to involve the group more, I announce each person can read a chapter. My bossy side kicks in.

Clearing my throat, I read, *"Chapter One. Life is Messy. 'There*

is a way that appears to be right, but in the end, it leads to death.'
Proverbs 14:12 NIV. Life is messy. Unexpected things happen . . ."

Cash curses, interrupting loudly, "In the end, it leads to death?!
You should skip this chapter. It's morbid. We be trapped. Really,
Sherry!"

"Calm down Cash," Rashida commands. "I actually remember
reading her *Life is Messy* article. As I recall, it is hilarious. It's about
Sherry changing her baby's diaper."

"Wow, Rashida. You're right. It is about the time my baby Drew
shot at me with projectile diarrhea during his diaper change. You
remembered this from my magazine article? Impressive!"

"Like mother, like son," Cash laughs, plugging his nose
theatrically. He scoots away from me, pointing at my poo bag in the
corner.

"Oh, I remember it distinctly. The infant exploding diarrhea
hit your hair, your face, and it even smacked your lips," Rashida
giggles. "I got twins. I know all about diaper blowouts."

"Do you remember the Bible application, Rashida?" I ask.

She does not recall the spiritual point.

Figures. Of course not.

She only remembers the funny illustrations, but not the Biblical
application.

Continuing reading from the top, we alternate readers for each
chapter until getting to the life-coaching questions.

The first question deals with our daily screen time. The girls
agree we lack balance, needing less time on Facebook and television.
Except for Cash. He wishes he could afford all the sports channels,
because he would be on them day and night. Caroline presses her
lips together, slanting her head.

I am convicted, again, from my own writing, to stop wasting so
much time on Facebook. I use it for encouraging others, but often I
spend more time on Facebook than I do reading my devotions. Out
of balance.

The book's question about reading through the Bible perks the
responses. Rashida tells us she used to read through the Bible every
year.

What???

An atheist who knows the Bible?! Carrie and I snap our heads up. I have a theory for the reason Rashida rejects God, but I don't know the details. I want the backstory for Rashida's attitude.

Carrie Rae tells how she reads the Bible every morning like I do. I recognize her kindred spirit. We make a witnessing team in this vault. We both grin from ear to ear.

Caroline says she wants to read through the Bible every year like Carrie Rae and I do. I sit up taller as my heart lifts. I love the passion of new believers.

Digging in my duffle bag, I pull out a New Testament Bible I give to new believers at events. Presenting the Bible to Caroline, I ask her to sign her name and record today's I-got-saved date.

We celebrate her spiritual birthday by singing happy born-again birthday.

Carrie Rae and I encourage Caroline to find a Bible-teaching church, to read her Bible daily, and to talk to God often. I suggest she start reading in the book of John because it explains her newfound faith well. Caroline hugs her gifted Bible, rocking it softly like a precious newborn. Carrie Rae hums a beautiful lullaby.

Silence stills the room as Caroline cradles her Bible gently, sharing details of how the abortion caused her infertility.

She takes a deep breath, saying she must confess about the abortion to her husband Sterling.

It will be a brutal conversation emotionally.

When we get out of here, Caroline will need our support on her newfound-faith journey. Carrie Rae and I embrace Caroline, cuddling her Bible and bowing her head. We caress her shoulders lightly, praying earnestly for her upcoming deep talk with Sterling.

Rashida sits quietly on the sideline.

She does not interrupt.

Is Rashida softening to spiritual things? At least Rashida does not mock us this time.

As we discuss the remaining questions, we laugh about how ironic it is to be asked about being in a situation out of our control . . . while trapped in a bank in an out-of-control situation.

Ha!

We girls agree we make the best use of our time here in the

vault discussing life-coaching questions. I admit to the girls I can overreact to my son Drew's autism flare-ups. Often, I need patience like my husband. I think of myself as goal-oriented and motivated, but I wonder if bossy and demanding describe me more accurately?

We self-examine our lives.

Rashida shares the daunting transition of raising twins on her own in a new town. Head circling and finger snapping accompany her talking. I cannot imagine being a single mom of twins. I understand her assertive nature.

Carrie Rae does not interject much into our discussions. She listens mostly.

When we talk about the 48-hour-kindness-challenge question in the reading, we crack up thinking of Cash. He could never make it 48 hours straight without saying a single mean, snide, or nasty remark. No way! Cash cusses more than anyone I have ever heard. But we gals confirm Cash has a lovable side under his tattooed-flexing, profanity-flying self.

As a group, we decide to try going two days without a critical attitude, without a sarcastic eye roll, without a mean word, and without gossiping. We resolve to only speak kind words and let no unwholesome word out of our mouths. We accept the life-coaching question challenge to talk kind for two days. Gritting his teeth, Cash agrees to try it.

Yeah, Cash won't make it.

When we answer the humble servitude question, Carrie Rae seems to fit the description of a humble servant in my eyes. She helped me to share hope with Caroline. Even though Carrie Rae's shyness reigns, she knew singing her song would break the tension in the vault. She determined to give of herself. She stepped out of her box to offer her singing.

We discuss humility and servanthood, describing how we all want to improve.

Cash eavesdrops on the modest servant question and interrupts our book study. Pounding his upper torso, he claims, "I am pretty humble for as handsome as I am without my shirt."

He pumps up his chest, posing like a muscle model in a competition pose.

Oh . . . my . . . goodness.

Hooting and hollering breaks out in the vault.

Cash claims he is not in our book club, but he listens, chiding in regardless. In fairness, where else could the man go? Nowhere. He's stuck in a confined place with a pack of women.

Finishing the first set of life-coaching questions, we engage in supporting one another in our book club. Transforming into soulmates, we bond together, locking elbows arm in arm. We decide to exchange phone numbers, take cellphone photos, and plan to continue our book club when we get out. We turn off cell phones to save power between photos.

Cash demands I take a full-length photo of him kissing his biceps and showing off his tattoos. He wants his *Muscle Mania* wrestling pose as well. I oblige. Why? Like I will ever want these photos on my phone?! Whatever. Smiling, we take other group photos.

Cash gives us his girlfriend's phone number, asking us to include her in our book study. We agree. Then Cash tells us, with cussing scattered throughout, "Dani can learn a lot from you ladies."

Spattered with raw profanity, he says, "She lived a hard life. Her own dad forced her to prostitute as a kid so he could have da money for his drinking problem. He'd get her drunk and sell her off. I think she would fit in great wit you girls. You could help her."

Silent shock.

What??

My brain hurts from contemplating all that his girlfriend suffered. I shudder. This tops the most horrific personal story I have ever heard. I can't even wrap my mind around what Cash describes so casually. And Cash thinks his girlfriend will "fit in great" with us?!

Okay!

This stretches my church-in-America-suburbia mentality.

Oh, my. Lord, we can do this. I thought our book club group was about as misfit as it gets. It is going to get even more diverse when we resume outside this vault. Dani, Cash's girlfriend, or should I say fiancé, will be a unique addition to our already diverse group.

Huddling around the bowl with a few strawberries left, Rashida announces, "We need a name for our book club. Anyone got any ideas?"

We throw out all kinds of names. Cash suggests a cuss name featuring our "hot group of ladies" book club, adding many other inappropriate adjectives. Caroline gasps. I state Cash's name idea is too long and promiscuous.

I roll my eyes.

Oops. I need to start over on my 48-hour challenge with only kindness. I did not make it to an hour. Sarcastic eye rolls don't count as kind.

Caroline suggests *The Vault Book Club*.

Nah.

We're stumped.

Nothing seems to fit just right. Cash complains about running low on strawberries when Carrie Rae pipes in, "What about the *Bowl of Berries Book Club*?"

Yeah.

As we look at our variety of shoes circling the bowl of berries, we agree, "That's it!"

Bowl of Berries Book Club. The official name.

As a sweet-variety bunch of gals, the name fits. We anticipate reading through my book, *Invite Delight*, together. Our bonded group opened up deeply with our life-coaching questions. Who would have suspected this? Straddled by our jeopardizing circumstances, the book club distracts from our grave fears.

Will our plan to meet outside of the vault really happen? How will Dani fit in with us?

We should bring strawberries to every future meeting.

Lord, thank you for our *Bowl of Berries Book Club* and my precious new friends. As my eyes circle around the vault, I smile. I glance at our bowl with fewer strawberries, and my smile flips upside down to a frown.

Uh?

The bowl only has a handful of berries left. We will need to ration.

Will we run out of berries?

If I dwell on it, I will freak. Hunger pangs hit suddenly. My stomach growls.

CHAPTER 12

Listen to counsel and receive instruction,
That you may be wise in your latter days.
Proverbs 19:20 NKJV

What a miserable night. My stomach growls again.

One by one, we sit up, circling around our strawberry bowl. I ask the group, "What happened here? I thought we agreed to ration the berries last night."

All eyes turn to the large bowl with a single berry at the bottom. A lone strawberry with no chocolate. How strange. The bags are empty. The only remaining morsel is in the bottom of the bowl.

One berry.

Rashida glares. "Who ate the berries in the middle of the night?" she demands.

We scrutinize each other.

Mumbling, a grumbling fog clings to us.

Everyone denies the crime.

Rashida snarks, "Some jerk did this. It's not right. Who did this?"

She scowls around the circle, then stops directly at Cash. She darts him the evil eye.

"What? Why do you have to blame the guy? I didn't do anything," stammers out Cash, but Rashida and I notice the freshly smeared chocolate on the side of his mouth.

Umph.

We're a "hangry" mob of accusers, angry and hungry at the

same time. We pierce Cash with our glares until he throws his hands up and breaks.

"Okay, okay, okay. I admit it. I'm not the perfect hero y'all think I am. I'm a bad, bad guy," yells Cash as he looks at us, then looks directly at Rashida.

"If yo really knew the evil I'm capable of, you'd shoot me, Rashida. Yeah, I hungry. Cash does bad things. Cash takes what Cash wants. I ate the strawberries. I admit it. At first, I just took one. It tasted good, so I snuck another and another. Before I know it, I gobbled too many."

"At least you left one berry, Cash," says Carrie Rae in Cash's defense. She pulls out the water bottle from her backpack and holds it up. There is just maybe one more capful left for each of us.

"Cash did not drink any water in the night," she adds, trying to soften the mood.

Caroline, Rashida, and I glare at Cash.

The tension does not fade. Nice try, Carrie Rae.

"Yeah, but what's up with it not having any chocolate?" Rashida quips, giving Cash the evil eye. If looks could kill, Cash would be dead.

"When I realized I took the last one, I refrained. I stopped. I just sucked off the chocolate and put it back."

I palm smack my forehead.

The girls moan and groan.

Cash continues his sordid apology, laced with profanity and excuses.

"What do you want me to do? Say sorry? Soooorry."

Frowns and squints dart in his direction.

"No one's perfect. Look at Caroline. She's not perfect. We all got slop we try to hide. I just got caught this time. I never get caught. For 17 years, I ain't been caught. I hear all you goody two-shoes. My bros taught me different. It's only a crime, if you do the time. So, I don't get caught."

Rashida barks back at Cash with, "Wow, Cash. Leave Caroline out of this. Caroline's confession to us is private and confidential. That's why I don't tell people about my business. You're a scoundrel for bringing her into your sad, sorry apology. You best not bring up my letter in public. I shared too much. You got that, Cash?"

Rashida points her finger inches from Cash's face.

With intense eyes, she shouts, "And you got caught with chocolate on your face! So just shut up you . . . you . . . you pec-flexing, over-confident, chocolate-sucking, strawberry hog."

I want to stand up and give her an ovation.

I refrain.

Instead, I pray I can deescalate the tension.

"Okay, it's natural to feel tense. It reeks in here. We're starved, and we're thirsty. How about we read through the next chapters and answer a set of life-coach questions to get our minds off this?" I suggest as I open my book to the earmarked page.

Rashida injects, "We all know who needs life-coaching, Sherry."

She circles her head, points her finger, and gives Cash another glare, lecturing, "Cash, you best pay attention. You need serious help. What man hogs four women's food supply? My deceased husband would NEVER be such a weasel. NEVER!"

"So much for Rashida's 48-hour kindness challenge. She needs a do-over," Cash chides.

Oh, boy! What are we? Third graders fighting at recess?

To ease tensions, I read *Invite Delight* where we left off.

"Don't Swallow the Pill. "Get rid of all bitterness, rage, anger, harsh words, and slander, as well as all types of evil behavior. Instead, be kind to each other, tenderhearted, forgiving one another, just as God through Christ has forgiven you." Eph. 4:31-32 NLT. Have you ever felt the seed of bitterness grow inside you? Spit it out. Get rid of it. Period. It will devour, consume, and turn your face into a prune. Ugh! I have heard it said, 'Bitterness is the poison you drink yourself, trying to kill another.' Yeah, this may sound harsh, but it is true."

It's a God-thing on the timing.

Rashida snatches the book out of my hands shouting, "No way. You just added what you want to preach at us."

She scans the page.

"Whoa, that IS the next chapter," admits Rashida, her eyes opening wider. She shakes her head back and forth, digesting the reading.

"Would you like to continue reading, or should I?" I ask with a subtle gotcha smirk.

Rashida shoves the book back as if it contains cooties.

"You got this. Read on."

She replies with one eyebrow raised up, puckering her lips like she tasted sour lemons.

Finishing the reading, I hand the book to Cash, piping out, "Your turn, Cash."

Cash reads slowly, but loudly. We all look around as he reads because, once again, the title fits.

Cash reads, *"Are You a Giver or Taker? 'The one who blesses others is abundantly blessed; those who help others are helped.' Proverb 11:25 MSG. Do you walk into a room and make it all about you? Are you non-verbally projecting, 'Hello! It's ME. I'm here.?' Is it all about you, you, you? Or do you walk into the room, and it is all about others? Are you more like, 'Hello! It's YOU. So glad YOU are here?' Are you known as a grabber getter or a gift giver? Is it all about YOU, or is it all about OTHERS?"*

Cash continues to read with his bare back against the wall. All the while, we look around at each other, silently air-laughing. The entire chapter describes Cash's problem last night. He grabbed up and snarfed down the group's food supply. Selfish.

God's timing on the reading rolls in with perfection again.

Yeah, God!

As we pass the book and tag-team reading chapters, we belly laugh as Caroline reads the *Not the Shoes* chapter. She reads where I pee my skirt, dousing the fancy shoes with pee pee spraying out like a fountain.

Laughing, Cash pulls my stilettos out of the bag, and we toss the heels around the circle like hot potatoes contaminated with pee cooties. I do not know how Caroline can concentrate, but she reads on steadily with the shoes bouncing around our circle of sillies.

It's good to laugh and release the pressures of being cooped up.

The life-coach questions at the end of this section uncover profound emotion. We get deep into dialog. During the first question, we discuss bitterness. Rashida sits unusually quiet until she spills her guts about her deep anger and bitterness issues.

Is she about to reveal the death details?

Laura Loveberry

CHAPTER 13

Because your love is better than life,
my lips will glorify you.
Psalm 63:3 NIV

Rashida confesses she moved out of Chicago to protect her yet-to-be-born twins. Her head twitches and her voice builds in volume. She raises to vibrato as she ends up screaming, "Someone shot and killed my beloved Jonathon and our two precious boys in a drive-by shooting . . . as they were walking . . . up the steps . . . to enter . . . the church!"

The decibels of her volume equal the terror trapped in her darkest hour.

"My husband opened up the church every Sabbath morning with the boys."

Eyes flashing and nostrils flaring, she rages. "They would pray over the pews . . . for all who would come and sit during church . . . and some thug . . . evil thug . . . shoots them for no reason . . . NO REASON . . . NONE."

Rashida's chest heaves.

She gasps for air between words.

Her fists clench and her entire body trembles. She grits her teeth as saliva sprays out with each gust.

Finally, her rage dissipates. For now. She opens her mouth into an "O" shape, breathing several calming breaths.

Where are her tears? She has no tears, just anger.

After several slower, deliberate inhales and exhales, Rashida speaks with a lower volume and with control. "Now you understand why I formed a non-profit. I give ten percent of all my jewelry sales to support families of victims of violent crime. Trying not to be trapped in bitterness, I did something positive. I need to make a safe life for my girls, Jona and Jamila."

She looks around at her mute audience.

"Chicago police never found the killer," Rashida says.

I notice Cash's face. It's as pale as my notebook paper.

He hangs his head low, sniffling, and wipes his nose. Cash is visibly the most upset. That's a surprise for a "tough" guy from Chicago.

We wipe our tears. Except Rashida. She does not shed a drop.

We solved the mystery of why Rashida turned to atheism. Despite of her nonprofit organization, Rashida's bitterness grows because of the death of her loved ones.

And for this . . . we have Jesus.

But how do I help Rashida find peace in Jesus?

She's trapped in her own vault of vitriol for seventeen years.

She needs to find a key to open that door, but who can give it to her?

Jesus!

Jesus can open the door. We sit still in frozen silence. Except for Cash.

Cash reaches in his pockets, adjusts his pants, taps his foot repeatedly, and cracks his neck. Talk about uncomfortable.

Holding the book, Carrie Rae surprises us again by asking to jump down to the question about living in the land in-between. It's about the time in between the start of a trial and the triumph at the end.

She softly explains, "I live in the land in between. Like Rashida, I crashed into tragedy. My dad and my mom drove me to choir practice at church. A drunk driver smashed into us head on. We all wore seatbelts, but they never had a chance. My parents died instantly. I laid in a hospital bed for a week before my big brothers could bear to tell me."

We sat perfectly still. No one moved.

Carrie Rae speaks with a sincere smile. "My church family was and is wonderful. My dad was a leader in the church and a missionary with my mom. Everyone loved them and reached out to us. They brought meals, prayed over us, and to this day they still help us with bills."

She smiles, adding, "The church is a family to me and my brothers. We love Jesus, just like my mom and dad. I know we will see them again in heaven. Our worst day was their BEST day."

Cash scowls and blurts out with profanity.

After his cussing spree, he asks, "What does that mean? Worst day was their best day?"

"My mom and dad went directly to Jesus. BEST. DAY. EVER. For my in-love parents to see their Savior face to face was their most glorious day. It was our worst day ever, for sure, because we miss them. That's why I can relate to the 'land in between.'"

Carrie Rae makes direct eye contact with Cash.

"I experienced a tragic trial. I am living in between for Jesus, and I will see my parents later in triumph when I go to Jesus," answers Carrie Rae.

"Carrie Rae, you remind me of a verse in the Bible. 'Though You slay me, yet I will praise you.' It's something like that, but it goes back to trusting God when we do not understand his ways," I tell her.

Carrie Rae takes a deep breath. "Yes, Mrs. Strawberry. I said all this because I want to sing you the lyrics of a song that I wrote on my hospital bed. At my parent's funeral, I wanted to sing it. I choked."

She cleared her throat to compose herself.

"Some mean girls, who used to make fun of me for being a half-breed, showed up at the funeral. Back in school, they used to tease and bully me about my race and my singing. When I saw those upperclassmen whispering, my mind went back to the past. I convinced myself they were gossiping about me. I started to sing. Holding the microphone, I turned red and forgot the words. I dropped the mic and ran off."

Carrie Rae feels like God prompts her to sing it for us. Public singing terrifies her now, but her parents taught her to obey God even when it is hard.

Caroline and I smile at Carrie Rae to encourage her as she unveils her story.

The song came from Psalm 63. It's her favorite.

She quotes the first part, "'O God, You are my God; I shall seek You earnestly; My soul thirsts for You, my flesh yearns for You, In a dry and weary land where there is no water. Thus, I have seen You in the sanctuary, To see Your power and Your glory. Because Your lovingkindness is better than life, my lips will praise You. I will bless You as long as I live; I will lift up my hands in Your name.'"

I mouth along with her because this is one of my favorite Psalms, too. I think of lifting my hands in sign-language ministry with these verses.

"Sing for us, Carrie Rae," I request for our group.

Rashida stares downward.

"Yes," pipes in Cash along with his usual cussing.

"Oh, I would love to hear your sweet voice," adds Caroline.

The vault transforms to our church again. Carrie closes her eyes and sings tenderly.

"I will praise You as long as I live. In Your name . . . I lift up my hands."

As she repeats the chorus, she raises her hands high, opening her eyes, beaming a smile. Carrie Rae rises to her feet, making direct eye contact with each of us. Picking up the pace, she sings boldly onward, *"Whatever I go through, whatever I do, oo, oo, with singing lips, I'll glorify You."*

We join in, clapping to the beat.

She motions for us to stand with her and sing.

We all sing, *"I will praise You as long as I live. In Your name . . . I lift up my hands."* Now we are singing . . . and raising hands . . . and clapping . . . and dancing . . . and bouncing . . . and laughing.

I grab my phone out of my bag while still dancing, power it up and start recording our joyous party of praise. With a radiant smile, Carrie Rae sings the second verse. We dance around, bumping and boogieing in our tight quarters.

Cash jams on an air guitar.

Caroline gently bops.

Rashida blows away our impromptu dance-off with her rhythmic moves and head-jiving smoothness.

I crack everyone up with my 80s robot dance while filming with my phone.

Carrie Rae sings exuberantly, *"My soul thirsts for You, in a dry and weary land, because Your love is better than life!"*

Swept up in emotion, we all join in the party, dancing, bobbing our heads, giggling, and jiving.

Without warning, the vault door handle moves . . .

CHAPTER 14

Greater love has no one than this:
to lay down one's life for one's friends.
John 15:13 NIV

The massive vault door rolls open.

As I whip around with eyes wide open, my phone flies out of my hand. It smacks onto the plastic bags full of excrement in the corner. The recording light remains on.

Our screeching pierces the vault.

A big man, dressed in all black and holding an AK-47, blocks the doorway.

He wears a baseball cap under his pulled-up black hoodie. His beard and mustache dangle, obviously fake and glued on crooked. Duct tape holds on his black gloves at the wrists of his hoodie. He sweats profusely. I suspect he wears a bullet-proof vest under his bumpy sweatshirt. He sports a backpack, and he taped ammunition all over himself.

In a fraction of a second, he seizes Caroline by her blonde hair like a WWE wrestler, yanking her petite body against his chest. We shriek, jumping back against the wall. I snap my head toward Cash.

Cash understands we're counting on our shirtless bodyguard.

He addresses the gunman firmly, "You don't want her. She's got a bad case of diarrhea." I wonder where he got that idea?

Right on cue, Caroline grabs her gut, moaning. I'm an excellent teacher. The gunman jerks Caroline's head back, ramming the gun into her temple.

I scream, pressing my hands over my eyes and peering through my spread fingers.

Carrie Rae freezes. Both her hands cover her open mouth and her half-closed eyes. The whimpering starts.

Cash shouts confidently, "Take me!"

Cash points at his chest. "She's a mess. I'll cooperate with you as a hostage. You don't want her."

Caroline pees down her legs, spraying urine off her stilettos. She learned that slick move from me, too. Despite the grave danger, I pause, giving her a proud wink for using my trick.

My mind races, tumbling into haphazard thoughts.

The gunman looks down, grunts, and shoves Caroline to the vault floor. The empty berry bowl clamors around. Almost slipping, the disgruntled gunman kicks the tumbling bowl fiercely.

He waves the gun back and forth at us. Is he panicking?

A voice outside the vault yells, "Come on. Come on. What's taking you so long? Grab a hostage. Let's GO!"

Cash reaches in his pocket and throws his wadded marriage proposal note at me.

"Give this to my girl, Dani."

He winks.

I gasp as he steps right in front of the jittery gunman. Cash Jones steps up with his chest inches from the pointing gun barrel.

Are you kidding me?

Cash turns back toward us, stating bravely, "I got you."

He forms fists, pounds his *Cash-is-King* arm tattoo twice, and points at us, bragging, "Cash is King."

He turns back to face the gunman eye to eye and pressures him. "Go with it, man."

Cash raises his hands above his head in surrender.

"Come on, NOW!" shouts the deep voice of the man outside the vault. He's losing his patience.

The jittering gunman, under pressure, mutters, "This better work. You go first."

Cash struts out the door with hands over his head like a superman about to fly. He is a hero without a cape. Who knew Cash Jones would actually step up into danger to protect us?!

The gunman follows Cash, pointing the gun at his back. Cash keeps his hands above his head. The gunman tracks behind, jerking his head from side to side nervously, checking around him.

Rashida murmurs, "Not on my watch." She jumps up, grabbing one of the plastic bags full of urine and feces.

Caroline blocks Rashida with her arms and legs stretched out like a human fence.

"What are you doing?! Let the police handle this," Caroline insists.

Caroline grabs the door handle and pulls.

Carrie Rae remains stunned in the corner, pale-faced and immobile.

Just before the door shuts, Rashida lifts the plastic bag like she is an NFL quarterback. She lunges forward, sliding through Caroline's pee puddle, heaving the bag toward the closing gap in the door. With Rashida's precision aim and power, the bag of feces soars through the narrowing opening.

KERSPLAT!

It hits the target.

Bursting on the back of the gunman's head, the fecal matter splatters down his back just as the door shuts tight. We don't hear gunshots.

Phew!

I can't believe Rashida did that.

I can't believe Cash did that.

I can't believe Caroline did that.

Caroline shuts us back in the vault again. We look around at each other as Carrie Rae and I slide down the wall to the floor.

The color is gone from our faces. I quiver uncontrollably. Carrie Rae goes back to whimpering and rocking. Caroline paces. Rashida rattles her bracelets, nostrils flaring, glaring at the door.

I giggle a little.

Rashida whips her head around at me.

She peeps a giggle. Caroline's mouth curls to an unlikely grin. Unexpectedly, the girls join me in a growing "gigglefest." Terribly inappropriate laughter breaks out. Caroline and Carrie Rae lean over laughing. We all bust a gut, rolling around the urine-splattered floor. I smack my hands on the floor, splattering the pee pee.

We snap.

We lose it.

The pressure cracks us.

"Okay," Caroline speaks, bringing us back to reality. "They exited the building. Shouldn't we pray the snipers don't shoot Cash accidentally?"

"Yes, let's pray popcorn prayers right now," I answer, grabbing hands. We circle up, sitting on the dry part of the floor. Even Rashida holds hands.

"What is popcorn prayer?" Caroline asks.

Unexpectedly, Rashida answers. "Everyone prays one-sentence prayers in no specific order. You just pop pray quick prayers like popcorn in a microwave."

She shrugs her shoulders. "I know church, you all. Come on."

An atheist. Who knew?

Carrie Rae, Caroline, and I pray brief prayers for Cash's safety. Rashida holds our hands but does not pray aloud. At least she's in our circle of "sistas."

That's progress.

We plead to God on behalf of Cash.

We sing a glorious amen song.

"Let's get this vault cleaned up. I think we'll be out of here soon," Caroline says.

We put our purses in order. Rashida wipes up the floor with her scarf. It's our mop and bathroom door scarf. Rashida won't wear that again.

I find Cash's cell phone and slide it into my purse. I will give it to Dani when we meet her.

Noticing me, Carrie Rae asks to see his phone. She has a cord and connects it to his phone to make a copy of the recording Cash took of us singing and signing together. We guess his password, "Cashisking," on the first try. *Giggle.* We unlock his phone. She transfers the video to both our phones.

I notice my phone recorded all of our action when the gunman burst in the door.

"Hey, girls, check this out. My phone recorded from the floor. It caught the action of Cash standing up for us."

We gather around to watch the video. We hoot and holler when Cash said, "Cash got you," and "Cash is king."

Cash stepped up, making us proud. Here we thought he was a "weasel" like Rashida in her rant. It turns out weasels can wiggle their way to "herodom." Cash Jones became our hero.

Who'd of thought?!

As we all check for our letters we wrote to our families, I dig for my notebook. I sense a song flooding into my mind because we've become "sistas" in here. I find it.

I scribble out the words as quickly as they flow into my mind.

CHAPTER 15

Anyone who loves God
must also love their brother and sister.
1 John 4:21b NIV

The song lyrics pour from my heart to the paper.

"Through all of my brokenness and all of my strife, God blessed me with friends for life. And I thank the LORD for giving to me, my sisters in Christ who pray for me. I felt so lost and deeply scarred. At times, my heart felt so hard. She told me to go wherever Christ leads, even if all I can see are my own needs.

(Chorus) My sisters in Christ have stood by my side. She has seen me laugh and heard my cry. My sisters in Christ know God's in control. And when I'm feeling down, she prays for my soul.

I know God has a plan to strengthen our souls. Our family and friends play a part in that role, and when my candle hasn't burned all that bright, my sister shares with me a part of her light. (Chorus) I'm going to follow Jesus all of my days. I'm encouraged to do more when I see my sister going the same way. (Chorus)."

I read it to my vault sisters. They applaud, cheer, and shout their admirations for the lyrics. Carrie Rae comes up with a tune right off the top of her head.

Yeah!

She writes the guitar chords down on my paper. Crowding around the notebook with the lyrics, we all sing ecstatically through it acapella three times. We sing, we laugh, we create dance moves mixed with sign-language drama while giggling all over our silly selves.

Do we really want to leave? Vaults are for dancing.

Joy fills this jail.

I admit to the gaggle of girls, "I love you. I'm gonna miss you all."

Sweet Caroline adds, "Hey, we meet at your house when we get out, right? We can pray every day for Cash starting now. Nobody forget. And let's all pray about meeting Cash's girlfriend, Dani. I hope she joins us. And please, please, please, everyone pray for me. I cannot imagine how my Sterling will respond to telling my secret sin to him."

I remind her, "Hey girl, remember YOU . . . ARE . . . FORGIVEN. God cast your sin away as far as the east is from the west."

I swoop in a broad gesture like I am throwing away her sins.

"God remembers your sin no more. What's red as scarlet God made white as snow."

"I believe that, Sherry. Praise God. But will . . . but CAN . . . Sterling forgive me?" she asks.

Carrie Rae and I give her a reserved grin, raising our eyebrows with hopeful expressions.

Honestly, I don't know. But I don't dare say that out loud.

I remind her to keep reading her new Bible and the book of John. It will help her journey. We embrace in a group hug. I love our gaggle of girls. We look deeply into one another's eyes.

Clutching the group, my lip quivers. I start to cry.

"I know when we leave here . . . *sniffle, sniffle* . . . everything might change. We may just go back to our busy lives and not stay in touch. That will crush me . . . *sobbing* . . . I need our friendship. I don't want to . . . *deep breath* . . . leave all of you sisters. We're like a band of brothers, only we're a band of BROADS," I say.

We giggle.

I blow a snot bubble. It sticks on my nose.

Rashida pops it with her finger, commenting, "Only true sisters do this," and she winks at me.

Eew!

Caroline crunches her face. Carrie Rae hops around, face

scrunching and waving jazz fingers. Laughter explodes.

"Let's make a sisterhood alliance and pinky promise to meet each week. We can finish Sherry's book and do all the life-coaching questions together," Rashida says. Tears flowing, she adds, "And let's all include Dani, because she will need us whether or not she knows it."

After Rashida wipes off her slimy finger, we hook pinkies, linking our circle of sisters together.

My tears flow, nose running, but I don't care. I do not release my pinky to wipe my face. Gazing around the circle of happy-tear-drenched faces, I beam my broadest smile. Joy floats around our prison vault like a pleasant aroma, despite the urine smell.

Carrie Rae Hucklenuckle . . . *giggle* . . . starts singing her song titled *Praise Chorus*. We all join in, swaying side to side, dancing to the feet-tapping beat.

"I will praise You as long as I live. In Your name, I lift up my hands. Whatever I go through, whatever I do, oo, oo, with singing lips, I'll glorify You . . ."

Wrapping arms around each other's waists, we form a circle scarf of sisters woven together. We resemble Paul in prison when he wrote, "Rejoice in the Lord always; again, I say, 'rejoice!'"

I sense the same joy Paul, author of Philippians, felt in a Roman prison over 2000 years ago. We smile radiantly, praising God in our prison. Our vault is a prison, but nothing can stop our praise!

I don't want it to end.

Carrie sings the chorus beautifully.

Caroline glows.

Rashida smiles.

I breathe in the moment of perfect peace, looking around our sacred circle of soulmates. In a complete mess, we are blessed. I breathe in deeply and exhale. I am both exhausted and refreshed.

Suddenly, we hear the door opening slowly. Who breaks up our precious praise moment? Is it the good guys . . . or the bad guys?

Eyes widen, and eyebrows raise staring at the creaking door.

CHAPTER 16

I will praise you, Lord, with all my heart;
I will tell of all the marvelous things you have done.
Psalm 9:1 NLT

The door slowly opens as a barrage of warriors dressed in all black implode through the doorway, pointing big guns. It's like an alien invasion of soldiers in black helmets with cameras on the front and flashlights. They wear side microphones and black boxes strap around their arms, legs, and chest. Black kneepads protrude with their pant legs tucking into army boots. Their armor and bullet-proof vests bulk them up like the Hulk. They look like *Star Wars* storm troopers in black.

We shriek, jumping back, clenching each other and plastered against the back wall.

I squeeze my interior muscle to prevent peeing. That trick won't work with these big bad boys. This legion of combatants means business.

Are they the good guys . . . or bad guys?

"Hands up!" the leader shouts.

We instantly throw our hands in the air.

I glance frantically at Rashida. Don't even consider tossing another bag of feces, girlfriend. Thankfully, Rashida complies like the rest of us trembling chicks.

"Is there a perpetrator in here?" barks the leader as we hold our hands high.

"Only you guys," Rashida quivers.

We don't know if they are the good guys . . . or the bad guys.

They appear highly trained with their gun handling and teamwork.

"Hallway clear, Sarge," a voice from outside the vault reports.

Escorting us to the hallway, they permit us to lower our trembling hands. We cluster together again as I notice Carrie Rae bending down, fixing the moss at the base of a fake tree. That's odd. They separate us, spreading us all out. After a quick frisk of each person, we huddle back together.

"We're FBI. Our SWAT team is scanning the remaining building for explosives," he states matter-a-fact. "Gunshot damage to this vault set back your release."

"We will take you to the hospital for medical treatment. We'll get your info, and your families will meet you at the hospital."

He pauses, lifting his helmet shield, holding back a smile and stating, "You're safe now."

We smile, breathing in a deep sigh in unison.

It's finally over. It's over. Our questions fly at the officers.

"Is Cash safe?" Caroline asks.

"Are the police injured?" Carrie Rae asks.

"Is anyone else trapped?" Rashida asks. "Did you catch the bad guys?"

The relief melts my legs as tunnel vision fogs my view. My eyes retract to darkness. I fade downward. Fleeting white spots of light spin in the darkness of my clouding view. My arms feel like lead.

I dissolve onto the floor . . .

****

I hear a siren in the distance and voices as I blink my eyes. The jarring from the ambulance gurney jolts me back into reality. A team of medical staff surrounds me as I gaze at the IV equipment leading from the tubes taped to my arm.

"You're dehydrated, Honey. You fainted. We're going to take care of you," the medic says, rubbing my shoulder in a soothing manner.

"You've experienced a big ordeal."

"Where is my bag? Where are my strawberries? I have a speaking event to get to," I say to the medical team.

They glance at each other, raising eyebrows.

Maybe I am being ridiculous. I read the expressions passing back and forth. Okay. Perhaps their diagnosis is legit. I sit up, looking around the ambulance. My head spins. They ease me back down gently.

Yep. I'm a mess.

Where is Kyle? I bend my elbows to clutch my strawberry earrings. I need Kyle.

****

I wake up again with a tender kiss on my forehead. Aww. I know those soft lips anywhere.

It's Kyle.

Am I dreaming or am I still trapped in the vault?

Pinch.

Nope.

This is real.

My Kyle and I touch noses as he moves the loose hair back from my face. My breath must be horrible. I did not brush my teeth in days. Moving my head to the side, I wrap my arms around his neck. What? I still dangle with IVs attached to my arm.

We are in a hospital room.

"I love you. Praise God you're safe. We prayed all night in a vigil at church. Everyone's thrilled you're safe," he whispers between kisses, snuggling my cheek. "And Drew can't wait to see you."

I turn my head to take a deep breath near my armpit area. Someone gave me a sponge bath and washed my hair.

Ahhhh!

I am clean in my hospital gown. My skin feels soft and fresh, like a newborn baby. I wondered if I would ever see this day.

Pinch.

It's real.

I hear a knock at the door as two police officers enter. Captain

Thomas Miller introduces himself and his partner, flashing their badges.

"Do you mind if we speak to Sherry Kay Strawberry? We need to get as much information as we can while it is as fresh as possible. You are the last of the hostages to interview."

"Are the other girls here, too?!" I interrupt in a perky voice. "I can't wait to see them. Are any other bank patrons injured? Did ya nab the bad guys? How's Cash? Is he here? What about . . ."

"Slow down. Let's get our interview done, if you are up to it. Most of the other bank patrons escaped in the chaos. It's going to take time to recall the events of three days," the captain says.

"You girls may get together AFTER our second set of interviews wrap up. You might remember more details later to help locate the hostage, Cash Jones."

"WHAT? You mean you did not free Cash or catch the bank robbers yet?"

I interrupt him again, furrowing my eyebrows. My eyes pierce. I continue scowling as he replies.

"Ma'am, this is an ongoing investigation. Cash Jones has not been located. We will interview each of you today and tomorrow for additional details. You can call me any time of the day if you remember anything you left out," Captain Miller says, handing me his business card.

"Don't listen to social media and the news. If you accidentally hear something, take notes on where you heard it. You are the key witnesses to this crime. The suspects are at large and with a hostage. We need this case solved, and Cash brought back ASAP. If you girls get together after all the interviews, do not discuss the case."

"Can Kyle stay with me?"

Kyle squeezes my hand like he never wants to leave me.

"We are going to ask him to leave for the interview. At any point, if you feel too tired to continue, we can take a break. We would love to get information now while it is fresh in your mind. I will record everything on a voice recorder and video."

His partner sets up the camera on a tripod near the bedside. I push the button to raise the head of the bed.

"Is my purse in here?" I ask Kyle. "Nobody wants to be frightened seeing me without makeup,"

"Honey, you look fine, but here's your purse."

I rummage, searching desperately for mascara and lipstick.

"Am I the only one objecting to the filming without makeup?"

"Just you and Mrs. Caroline Forbes-Radshaw," the officer states, half grinning.

I snicker.

Kyle cradles both sides of my face, kissing me on the lips. A loud smackeroo sound reverberates.

Whoa!

He must miss me to smooch like this in front of strangers. Kyle blushes three levels of red. He did not expect the volume of his smacking kiss.

"Did ya get my hot hubster's smoochie on film?"

I giggle as Kyle strides out of the hospital room, hand covering his face. The police detectives don't crack a smile. *Sheesh.* Lighten up fellows.

The interview starts with, "Tell me about the day before you went to the bank. Give me step by step from the time you got up and dictate the entire day."

Yeah. It is going to be a long interview. If it helps get Cash back, I'll give them every single detail from Friday to today.

Here we go.

After my play-by-play of my last few days in sequential order, they ask me a series of detailed questions about what I just told them. They each take notes as they record my answers. On top of this, they ask me to provide a written statement of the events that transpired.

I hope the girls can meet after these intense interviews.

The officers return my cell phone they took to make a copy of our vault videos and photos. They keep Cash's phone. You would have thought they won the lottery when receiving his phone.

The detectives reluctantly agree that we can convene our book club after our statements are in and the interviews completed.

We get to meet for the *Bowl of Berries Book Club* next week!

Yippie Skippy!

The first meeting with our bonded sisters will be at our house. I plan to prepare strawberries for refreshments. I hope Dani, Cash's gal, will be brave enough to come.

How is Rashida handling the post trauma for a second time in her life?

Questions spin a hundred miles per hour. The captain said I could not LISTEN to the news and social media. But he didn't say I couldn't POST Carrie Rae's and my duet video or shirtless Cash's hero moment video. I can post these, right?

Click. Done. Posted.

All I want is to be in our bed tonight snuggling beside Kyle.

But where is Cash? Is Cash alive ... or dead in a ditch somewhere?

CHAPTER 17

Bear one another's burdens...
Galatians 6:2a NASB

My cell phone chimes.

I hope it's Dani, Cash's girlfriend. Cash gave me her number, insisting we include her in our book club when we get out. I finally got ahold of her and invited her to the *Bowl of Berries Book Club.* Dani said she would let me know.

"Hello."

"This is Captain Thomas Miller."

Doggone.

It's not Dani, but my heart stops. I hold my breath.

"We scheduled a press conference to get Cash's face out there in public and answer questions about the case."

Rats! Cash remains missing. I exhale at the bad news.

The captain explains we can debrief two hours before with the released hostages. Then we have the option of talking with the press at a podium set up in front of the police department. The more publicity, the better the chances of solving the crime and getting Cash back.

The captain says we need to glance at the prosecutor first before answering any question publicly. If the prosecutor nods, we can answer. If not, we reply something about not being at liberty to answer the question.

I jump up and down doing my 80s robot dance, beaming a smile after I hang up. The girls are getting back together . . . *whoop, whoop* . . . and we can DO something constructive to help find Cash Jones. It feels helpless not doing anything. Finally, we can take action.

****

We run to each other, smashing hugs and bouncing up and down joyfully as each former hostage sister arrives. You would have thought we were lifetime best friends. I suppose being locked in a vault 24 hours a day for a weekend constitutes a lifetime together. We laugh and love on each other as we turn around and see her.

"Is that her?"

"That's got to be Dani."

"I hope she likes us."

"She does sport blue-tip hair."

"I'm nervous. What if she doesn't want to come to the book club?"

As our gaggle of gals continues whispering questions, I approach the woman in faded jeans, biker boots, a wrinkled black t-shirt. Timidly, she smiles, revealing several missing teeth. My eyes go right to her teeth as I introduce myself. Her teeth display black decay and gaps. Each person in life is unique.

Dani confirms this.

"Hi," says Dani with the low and raspy voice of a smoker. Her hair straggles. She looks tough. And from what Cash told us, she lived the hardest life I can't even imagine. My mind flashes back to Cash in the vault talking about her being sex-trafficked.

I wipe the pity off my face.

"Yo. Thanks for calling me, Sherry. I recognized yo name from the sign on da edge of town. It's a . . . um . . . heck of an honor to meet yous," Dani says.

Dani rambles on nervously, peppering her sentences with swear words, then pausing and apologizing.

I can hear Cash in Dani's voice. They may talk slightly uncouth, but are a likeable match made to be together.

Slapping her hand over her mouth, she opens her eyes wide, saying, "I'm so sorry. I be tryin' not to cuss if I come to you's all

100

book club. I gots a bad cuss habit to break. I'm gonna stop drinking, too. At least, I'm gonna try. I want to come to yo group. If Cash wanted me to come, then I best be joining yo gang."

"Thank you for accepting our invitation to the *Bowl of Berries Book Club*. Cash definitely wanted you to be a part of us. We're thrilled you will join."

I walk her back to my cheery girls with their friendliest of faces grinning toward her. We embrace Dani in a grandiose group hug. Since we've prayed for her, we bond with Dani naturally. Hugging her somehow feels like embracing Cash. Does Dani sense our loyalty to her? Who knows? But her radiant gap-tooth smile tells me love surrounds her. She beams amid her sadness.

Twenty-five different microphones jam together in front of the podium. Captain Thomas Miller steps up, commanding the crowd's attention.

He shares how the police officers performed with excellence, freeing most of the bank employees and patrons. The heist could have been worse. He explains how the suspects entered the get-away van using Cash as a human shield. The megaphone negotiations did not work. The SWAT snipers did not have a secure shot, and the police prioritized the safety of the hostage.

He glances over at Dani, assuring her with a nod.

The captain explains the low-riding escape vehicle had no windows behind the front seat. The criminals executed a well-conceived plan to slip down through a pre-cut hole in the van's floorboard and escape. They discovered the suspects lifted the manhole cover and lowered themselves down through the street sewer system beneath the road.

He shared how the negotiation team worked the megaphone to encourage a surrender as the fugitives fled the scene underground.

A second vehicle waited nearly a mile away. There is no description of the escape vehicle. The captain describes the three suspects as armed and dangerous. He warns the public not to approach the suspects, call 911, and keep a distance. Cash Jones' whereabouts—unknown. Police assume he remains a hostage.

They need tips in the case. Captain Miller said Jones risked his life to spare Caroline from being a hostage. The captain holds up a recent photo of Jones.

The crowd cheers.

Dani's eyes fill with tears.

We instinctively hold our hands over our heart.

Miller states his gratitude that no one was seriously injured. But he wants Jones spared from any harm and the suspects apprehended. He looks compassionately toward Dani each time he mentions Cash's name. Dani nods her head in agreement with the rest of us behind the podium. Rashida and I rest our hands on Dani's shoulders, squeezing her gently.

Miller adds that many may have already seen the viral internet video of Cash Jones in the vault.

Cheering and robust applause break out.

After the crowd quiets, he verifies the authenticity of the video filmed with Sherry Kay Strawberry's cell phone. Captain Thomas describes how the phone video stayed on when the suspects opened the vault door, nabbing Cash Jones.

Leaning her head against mine, Caroline whispers. "It's just great knowing the world observed my overflow spraying on my stilettos." She drips with sarcasm, scrunching her face.

"I trained you well," I smirk back at her under my breath. "We got skills."

Giggle.

Listening, Carrie Rae leans in, saying under her breath, "The video of Caroline peeing just pinged over 300,000 hits. It grows in viewers as we speak."

"You're not helping my self-esteem, Carrie Rae," Caroline mutters.

The captain gives kudos to his police officers, the bank employees, and the patrons who escaped. He thanks everyone for their patience and prayers in the volatile situation. He opens up for questions from reporters. The press asks to talk with Dani Jones, the girlfriend of Cash Jones.

Dani marches up to the podium, rather manly.

CHAPTER 18

For the life of every living thing
is in his hand and the breath of every human being.
Job 12:10 NLT

Dani explains how Cash has the same last name, but they're not married. She blushes, attempting to talk without showing her teeth, not opening her mouth wide. She explains they moved here recently, trying to start a new life away from the crime in the big city.

She smiles a huge toothless smile as the cameras focus on her. Dani announces this small town is best for them since she is pregnant with Cash's baby.

Cameras flash.

The crowd buzzes.

Gasp!

"Whoa!"

"Oh My!"

The crowd energizes with the hottest news. Exclamations repeat throughout the large gathering. My girls surround Dani, bouncing up and down like in a dance mosh pit party.

"Congratulations!"

"This news blesses us!"

"Dani, we're so excited for you and Cash!"

The captain raises his hands, stepping back in front of the podium. We bounce in our huddle hug of pandemonium, celebrating the life within Dani's womb.

My eyes meet with Caroline's momentarily. I wonder if her heart stings a little over the announcing of Dani's pregnancy.

I wink at Caroline in the chaos. She knows I understand her barrenness and ache. We keep dancing. No one notices our glances.

We stay wrapped together. Captain Miller addresses the onslaught of questions from hand-raising, shouting reporters.

"How far along are you, Dani?" a reporter yells.

Stepping back up to the microphones, Dani answers, "I just found out. Cash doesn't even know yet. Let's bring CASH BACK!"

Behind the reporters, the crowd chants.

"CASH BACK! CASH BACK! CASH BACK!"

The volume escalates. Soon all the crowd yells in unison. Dani flashes her gap-filled smile, throwing her hands up in the victory pose as we lift her in the air. The cameras flash, pop, and snap. I am certain this scene will make national news.

I am right.

****

One day later, the village of Villa flutters with wide green ribbons.

Trees down main street dance with plastic green ribbons wrapped around their trunks. New lawn signs state "CASH BACK" as if Cash runs for political office. Reporters interview people on Villa streets. Excitement stirs for the safe return of Cash Jones.

Our little community of Villa is the talk of the nation.

Reporters refer to the citizens of Villa as the new *Village People*. Newscasts show neighbors on the street dancing the *YMCA* song with arm motions.

Cash's shirtless video goes viral.

People around the nation tattoo "Cash is King" on their arms replicating Cash's now famous tattoo. Some brand themselves permanently with "Cash Back" on their forearm. I can't imagine the *World Wrestling Entertainment* moves Cash would do if he saw this celebration and heard the pleas for Cash to come home.

Churches open their doors for prayer vigils. People hold up and wave dollar bills representing Cash's family as they pray "Cash Back" pleas to God.

The village of Villa comes together big time for Cash.

But not only for Cash.

Last week, I posted the duet video of Carrie Rae and me with her beautiful voice and my sign language drama. It went viral after the news conference, too. Who imagined Carrie Rae and Sherry Kay would become household names? My speaking schedule grows as I get phone calls for gigs non-stop. I am scheduling way ahead for speaking events in churches around the nation.

At the press conference, Rashida shared how we bonded together, reading through several chapters in my book, *Invite Delight*. Since Rashida's promotion for my book with the press and her praise for the life-coaching questions in the book, everything explodes. Who cares I missed my book launch during the bank robbery? Now I receive more book orders than ever expected.

We self-publish so I can afford to give away more books for free. I place new orders for more books, filling our garage as we process the distribution. These need to go out pronto. I hire an employee to keep up with the demand on my website.

My Amazon-listed books roll off the press. These books hit one-day-record highs for Amazon. Book sales boom, growing in numbers.

I need to keep a level head.

Stay humble Sherry Kay Strawberry. Don't touch the glory. I am not all that. It's just a prime advertising moment gone viral. Focus on God.

I need not become all uppity over this. I must give God all the glory because my books point to Jesus as our source of strength. Stay underneath all this because it is God allowing the book to flourish, not me.

A spiritual revival grows.

What could stop the Spirit of God? We will meet later today for our *Bowl of Berries Book Club*. I flurry around in my usual rush because I'm hosting the book club. Dani plans on coming, too.

The Holy Spirit moves in our village.

Nothing can stop my spiritual joy. It overflows!

We will gather and pray earnestly for Cash's safe return. This emphasis on prayer inundates Villa, Michigan and the nation. Will this uplifting energy continue to flood the land, springing forth from our one-stoplight village? Will our press conference help police find clues?

What will next week bring?

CHAPTER 19

Your eyes saw my unformed body;
all the days ordained for me were written in your book
before one of them came to be.
Psalm 139:16 NIV

Our Victorian home lights up with candles in every window to welcome our *Bowl of Berries Book Club* members. What's for the snack? You guessed it—strawberries. The mini-chocolate fountain set up in the kitchen flows with milk chocolate for the berries on the skewer sticks. There's an empty basket on the kitchen counter for all our silenced cell phones.

I smile radiantly, knowing Dani accepted our invitation to join the group.

Cash gave me Dani's phone number. It made it easy to connect. She fidgets, but stomps courageously through my doorway.

I greet every "sista" with wrap-around hugs, kisses, and bouncing joy. Even Caroline loosens after the vault bonded us. We squeeze bearhugs, and I lift her off the floor.

Giggling ensues.

We fill our snack plates of chocolate-covered strawberries, circle up in the living room, and pray together to start off the meeting.

Rashida does not pray, but she holds hands with us. Progress.

The girls smile when I pass out gift-wrapped books. After opening their own personalized *Invite Delight* book, the mayhem begins. They hug their paperbacks like newborn babies. We dance around the living room, laughing, before settling back into our circle of friendship.

With books in hand, we take turns reading out loud through the next chapters. Dani struggles to read, so we help her with the occasional word. She concentrates, plowing through with a focused intent.

The life-coaching questions affect us again.

The questions apply to our season of waiting for Cash to come back. We feel undone, unfinished, and uncalm. We bask in the growth of ministry opportunities of sharing our faith publicly and trusting God. In our struggles, we praise uninterrupted. But sometimes I wrestle with God over the fact that Cash Jones is still missing. Rashida nods emphatically after I admit this.

Carrie Rae fidgets, stuttering as she mumbles about one of the life-coaching questions impacting her the most. The question, "If someone did not judge you critically, what area would you love to live with no restraint, and why?"

We all assume Carrie Rae references her singing ability. She reveals more. Under pressure, she struggles to stand firm. She freezes. With her head hanging low, she admits she dishonors her Cherokee heritage by cowering in stressful moments.

"You're young, Carrie Rae," Rashida says.

"Do it afraid," I say. "That's how I developed into a national speaker. I did it, shaking in my stilettos. I kept doing it. My voice quivered in the beginning. Eventually, I grew into my calling. You will, too."

"You don't understand how cowardly I am."

Staring forward, not making eye-contact with anyone, she apologizes to Dani. She confesses to having her concealed-carry gun when she entered the bank that dreadful day. When the robbers held both Caroline and Cash at gunpoint, she froze, and did not pull out her gun to rescue Cash.

She did not stop the robbers when she had the chance. She sobs, grabbing the hair on top of her head, trembling.

We sit in confused silence.

Carrie Rae explains, "Concealed-carry laws ban guns on bank property, so I hid my gun from police after leaving the vault."

Caroline asks how the police missed her gun when she got frisked in the hallway.

Carrie Rae's neck splotches with red spots and her forehead vein pops out as she explains. Her gun was under her pant leg in an ankle holster. When we came out of the vault, she bent down, pulling her gun out of the ankle scrap carrier. She slipped it in the metal pot with the fake tree right outside the vault door.

We huddled together, blocking the view of her bending down from surveillance cameras and from the police. Police frisked her moments after hiding the gun. Because they searched the area prior to her slipping the gun down in the moss, they did not find it.

What a close call for Carrie Rae.

Rashida knows gun laws and agrees they could charge Carrie Rae for bringing the gun into the bank. She could lose her privilege to ever carry or own a gun. Carrie Rae's prints will be all over her registered gun. She holds her head down, slumping her shoulders.

"Could I do jail time for this?" she whispers from behind her hair.

Caroline clears her throat, "Um . . . I am going back to work tomorrow. I think I will sell off the old décor in the bank. Don't you think we need a fresh look? Why don't you come into the bank tomorrow, Carrie Rae? Buy the TREE I am selling for cheap."

She winks at Carrie Rae.

"Wouldn't it be best to come forward explaining everything to the captain?" I ask.

I use my life-coach questioning technique to guide the girls toward a healthier response. Caroline, a new believer in the faith, battles her natural instinct to hide sin. The two girls discuss the matter, deciding to go forward with their gun retrieval plan.

I wrestle with how I handle this. I determine to pray about the incident and allow the Holy Spirit time to convict them.

Kyle teases me about being Holy Spirit Junior. I'm giving the girls time to grow in this area. If authorities ask about this, I must tell the truth because withholding information on hiding the gun makes me complicit.

Oh, what to do? What do I do?

Deep in thoughts, I wish I never heard the conversation. Loyalty to friends does not trump doing the right thing. I am bathing this in prayer. We vowed earlier to keep our conversations confidential in our *Bowl of Berries Book Club*.

Oh, my! What will I do?

Rashida changes the subject. She addresses the life-coach question on developing empathy for people who went through a similar hardship.

She looks at Dani, hardly showing her pregnancy bump. Rashida shares her victim-of-crime story of raising her twins alone.

"I have been where you are, and I started a *Go-Fund-Me* page for you and that baby," Rashida says.

She runs into the kitchen to pull out her cell phone, showing Dani's fund rises to $49,190!

That's a lot of money.

We shriek with joy, hugging Dani. God takes care of Dani financially through Rashida's idea.

Caroline grabs the *Go-Fund-Me* idea and draws up a plan for a retirement account, a college fund, and Dani's down-payment when she finds a house. The phone pings. The funds grow as we speak.

Dani shakes her head repeatedly in disbelief.

"Meeting you gals is da best . . . oops . . . I almost cussed. I mean best DOG GONE thing ever to happen," beams our Dani. "What will Cash say?!"

She tries to hide her teeth. I say nothing, but shouldn't she fix those teeth first thing? I would. Is this just me being judgmental? Yep. Do I fret about outside appearance too much? Evidently. Forgive me, Lord.

Carrie Rae speaks up again with her shyness fading.

"What about the next question? *'Describe a time when you got knocked over, but you got back up, adjusting and growing from the experience.'*" She reads from the life-coach question.

"I will get back up, adjust, and grow because I am going to Nashville to record an album!" Carrie Rae states.

What?!

We beg her to elaborate.

"Some bigwig producer offered to pay my expenses. They invited me to record an album in Nashville."

"Congrats, giiiiiirl!" Rashida says.

"No . . . um . . . I mean to say NO WAY! That's cool!" Dani shouts.

I think Dani stops herself from cussing again.

Carrie Rae is on her way!

Taking a deep breath, I look around. I am a skeptic who doesn't want Carrie Rae scammed. I ask if she googled the producer's name.

Caroline cuts in, explaining Carrie Rae asked her to check the whole thing out. Caroline made contact, talked with her bank lawyers, and confirmed the legitimacy of the offer. It's a solid proposition from one of the major Christian recording studios.

Are you kidding me?!

"In case you be famous, what is your last name, Carrie Rae? I never heard it yet," Dani asks.

Rashida, Caroline, and I attempt to squelch our smirks. There's a pause. I grin sideways toward Carrie Rae.

"It's Carrie Rae . . . pause . . . Hucklenuckle," Carrie Rae says reluctantly.

We all burst out in laughter. Even red-faced Carrie Rae giggles as we all flop on each other with out-of-control fits of hilarity. As the noise subsides, Dani asks again.

"Seriously, what is your REAL last name?"

Ba.Ha.Ha.Ha.

I can't even breathe. Poor Carrie Rae Hucklenuckle. She may want to come up with a stage name by this weekend. We roll over giggling, explaining to Dani it is her actual name.

"Oh. Nice name. I like it," says Dani.

This time we just snicker, leaning in, hugging on poor Carrie Rae. I bump her head accidentally. We smile around the circle of sisters. We grow from friends to family. God blesses our group beyond measure.

Carrie Rae Hucklenuckle is going to Nashville.

Pinch.

It's real.

What more can blow us away?

Nothing.

My mind overloads with excitement. Carrie Rae raises her

eyebrows, holding a hopeful grin. We turn back to the questions. I giggled when we bumped heads. I hit Carrie Rae's eye hard. It turns red, swelling a tad.

Dani asks for an explanation of the next life-coach questions, *"How is adversity best approached? What impedes you from overcoming?"* After we simplify the questions, Dani takes a deep breath.

She shares her horrific story of how her own father sex-trafficked her for money. He needed it for his drinking habit. She describes her dad as an alcoholic who got her drunk to comply with his money scheme. He also abused her. I wince.

What a schmuck!

It's the worst story I ever heard and gets even worse.

CHAPTER 20

But you, God, see the trouble of the afflicted:
you consider their grief and take it in hand,
Psalm 10:14a NIV

Dani tells how she got pregnant. Her relatives sent her away to birth the baby. At 13 years old, she gave the baby to an adoption agency. The agency must have reported her abuse to the police. Shortly after she delivered the baby, they scurried Dani back to Chicago. Child Protection Services came and got her. She passed from foster care to foster care home until she aged out of the system.

In awkward silence, we glance around the circle.

Dani stares at her shoes.

Tears stream, noses drip, and stomachs churn. An array of emotions affects our circle of sisters. My breathing labors as I wipe my tears. Dani's story crushes us. No one speaks.

I have never heard such a tragic tale.

But it's not a tale.

It's true.

We sit dumbfounded, staring into the abyss of her life.

Dani lived a hell-like childhood on earth. Through my tears, I struggle to wrap my mind around it. We pass the Kleenex box around our circle, drying our watery eyes.

Dani breaks the silence by adding details.

"Jan 22 is my baby's birthday. Every year my heart aches on dat day. They never let me hold my baby. The doctor said it be best if I didn't bond," says Dani in a trance-like stare. "But I saw his beautiful dark skin. He had dark knuckles and ear tips. I knew he be bi-racial."

She looks down at her plate of strawberries, saying, "I be rolled out of the hospital in a wheelchair. No baby. In my arms, I cradled a box of chocolate-covered strawberries. Can you believe we got chocolate strawberries for snack right now? They reminded me of da story."

She pops a chocolate strawberry in her mouth, saying, "It feels like a hug when I eat these. Not like a horrible hug from men I don't know, reeking of alcohol, stinking like fat pigs covered in sweat. Nope. Chocolate-covered strawberries remind me of da real love. Like da hug from a kind nurse and a beautiful love letter from adopting parents."

I find it hard to breathe. My chest lifts and lowers rapidly.

More tears roll down as Dani goes on, "Yep. One nurse spoke kind to me. She looked deep into my eyes, talkin' to me. She cared. The only one. She squeezed my hand tight during da labor."

Dani says, "Dat nurse said she met the adoptive parents. She told me dat they tried eight years to have a baby. My baby will 'fill their empty arms' is what dat nurse said. I remember dat part. These adoptive parents asked dis nurse to tell me my baby boy be the greatest gift they could ever imagine. I think about that. It helps me."

Dani smiled faintly.

I grab my heaving chest. I feel lightheaded, beginning to tremble.

She continues speaking through her tears.

"Miss Nice Nurse snuck da thank-you letter and da box of chocolate-covered strawberries to me from the couple adopting my baby. The nurse slipped me dis long letter secretly because I ain't allowed to meet with da adoptive parents."

My head spins. I pant in shallow breathing. Could it be possible?

"My dad made it clear I ain't meeting whoever gets my baby. He be angry wit me. He made me lie and say my baby was by a boy I didn't know dat moved away. Everyone else be thinking the berries were from the nice nurse. They never knew about da special letter I done hid in my pocket and reread over and over. I kept it until it crumbled into pieces."

Dani takes a deep breath to gain composure.

I breathe deep and exhale, too.

She said, "As we be in the car, turning the corner by the hospital, I saw a couple coming out of the hospital together. The husband's hand be around the new mom's shoulder as she be wheeled out of the hospital by da nurse. They be smiling down at dat baby. They tied balloons to presents. I guessed it be my baby wrapped in dat blue blanket."

More tears roll down her cheeks, splatting onto her wringing hands. "To dis day, chocolate strawberries remind me of dat one nurse who showed me kindness and the letter she snuck to me."

She takes a deep breath. A slow smile spreads across her face as she ends her tumultuous testimony saying, "Strawberries make me feel love like I feel with all yous new friends."

She studies a strawberry and smiles at us. We smile back, sniffling. We each pick up a strawberry, holding it like a glass at a wedding toast.

Shaking, I pronounce boldly, "To Dani, our new *Bowl of Berries Book Club* member. May each chocolate strawberry we eat taste like a loving hug from one another. To our sisterhood."

We raise our berries in the air, touching them like stemware glasses, tapping in a formal toast. We take a big bite to our sistership.

It tastes like a group hug.

I breathe deep.

Did she really say January 22? No way?! I can't breathe. There are lots of blue blankets and balloons, but who else would give strawberries to the birth mom of their adoptive baby? This cannot possibly be . . . or could it?!

Dani continues, "Back then, I drank alcohol. Later, I learnt in health class about not drinking when yous pregnant. When I was prego, I messed up by drinking. I didn't know a baby lived inside me until right before my baby be born. I had troubles."

We give her lots of time to talk.

She pours out more details of her soul secret to us.

"Dis time I'm gonna learn from my past. I crave alcohol, shaking a little since I stopped drinking after I took the prego test. I started

AA, but I don't know if I can do it. What's dat word? Adversity? I gots trouble before and want to beat it dis time. I want to be better for my baby."

She holds her abdomen, smiling. She doesn't look pregnant yet.

Looking around at our red-eyed group, Dani continues, "To be truthful. I ain't no good wit babies. I thinks I can break 'em. Nope. Give me a room of deadbeat teens, and I be in heaven. Because of my past, I love to help messed-up teenagers. When I help losers like myself, I feel like a winner. I'm happiest helping foster care kids in trouble. I was a good big sis to foster care kids."

As if right on cue, my son Drew busts in the door, waving a toy car in hand. He's upset.

"Momma, my boss is mean again. He tried to take my car away. I was working, and he just tried to take it," Drew complains, oblivious to our private book club meeting. He paces around the room back and forth, holding his toy car.

Drew struggles to live on his own. Often, he comes over from his nearby apartment. His boss at the special-needs workshop has his hands full. I get it. I puff out my cheeks, moving towards Drew to help calm him.

We go through this often.

I take in another deep breath.

Dani responds before I make it half-way up. She rushes to Drew, telling him the exact make and model of the metal car he clutches. She tells him it is her favorite car. As she gives car statistics, Drew calms down, spewing out all his car knowledge to her. Dani appears honestly interested.

Drew settles right down with Dani.

Well, I'll be doggone!

Who knew those two would hit it off so well? And they both have similar mannerisms. They almost look related. No way? There is no way? Or is there a way?

"Hey Dani, what city was your baby born? I'm just curious."

"Um, I don't really remember. Oh, um, maybe Stu . . . Stur . . ."

"Was it Sturgis?" I ask.

"Yeah, that's it. How did you know?"

"Er . . . it's . . . it's sort of close to Chicago where you are from,"

I answer.

My face turns red now. I'm burning up. Is this even possible?

"They threw me in foster care homes all around Chicago. I'll never forget them coming and taking me away. I cried, clinging to my dad, but they pulled me away, screaming."

Dani apologizes for talking about it in front of Drew. Drew's clueless. He focuses intently on showing his new best buddy details on his toy car.

Dani and Drew bond like family.

My head's going to explode.

"Oh, before we leave, I forgot my other big news. I met the singer Queen Gina during ministry years ago. She called me today, asking me if I thought Carrie Rae would perform an opening song at her upcoming concert in Fort Wayne. Just one song. It's at the Coliseum and nearly sold out. I said I will ask. Carrie Rae, do you want to test out your doing-it-afraid progress? The concert is . . . this weekend."

Carrie Rae's eyes widen. She freezes.

We wait.

My head races. I contemplate my suspicions about Dani. We swore to confidentiality, but dare I discuss this meeting with Kyle? First, I need to talk more with Dani Jones.

Hugging our goodbyes, Rashida says, "Hey! Will you girls pray for the Chicago police to find my family's murderers? I got nightmares again like I did 17 years ago. I don't want to worry my girls. Last night, I woke up screaming in a terror. Please pray for my case to be opened up and additional evidence found to convict the killer. I need him slammed behind bars. I need the killer or killers in prison. We need to feel safe."

We stop dead in our tracks. Our atheist friend just asked for prayers. I suppress my shock.

"Let's pray over our sister now," I suggest.

Carrie Rae, Caroline, and I lay our hands on her shoulders, crying out to God in prayer.

After our prayers slow down, we lay hands on Dani, thanking God for adding her to our group. We pray for healing for her childhood scars. We layer her in prayer after soft-spoken prayers.

Then we slide over to Carrie Rae. We pray for her courage, for her gifted singing voice, and for wisdom as she moves forward, afraid.

All these prayers raise up to God from our doorway.

I look at Caroline, asking her how the conversation went with her husband Sterling. She asks for prayers for courage because she cannot quite tell him yet. Immediately, we pour out more desperate prayers for her strength. Carrie Rae and I mix Bible verses into our prayers. We praise the Lord for being our stronghold in time of trouble and for helping us climb mountains like the feet of a deer.

I remind them God calls us to carry each other's burdens in the book of Galatians. That's how our *Bowl of Berries Book Club* rolls. We bear each other's burdens.

Here I thought we ran out of time, and God allows our atheist friend to remind us to make time to pray again.

Yep. God must be working on Rashida.

We need prayers because there are many unanswered questions. How will Sterling respond? Will Carrie Rae take the stadium-sized singing opportunity this weekend? Is my adopted son's birthdate just a coincidence to match Dani's adopted-out child's birthdate? Will Rashida's night terrors subside? Will she return to God?

Every day that passes, the chances for a safe return for Cash plummet. Where are you, Cash? Will we ever see Cash again, alive? I fidget as my anxiety increases. God, please let my brain rest.

I need a mental break. Is it too much to ask for a little calmness, Lord? I would really appreciate a less stressful week.

Will my mind get the much-needed rest?

CHAPTER 21

The Lord upholdeth all who fall...
Psalm 145:14a KJV

It's going to be an uplifting day. I just know it. I need a smooth day after the rough night I spent in my son's apartment complex. Needing to check things out, I slept there overnight. It just isn't working there for Drew.

I pray, "Lord, I would love a calm day after my restless night."

Ping.

My phone pings away with text messages from the *Bowl of Berries Book Club* sisters. The *Go-Fund-Me* page shows over $145,000 for Dani.

What?! That's crazy money.

Carrie Rae accepted the singing offer to open for Queen Gina at the Coliseum. I hope Hucklenuckle nails it. She's coming early before the afternoon concert. She wants my special make-up skills for her stage debut.

She has a surprise for me, too. What's that about?

The rest of the book clubbers will meet here, and we'll drive together for Carrie Rae's big solo day. We wouldn't miss her debut for anything.

Carrie Rae needs to leave four hours earlier than us because she's got sound checks. I'm glad she will stop here first for makeup. I'll share my calming techniques and pray over her.

Knock. Knock.

Carrie Rae even knocks quietly.

"Hey, super soloist! Giiiiiiirl. you are gonna kill it this afternoon. Wait. What is THAT?" I squint at her eye. Uh. It's not good timing for a . . . black eye!

This must be my surprise. She's got a shiner.

"I know. I know. I put ice on my eye, but it keeps getting bluer and bluer. Can you believe this?"

"Okay. I can fix this. I've dealt with black eyes before. Makeup works wonders. Um . . . Did I cause this in our group hug and laugh fest over your last name? I am so sorry I bumped your head, Miss Hucklenuckle."

My desperate attempts to lighten up her mood fail.

Carrie Rae Hucklenuckle is off her game. I apply makeup to hide the black eye, show her my calming breathing techniques, and pray over her for confidence. Now's the time to be strong and courageous.

She's weak and shaking.

Covering her mouth with her hand, Carrie Rae dashes into the bathroom. I grimace outside the bathroom door, hearing gags and puke splatting into the toilet.

Splat. Splat.

Shuffling out, her face washes white as a sheet. She's a wad of nerves. Except for the darker makeup attempting to hide the peeping-through-blue bruise, she is one pale-faced Cherokee. Shaking, she cowers near the restroom, a nervous wreck.

Oh my.

I remind her this fear is not of the Lord. Her hands continue to tremble. I tell her all the vault buddies will be there to support her in the audience. She says her whole church plans to come.

This opportunity to shine for Jesus with singing grows humongous.

Carrie Rae's natural beauty peeks out behind her dark Indian hair despite her blotchy hives, black eye, and nervous barfing. She inhales deeply, heading to her car alone. I hope she's got this.

I scratch my arms.

Am I getting nervous about her breaking out in hives, too?

Earlier, I noticed her neck blotching. My neck itches now. This day grows my prayer life. Carrie Rae heads out of my driveway, down the road to her biggest day ever. I shake my head, scratching my neck saying another prayer.

Standing in the yard waving goodbye, I notice all the green ribbons for Cash's safe return waving in the wind, too. Our village community supports Cash Jones coming home. I count thirteen "Cash Back" signs on the neighbors' lawns just looking up and down my road. I smile. I love the community backing for Cash and Dani Jones.

Ping.

I glance down at a text. Dani's *Go-Fund-Me* hits almost $250,000. BOOM! God is good. He takes care of Dani's finances. She lived poverty-stricken her entire life until now.

Yeah, God is good, but I've got something bad happening.

My mind flashes back to when I spent the night at Drew's apartment. Those low-income apartments bless people in poverty, but the negative influence on Drew troubles me. Some druggies pounded on his door in the middle of the night. I shooed them away.

Because of Drew's social ineptitude, it's hard for him to fit in. Some take advantage of Drew's disability. Drew's gullible. Unscrupulous people take advantage of his autism. This low-rent apartment complex might not be the best solution for Drew to become independent.

I scratch my arms.

Come to think of it, ever since I stayed the night, I itch all over. That's odd. I need to pick up the rest of the gals in three hours. Why in the world am I welting up and scratching incessantly? My neck, my ankles, my arms, and back all welt up. I rake the welts, feeling as though my skin crawls.

That's it.

I throw my hands in the air. Enough is enough. I'm squeezing in an emergency doctor visit to find relief before the concert. Maybe a prescription crème will fix it better than my over-the-counter tube of anti-itch creme.

I scurry to squeeze in the doctor visit.

In the office, my fear comes to fruition.

Laura Loveberry

CHAPTER 22

In this world you will have trouble.
John 16:33b NIV

Bedbugs! You've got to be kidding me?! Evidently, I'm highly allergic to those nasty parasites. Surmising Drew's apartment crawls with these little creatures, I shriek in the doctor's office. I CANNOT DO THIS! I shake my head back and forth again and again.

I pray my house does not have a bedbug transfer. Please, please, please don't let my home have a single bug. They lay 250 eggs. I heard how costly and troublesome this process of elimination can be. Please don't let these buggers be in my home, too. And help the apartment complex get rid of these creepy crawlers.

I call the dog-sniffing bedbug detector company before I even leave the office. They will be at my home in the morning. In the meantime, I notify the apartment complex. Ugh.

The doctor crème does not seem to calm the itching sensation yet, but the steroid shot in my buttocks should take effect soon. The doctor never saw such a dramatic reaction of welts. At least I am a human detector for finding those rascals. The size and intensity of my welts shock Kyle.

It's like I've got the plague.

This is my secret. Nobody needs to know. Not even my book club gals. When I pick up the girls for the concert, I switch cars with Kyle in case bedbugs lurk in my car. *Shiver.*

As we drive the back roads, we spot many "Cash Back" signs

in lawns along the way. We start a game, yelling "Cash Back" and counting our points at each sighting. Our whole county sprouts with random green ribbons wrapped around trees. Passing each one, we honk, hollering out the window at the top of our lungs, "Bring Cash Back!" What a silly ride with my sisters! Along the route, we smile, laugh, and high-five.

My itching subsides, and no one notices my welts hidden by my clothing and hair.

We enjoy our jolly ride to the fullest.

Pulling into the parking lot, we say a quick prayer for Cash to be returned and for Carrie Rae to be brave. Telling the girls about Carrie Rae's black eye, Rashida nicknames her Carrie "Sugar Ray" Hucklenuckle after the famous boxer. We just hope she can fight through her fear on stage.

As we stroll in arm in arm, the coliseum booms with energy.

We squeeze through the crowd to our upper balcony seats, gazing around at the monumental space. I squint my eyes to see the musicians. Watching the big screens will be our best bet to see Carrie Rae because we are so far back. Conversations blend in a loud murmur. Beach balls bounce around the crowd. This is the big league. Holding hands again, we lean in, praying for Carrie Rae to be brave.

I quiver inside with anticipation.

As the lights dim, spotlights fly around the crowd. A deep voice sounding like a WWE announcer booms out, "Ladies and gentleman, welcome to the Fort Wayne coliseum. . .. *feet stomp . . . thousands applaud* . . . Opening up for Queen Gina . . . *clapping . . . roaring . .* . is a newcomer on the music scene. Her video in a bank vault went viral. *. .. raucous applause* . . . She's here to perform a one-song solo debut to open for Queen Gina. Please welcome . . . Carrie . . . Rae . . . Hucklenuckle!"

As the spotlight follows Carrie Rae's entrance, laughter mixes with cheers. The crowd murmurs, repeating her name, laughing louder. We turn with a snap to look at each other. Rashida's eyebrows raise.

Will this laughing at her name throw Carrie Rae off completely? Stop laughing people. She could go freeze mode. Or flight mode.

Please stop laughing. Please stop the giggling now. Instantaneously, we slap our hands over our faces, peering through our fingers with our mouths dropped.

Will Carrie Rae freak?

On cue, Carrie Rae scampers out on the stage, halting when the laughter starts. Holding her mic, she whips her head around, staring out at the crowd. The spotlight beams on her alone. I don't think she can actually see the audience, but I know she hears their laughter. Oh. My. Stars. The intro of her song blares.

Carrie Rae just stares.

She misses her cue to sing. The song stops. The crowd quiets. Carrie Rae freezes in her typical freak-out frozen pose. Random voices in the crowd shout.

"You can do it."

"You got this."

Then someone shouts loudly, "You got this, Hucklenuckle!"

Giggling starts in the crowd at the mention of her last name. Crowd clapping attempts to encourage Carrie Rae.

It's too late.

Carrie drops the hand-held mic, running off the stage covering her face.

"Come on, sisters!" I grab Rashida's arm just like I did when we ran into the vault. We all jump up, gathering our stuff, and rush to find Carrie Rae.

Dashing through the crowds, we hear "Carrie" chants roaring, attempting to call her back. Her name is Carrie Rae, NOT Carrie. Rashida and I gnarl our faces as we sprint through the crowd. Caroline puffs to keep pace in her stilettoes.

With me leading the hustle down the steps, my shoe slips off. I stop abruptly. The girls pile up behind me. I turn around frantically, finding my shoe. Our mission hastens us. Our rushing entourage perspire beads of sweat, running to reach our wounded princess. After hustling down endless stairs, slipping past gates and a debacle of persuasion, we finally slide into Carrie Rae's dressing room.

Carrie Rae wails in the fetal position on the floor, gasping deep sobs.

Um.

There is no coaxing her back out. Mascara runs down her face. A
fake eyelash dangles off her black eye. Her eyes puff nearly closed.
She looks like she ran into an oil painting and it smeared all over
her face.

She's not going back out.

No way.

The entire crowd laughed at her last name. Official-looking
people with lanyards and head mics peek in the door. We don't say
a word when our eyes meet. They raise their eyebrows with an is-it-
a-go asking expression.

We girls shake our heads emphatically, shouting nonverbally,
"NO WAY!"

When Carrie Rae composes herself enough to leave, Caroline
and Dani drive Carrie Rae's car to go home. Hucklenuckle is not
emotionally fit enough to drive after this catastrophic trauma. I drive
with Carrie Rae and Rashida in my car.

What a dichotomy with the ride to and the ride from this event.
I scratch my bedbug welts discreetly. Could this evening get any
worse?

The bummer of this night just begins.

CHAPTER 23

The LORD is close to the brokenhearted;
he rescues those whose spirits are crushed.
Psalm 34:18 NLT

We drive in silence.

Carrie Rae rocks in the passenger side while Rashida and I contemplate how to encourage her. We follow the lead car with Dani and Caroline.

After a time, Rashida and I softly whisper to Carrie Rae that she will get past this. She will survive. I attempt to encourage her biblically, sharing how this too shall pass. It came to pass. Rashida tells Carrie Rae how it may feel like the end, but she can make it a beginning. She will pick up and carry on.

Our widow friend shares how she picked herself back up after the murder of her husband and sons.

Rashida's past gives perspective.

Carrie Rae hangs her head low, twirling her hair.

Humiliation oozes out of her. Her rocking slows. I share an embarrassing story of getting stuck in a traffic jam on the way to a speaking event. I tell her how a friend drove for me.

I say, "I rocked back and forward, trying desperately to not wet my pants before we made it to a restroom. Finally, traffic moved. My friend jumped a curb with the car while whipping me into a fast-food joint, and I leaped out.

I rushed to the bathroom, but by the time she parked the car and checked on me, I had washed and rinsed out my undies in the sink. I stood there blow-drying my underwear with the hand dryer when she entered. Ugh. When the event planner called asking why we were late, I told her. Embarrassing!"

Winking at Carrie Rae, I say, "Humbling, right?"

I get a smidge of a grin.

Maybe I'll get the other corner of her mouth to crack a smile? I remember another story of teaching my art class years ago, and my stomach churned. Carrie Rae surmises where this story ends.

"I called my principal to tell him I needed a change of clothes because I had an accident. He asked me what kind of accident. I simply told him I did not make it to the restroom. Seriously, what am I, seven years old? Who does this as a teacher? I did. My art class figured it out when I came back in a different skirt and red-faced."

Carrie Rae says, "At least I didn't pee on the stage."

We giggle.

I continue, "Later that year, there was a student who refused to leave the restroom because she soiled her pants. No one could convince her to come out of the stall. She remained for half the day. When I heard this, I entered to chat with her. Telling her she joined my club, I informed her I pooped in my skirt the other day. The principal covered my class."

Carrie Rae smiles out of both corners of her mouth.

"I got the elementary kid giggling coming out of the bathroom. She told me later she felt better because she belonged to my special "oopsie" club. Who knew my not making it to the restroom could encourage someone that week? It did."

Carrie Rae slightly smirks.

I tell her, "All things can work for good when we love God and are called for his purposes. If God calls me to share my embarrassing story for the sake of a poopy-pants girl in the bathroom, then so be it. If God can use the story to help another, then good. Count me in."

Carrie Rae's head raises up.

I add one last story. Speaking at a women's event, I stop in the middle of my talk. "I tell the audience to hug the person beside you and tell them, 'Jesus loves you.' I scurry to the restroom to remove my pantyhose. Yep. Back in those days, we wore hosiery. Mine lost the elasticity in the middle of my speaking to the audience. My nylon waistband slid down below my skirt hem.

I dashed to the restroom, the hosiery gathering at my knees and bagging at my ankles. Are you kidding me? It was like trying on shoes in Walmart with the plastic tag holding the pair together. I stutter-stepped shuffled. It's hard to walk with nylons waded at the knees."

Carrie Rae breaks into a giggling smile.

Rashida slaps her legs, bellowing.

"After removing my hose in the restroom, I strutted full stride back to the ladies. I told them what happened. They hooted and hollered when I held the hosiery in the air like a trophy. I made the best of the moment. The ladies related to the rest of my message on faith."

"After the message, one lady told me she's a widow new to the town. No one hugged her in weeks. The best part of the meeting for her was the spontaneous hug and Jesus-loves-you statement from the person next to her in the audience."

Carrie Rae says, "Your incident ended up blessing her."

Carrie Rae's shyness gives her compassion for others.

"I appreciated God using the hosiery-fail fiasco for one lady who truly needed a hug. Things happen for a reason. Carrie Rae, you may benefit others by telling your story of total humiliation, if you rise in the future and overcome. You will inspire others."

I go on, "What embarrasses or humiliates us most makes us relatable to others. God can use this awkward situation in your life for his purposes. You can either quit and never try again, or you can choose to sing for God's glory."

Glancing at her, I ask, "Will you try again?"

"This can boost your courage if you determine to learn from this, draw strength from God, and do things trembling. Do it afraid. You have a strong heritage. Will you serve the Lord with your gifts after this setback?"

Rashida says, "Setbacks are setups for step-ups. Remember, we do hard things. That's how we women roll."

Raising twins as a widow must have been the hardest of hard. Advice from Rashida holds weight.

Carrie Rae and I both nod our head.

"And you, sister, sing with a heartfelt voice." Rashida elbows Carrie Rae. "It is a gift not to be wasted."

Carrie Rae cracks a full smile, though hiding behind her hair. She takes a deep breath, looking at Rashida and me.

"Thanks for supporting me. I will do better if there's ever a next time. I don't want to fail God again. I don't want to let you down either or my church folks who came or my Cherokee tribe. Cherokee women do hard things. We learn from hardships. With God, all things are possible, right?"

We nod. I fist pump the air.

"I love you girls," Carrie Rae says with a soft smile.

I witness Carrie Rae rise out of her slump, brushing the hair out of her face. She sits up taller.

Driving onward, I notice many of the signs for Cash are gone. Weird. Even the green ribbons are gone. What? Squinting, I focus on a "Cash Back" sign with painted words over it. Spray paint spells out "Con Man" covering the sign like graffiti.

What's up?

I call the other car to ask if they're seeing what we see.

"What is going on?"

CHAPTER 24

. . . who comforts us in all our troubles,
so that we can comfort those in any trouble
with the comfort we ourselves receive from God.
2 Cor. 1:4 NIV

Caroline's quivering voice says, "I don't believe it. The radio just announced the suspected bank robbers were possibly former childhood friends of Cash Jones. They suspect Cash might be an accomplice in the robbery and NOT an innocent hostage hero. All three remain at large, but Cash is a person of interest in the case now."

"I don't believe it. Cash would not do such a thing," I say out loud to her, wondering inside if he conned us all. "What does Dani say?"

"Cash is NOT a bank robber!" shouts Dani in the background.

"And to top it off, I am taking Dani to the ER in Coldwater. She started cramping and writhing in pain after she heard the news report. With this stress, Dani could lose her baby. We need to get her to a doctor fast," Caroline says, attempting to sound calm, but I hear the strain.

"Put on your flashers. Drive fast, but safe. We'll meet you there."

Grabbing my phone, Carry Rae says, "I am going to pray. Ya got it on speaker?"

"Yes. Pray away. Dani can hear you."

"Oh God, right now we cry out to you. Everything's going amuck.

We need you, Lord. Please wrap your love around this precious baby inside Dani. Please help Caroline drive safely. We love you, God. Amen. Oh, and . . . help me . . . get past my humiliation, too. Sorry I failed you, God. Amen."

"Thank you. I'm putting both hands on the wheel now. See you at the hospital. I'm hanging up," Caroline says, speeding up.

My welts fester. I dig at them as I drive, trailing behind Caroline and Dani.

After flying down the back roads, we finally arrive at the hospital. Dani can only have one visitor go back in the room with her. We all volunteer. Dani asks for Carrie Rae. Good choice.

In the lobby, the rest of us hold hands, praying earnestly for Dani, her baby, and Carrie Rae. When our praying eases up, I ask Caroline if she revealed her secret to Sterling yet.

"Yes, I told him my horrid secret. It went . . . um . . . Let's just say he sleeps in the guest room. He does not speak to me. 'Pass the salt.' That's it. I'm giving him time. It is a lot to digest."

Caroline grabs a tissue, crying, "Oh, what have I done? I killed my baby. Now I'm losing my husband."

She folds over, weeping on my lap.

"And my night terrors aren't gone. It looks like your God sleeps on the job again, Sherry," Rashida says, glaring at me.

We both put an arm around our hurting friend. I look at my arm with welts puffing up.

Is this what Job, the character of the Bible, felt like? Rashida challenges me right when I don't need it. My skin welts and itches nonstop. And this baby struggles to live inside Dani's womb. I roll my eyes, shaking my head.

The night drags.

Carrie Rae sneaks Caroline and me into Dani's hospital room. Thank goodness Covid's restrictions are over and done, because the nurse lets us stay. As Rashida goes home to check on her teens, Caroline and I scrunch in the cold bedside recliners. Carrie Rae crawls in beside Dani in her hospital bed, hooked up to tubes attached to bags. Dani wears a belt monitor wired to machines. It's 2 a.m.

We can be here for Dani. Thank you, Lord.

When I call, Kyle supports me staying for Dani and Carrie Rae's mental health. He asks if he should start the church prayer chain. Dani doesn't want anyone to know her business after all the trash talk on social media. I understand. We'll keep this private.

I read Psalm 46 to the girls for our wee-hour devotions. We memorize verse one. *"God is our refuge and strength, an ever-present help in trouble."*

We definitely need help in our troubles.

After spotty sleeping, a barrage of testing, and the painful prodding; we await the news of the baby's fate. I suspect the worse when the nurse keeps checking and adjusting the monitor strapped around Dani's belly. Through our exhaustion, we perk up when the doctor enters after speaking with the attending nursing staff in the hall. Chart in hand, he pulls up a chair, looking eye-level at Dani.

I stretch to eavesdrop. This can't be good.

"No heartbeat," he says.

Dani will need a D & C.

Caroline bursts out wailing, collapsing on Dani.

We all lean in, gently caressing Dani as tears roll down her face.

We snuggle around her as I pray out loud, "Lord, please give Dani the peace surpassing all understanding, because we don't understand this. Be with Dani's breaking heart. Though you slay us, Lord, we will yet praise you. Give us wisdom to help Dani wade through this river of pain. It's too much to bear. Dani's precious child is with you, God. Hold this baby close in heaven. Please give strength for Dani's days. In Jesus' name, we pray, Amen."

As the medical staff snaps through their flurry of prep work, Carrie Rae sings softly with her eyes closed. The slow and quiet ballad gives a confirmation for our feeling as she sings, *"It's two o'clock in the morning, but I am not asleep. I'm floating down a river of hopelessness and defeat. The world's pain pouring in, I am holding on with all my strength. I need shelter within."*

Rashida walks back in with a questioning look. Our eyes meet and my sad head shaking signals the fate of the baby. Rashida's eyes well up as Carrie Rae sings the chorus.

"There's a hand that can reach me and pull me from this rapid flood, because I am a child of God, bought with His life-saving blood. Jesus, I've not understood. But I've seen in your Word, you

work all things for my good. I will cry out for you on this night, and grasp your strong and gentle hand. You're my rescuer, my defender, Lord, my deliverer in this land."

Carrie Rae opens her eyes, looking at Dani and repeating the chorus. She sings the next verse, *"You are my ever-present help when I am sinking. From this night I will recall how I'm saved by grace. You are my mighty rock, my refuge, and my all."*

Carrie Rae rises to her feet, raising her voice and repeating the next line three times, *"God pour out your comfort, flow over me. In your spring of living water, rescued I will be."* The nurses' eyes well up as they continue to work briskly in the background. I place my hand on my heart. It's pounding. Carrie Rae's heartfelt voice echoes down the hospital corridors as she builds powerfully in volume. The spirit of God floats away the dread and sadness through the beauty of her voice.

Carrie Rae sings while holding and caressing Dani's hand.

In a crescendo, Carrie Rae whispers the next lines, swelling from soft to bold, *"Wonderful Counselor, Ever-present Help in Trouble, My Savior, Shelter in the Storm, Prince of Peace, God of All Comfort, God Almighty, God Who Saves Me, Emmanuel, God with Us, King of kings, LORD of lords, God our Strength, LORD God Almighty, The Great I Am, King of Glory, GREAT, MIGHTY, and AWESOME GOD!"*

Boom!

Our spirits lift with the relatable lyrics.

They point us back to the perspective of God's light shining with an anchor of hope in our dark night storm. We hug, wrapping our arms around Dani and Carrie Rae. I marvel at how God uses her beautiful voice to minister to us precisely when we need it. Carrie Rae possesses a gift like David in the Bible, soothing others with his musical skills. Did Carrie write this song in the darkness like David wrote in caves 2000 years ago?

"Carrie Rae, did you write this song?" I ask.

"Yep. Around two-thirty, while everyone tossed in their sleep."

We rave about the power of her song. It penetrates into Dani's deep pain and begins lifting her out of the pit. We smile again, renewed. As we thank Carrie Rae for singing, the nurse announces it is time for the operating room.

We girls clasp tighter onto Dani's outstretched arm as our fingers slowly slide apart. We continue to reach toward Dani as the gap widens between us. They roll her on the gurney, down the hallway, and around the corner. With Dani out of sight, our hands remain outstretched towards her. We hear the nurses' steps echo down the corridor and fade.

Our hearts go with Dani.

I breathe in deep and exhale slowly.

How will Dani handle the weight of all she bears?

CHAPTER 25

Rich and poor have this in common:
The LORD is the Maker of them all.
Proverbs 22:2 NIV

After a couple of weeks of cancellations, I thrill to pick up Dani for our *Bowl of Berries Book Club*. We head to Caroline Forbes-Radshaw's home. We both gasp, holding our breath with eyes the size of quarters.

This is no house.

It's a mansion on the lake.

We approach the circle driveway landscaped with well-manicured hedges, beautiful gardens, and flowing fountains. Our eyes pop as our amazement grows. Stone steps lead to the three-story, stately brick home, adorned with massive windows and a double-tall, double-door entrance. Dramatic.

"Caroline Forbes-Radshaw is flippin' rich!" Dani says.

Profanity flies out of Dani's mouth as she describes the estate.

She slaps her hand over her mouth, saying, "I apologize for letting those words slip, but doggone, I ain't never been to a flipping castle. I don't belong here."

"Yes, you do. We're soul sisters, remember? Plus, you've got over $250,000 from your *Go-Fund-Me*."

"About that. I am giving it all back. My Facebook blows up with people demanding their money back. I shut off my phone. I'm talking with Caroline about this today."

"What? Let's just take this one thing at a time. Remember, Caroline's got her own struggles with her Sterling not speaking to her. If you lived in a big gorgeous house, but lacked love, I wouldn't say you're rich. Caroline probably feels broke and needy right now."

I look over at Dani, adding, "Adversity smacks us all in the face . . . although you've had more than your fair share."

I smile compassionately at Dani, who gapes at the manicured grounds. Like tourists at the Louvre in Paris, Dani clicks away, taking photos with her cell phone.

"We all need dis sister club because Cash be missing. Sterling ain't talking to Caroline. Carrie Rae crashed and burned in da arena. That's going viral on Facebook. And my baby, you know, got scraped out."

I wince.

"We all need a little hope in our despair. Let's go in," I say, wrapping my arm around her shoulder.

"I'll bet she's got nice strawberries for the snack, too."

In awe, our heads tilt back as we cross the threshold. Our shoes click on the marble floors as we walk, gazing up the grand spiral staircase. Caroline's chandeliers cost more than my house. Dani snaps photos of the dramatic entryway. Caroline invites us into her pristine kitchen, requesting we put our phone in the empty bowl on the counter.

"Are you flippin' kidding me?" Dani shouts, spotting the food display.

Rows of strawberries sliced into perfectly formed roses poke onto skewer sticks. Green honeydew melon slices form the leaves for each cut berry carved into a flower. A three-tier chocolate fountain flows. Pineapples, kiwi, melons, cheese, and nuts fill an array of silver trays arranged across the white marble countertop.

What a melody of delectable delights!

Giggling and marveling, Carrie Rae and Rashida stumble in the front door left open.

"The gardens look like a national park, and the house is a fancy museum," Rashida says.

I agree. Their eyes light up as they spot the gourmet spread of fruit, crackers, cheeses, and dips.

First, they bounce up and down, and it leads to a dancing celebration. Rashida announces every meeting will be here from now on. We laugh, hug, and giggle while nibbling a variety of morsels. High fives and smiles abound.

I hold up a rose-shaped strawberry skewer to make a toast. The girls interrupt, holding the roses like they are going to a wedding march. Carrie Rae hums the tune to *"Here Comes the Bride."* We giggle away in silliness, filling our plates.

"Oh, this reminds me. I forgot to give Dani this note from Cash. The timing is perfect now," I say, pulling the note from my purse. "I should have given it to you a long time ago."

We all quietly hum the wedding march with glowing smiles, watching Dani's eyes labor over the words of Cash's letter. She grins. This is Cash's wedding proposal letter with his unique poem he wrote while trapped in the vault.

She laughs, then bursts into tears.

Privately, doctors told Dani she won't be able to have children ever again. There was too much damage from the abuse when she was younger. It shocked the doctor she carried her first pregnancy to full term when she was thirteen. As Dani shares her broken heart, we all tear up.

How unfair?!

Instantly, we go from hand-raising joy to shoulder-dropping sorrow.

Life is cruel. Dani's afraid Cash won't want to marry her if "she be broken and can't have no kids." We weep. Dani weeps.

I understand her struggle and feelings of inadequacy. There's no ache like a barren woman's empty womb. The Bible compares it to a grave, a thirsty desert, and a blazing fire with an unstoppable burn.

It's true.

I know.

Breaking the silence, Caroline suggests, "Let's get out our books to find encouragement."

We search a place to sit in the living room. Dani asks to use the "can" as Caroline smiles kindly, leading her to the powder room. Does Dani need to cry alone for a moment?

Just as we settle in the formal living room, we hear Dani shout at the top of her voice, "I got GOOSED!"

What?

Rashida leads the way as we rush to the restroom. The bathroom looms bigger than most living rooms, so there's plenty of space for all of us. The toilet has its own special room inside the bathroom. Imagine that?

Talk about luxury. This is the Taj Mahal of potties.

Buckling up her pants, Dani explains, with arms flailing. "This contraption goosed me. Then I turns around and checks to see if I done broke it. When I push it again to test, I gets shot in the face wit toilet water."

She cusses her head off.

"What kind of fancy pansy toilet is dis, anyway?" she asks, puffing a strand of wet hair off her dripping face. "Excuse my French."

Toilet water drips off her hair, nose, and top lip.

We burst into hilarity. *Ba.Ha.Ha.*

"We worried about you. We thought you had medical complications," Rashida gasps between laughing bouts. "Now this is funny."

We all laugh out loud as Dani joins in with a soggy smile.

Caroline giggles with us, explaining the proper use of the bidet attached to the toilet basin. She points out the heated seat, nightlight adjustments, water temperature control, and spray pressure button. Nice features, huh?

Who knew rich people poop so upscale? No wonder their poo doesn't stink. Not with this royal flush.

It sure beats our plastic bag toilets in the bank vault. *Ha.*

One at a time, we each take turns testing the bidet personally behind the latrine door. Every time the button gets pushed . . . *whoopie* . . . giggling follows, announcing the gush of a warm water squirt to the derriere. The laughter outside echoes the laughter in the toilet cubical. Dani calls it the "lottie-dottie face flusher."

We're ridiculously entertained . . . by a toilet.

Am I missing out on life because I don't own a light-up, heated toilet seat with an adjustable five-pressure spraying bidet?

And will Caroline ever have us back again to her sophisticated home?

Maybe not. But she is more down-to-earth since her conversion in the vault. She laughs, leaning forward and holding her gut. She's one of us . . . just with a slightly bigger budget. Okay, perhaps a whopping better budget.

Dani says, "This is high class fo your . . ."

We hear a man clear his voice outside the door.

Uh. We quiet abruptly. Thankfully, Dani didn't finish her sentence. She almost spewed a derogatory word. Bless her heart. She tries not to cuss.

Single file, we shuffle out. We hold our heads down and giggles back. With our mischief under control slightly, we grin a hello to the man observing us leaving the powder room.

He stands tall with proper posture, folded arms, and one eyebrow raised. He smirks, but I can't quite read it. I don't know if he judges us or half grins with us. Caroline introduces us, formally apologizing for interrupting his studies.

"So, these are the lovely ladies who turned my wife upside-down."

Awkward silence.

What does that mean? Is this sarcasm? I can't tell, but Caroline's face flips to five echelons of red. Apologizing politely to him again, she ushers us back to the living room.

Rashida whispers underneath her breath she will host the next book club. Sheesh. We glance at each other, checking to see if anyone else feels uncomfortable around Sterling. Something wads him uptight. Persnickety fits his description.

After Sterling returns to his study, I tell the group I've got two astronomical announcements before we get started. I explain one concerns Dani. Dani may need to use the bidet again after I reveal my 21-year-old secret.

The other announcement involves a ministry opportunity for Carrie Rae. She can do it. I lean in, spreading my arms wide, describing my coming announcements as E-P-I-C, EPIC. Their eyes light up. The girls lean forward. Rashida rubs her hands together in anticipation. Carrie Rae bounces in her chair.

"Dani and I have a humongous announcement, too," says

Caroline, beaming at Dani and opening her arms wide to signify their staggering news. "Our proclamation impacts Sherry and her son, Drew. We think you'll love our idea, Sherry."

"No, we don't. I changed my mind. I am giving everything back," interrupts Dani with a scowl.

"I thought you might say that, but it's too late. The contracts got signed, Dani. It's a done deal," Caroline says.

Dani slaps her hands covering her face. "I don't want da money if people don't trust me. And what be happening wit Cash?! I CAN NOT TAKE IT NO MORE! Plus, they done gave to support a baby and I ain't got one coming."

Caroline assures us. "They will find Cash and confirm his heroism. He's innocent until proven guilty."

We all agree.

I hope it is true. The folks who got "Cash is King" tattooed on their arms hope he's innocent, too. One guy even tattooed Cash's face to his arm.

My mind spins.

CHAPTER 26

They are plans for good and not for disaster,
to give you a future and hope.
Jeremiah 29:11b NLT

My mind won't stop twirling. How will it go with Dani, Carrie Rae, Caroline, Rashida, and Cash? Questions swirl. My ADHD mind spazzes.

"Girls, my emotions whirl. They're circling 100 mph. I can't believe I'm asking, but can we back off our big announcements and help me settle down first? My anxiety's kicking up," I say.

Rashida moans. She throws up her hands, rattling her bangles.

Carrie Rae places her hand on her chest with a sympathetic glance.

"Why don't we delve into the book study now? It might help Sherry calm," Caroline replies, making eye contact with Rashida.

Dani, Carrie Rae, and I nod in agreement. Majority rules.

So, in Caroline's mansion, we seek a bit of perspective by discussing this week's reading of *Invite Delight*. Carrie Rae, Caroline, and I agree the *WWJD* chapter grabbed our attention in our reading assignment. Joining the majority, Rashida shakes her bracelets, picking up her book.

She suggests we read out loud together because it's so thought provoking.

She reads boldly, *"What Would Judas Do? 'So, Judas came straight to Jesus. 'Greetings, Rabbi!' he exclaimed and gave him the kiss.' Matt. 26:49 NLT. What would Judas do? Sheesh! This catches me off guard. I heard a radio interview clip where an author wrote a book with this provocative title. Whoa! The question grips me. What would Judas do? We all hear, 'What would Jesus do?' The question prompts us to be more like Jesus in our actions. It directs us positively."*

"Does anyone still own a WWJD bracelet?" I ask. "I do."

Rashida reads on, *"But 'What would Judas do' jerks my mind around to downside-up thinking . . . ."*

"What if Cash is a Judas with fake love for us? Maybe he isn't a hero! What if he's a criminal getting away with crime?" asks Rashida, interrupting her reading.

"No way! I know Cash. He is NOT in on this robbery. He wants NOTHING to do with those bum thieves. Trust me. I know," says Dani confidently.

I hope she is right.

"If you know Cash is innocent, then why wouldn't you keep the donations given to you through the *Go-Fund-Me*? Those people gave it based on Cash being a hero and wanting to help you. If Cash is actually a hero, then shouldn't you keep the money donated?" I ask.

Dani cocks her head sideways, thinking this over.

"Here's a good time to share our news," says Caroline, raising an eyebrow at Dani.

A long pause fills the space.

Finally, Dani nods her head in agreement.

"A foreclosure came up through the bank. I showed it to Dani, and she bought it! We hurried for the deal. It is the five-bedroom house next to the carwash and four-bay garage on U.S. 12 in Villa. She owns it all. Dani, tell them your plans."

Dani takes a deep breath. "I'm gonna be da house mom for a home for young adults like Drew and like the younger version of me. It's for those who age out of foster care, feeling lost and need a little help to make it. They can live wit me in da big house. They can pitch in. We're going to run the carwash and a body repair shop. You know I love cars, and you all knows I be best with bigger kids. I'd be like a mom to the trouble kids."

"Do you know about car repair? What do you know about

running a carwash business? Do you know about meltdowns with big kids?" I ask. My life-coach thinking kicks in.

"We've got this handled. Dani took shop classes and knows more than most about car repair. She helped her fellow foster care kids calm down in her various homes. Plus, she's taking parenting classes at the local crisis pregnancy center. I will handle her paperwork, budget, and setting up the non-profit status. Will you ladies join our board? We meet twice a year," adds Caroline, sitting up tall.

"If we meet at your home with this food spread, we're all in," I say, winking.

"And, Sherry, done told me about da bed bugs at Drew's building. We want Drew out of da bugs, away from the drugs. We want Drew to be our first client working at the carwash and staying in da home. He'll love detailing and washing cars," says Dani, grinning ear to ear.

Carrie Rae rocks back and forth singing, "Working at the car wash, yeah!"

"They fixed the bedbug problem at the apartment for now, but the bad influence of a few renters lurks around the corner there. Your house and carwash concept are ideal for Drew. He lives and breathes cars, cars, cars," I say, throwing my hands in the air. "This is perfect. Drew bonds with you. He'll love this. This answers our prayers."

Dancing the twist in my seat, I say. "I can't wait to tell Kyle."

I look around our joyful circle.

Clearing my throat, I look at Dani. "You will not believe my astonishing news. I can't wait. It goes along with you being Drew's future house mom. Um . . . I'm not sure . . . how to even say this . . .. *Deep breathe*. You . . . well . . . Let me start at the beginning." I scratch my head, looking up to heaven for wisdom to proceed.

"Twenty-one years ago, Kyle and I got a phone call saying there was a bi-racial baby boy born and asked if we wanted to adopt. 'Yes,' we answered immediately with a shout and rushed to a hospital an hour away. A kind nurse told us a few details. She described the baby's birth mom as very young and with little family support. We prayed for the birth mom from that point onward. We never stopped praying for her to this day."

The girls hang on every word.

They lean in as I continue, "We have a prayer list with our family names and Drew's birth mom tops the list. For years, we prayed for her to find Jesus and that we could thank her personally despite the closed adoption."

Standing up, I say I need to use the bathroom.

The group moans, yelling for me to hurry back and finish the story.

On the way to the restroom, I grab my cell from the kitchen, calling Kyle. I ask him to bring Drew and the special gifts we prepared earlier. Kyle knew I might reveal our epic secret today and wanted to be there. I agreed.

Dani needs an example of a man who loves her in a healthy way.

I talk while sitting on the toilet throne in the fancy restroom. *Whoopsie. Giggle.* This bathroom cracks me up. My husband asks about the giggling. I tell him he'll find out later. He needs to hurry here, bringing the special shirts and gift bags.

He knew I might call him, so we loaded the car with the presents beforehand. I remind him to have Drew wear the custom shirt, and they rush over.

I jitter with anticipation.

As I rejoin the group, everyone motions for me to hurry.

They pat my chair, signaling me to sit and continue my Drew story. I elaborate on our details. "We called the adoption agency where our home study was done. They sent a social worker over. We wanted to buy some new outfits, give the birth mom money, and help her get back on her feet."

I describe how the agency lady shook her head vehemently.

"Evidently, exchanging any presents or monetary gifts—not permitted by law. We had no information on the biological mom except she was young and did not know who was her baby's father. We debated about how to bless the young lady who would give us the greatest gift ever . . . a child. We had to do something. She probably felt alone and hurting."

I share how Kyle and I wrote the birth mom a letter, "We made a copy of this letter to put it in Drew's scrapbook to give to his birth mom if we ever met her in the future."

I reach down into my purse, pulling out the copy of the letter dated Jan 22, 1998.

Laura Loveberry

CHAPTER 27

Hope deferred makes the heart sick,
but a longing fulfilled is a tree of life.
Proverb 13:12 NIV

All eyes focus intently on me as I read our yellowed letter.

"To our baby's birth mom, how can we thank you for the sacrifices you make to fill our empty arms? We don't take this lightly. You give us the greatest gift anyone ever could give.

We tried desperately to have a baby. Countless infertility treatments and numerous adoptions failed. We set up a car-themed nursery. We keep the door closed, because it is too sad without a baby. Tonight, we opened the nursery door, praying over the room before we scurried here to the Sturgis Hospital."

The ladies gasp.

I look around at the ladies. Everyone's eyes widen and their mouths hang open. A single tear brims over Dani's eyelid, rolling down her cheek. Caroline gently reaches over, squeezing Dani's hand.

They remember Dani's baby birthed at Sturgis Hospital, too.

I read on.

"We pray you will come to know and love Jesus as we do. Jesus loves you just as you are. You are God's beautiful masterpiece. Thank you for giving us the precious gift of your son.

You remind us of Jesus with your generous heart. We wanted to give you so much more, but the agency would not allow the exchange of monetary gifts. We are asking the nurse, who we think is a

Christian, if she will give you these chocolate-covered strawberries. Hopefully, this is not against the rules. They hint of who we are. The red of the strawberry represents our namesake, our love for you, and your love for your baby. The chocolate represents God is good, and YOU are giving us the sweetest gift ever."

Knock. Knock.

We all jump.

Sterling walks out of his office to answer the door. He invites Kyle and Drew into the living room. Drew holds his model car and a gift bag. He wears a shirt with "Dani's Son" printed on the front. Kyle's eyes fill. He holds the other presents.

Sterling cocks his head. He's dumbfounded.

I read on, "Thank you for . . ."

Dani blurts out, preceding to quote the rest of the letter verbatim from memory, *". . . giving so much of yourself. You are the answer to our prayers. You will always and forever be his momma. He has two moms now. You are family to us, and I pray we'll meet someday to thank you for the greatest gift of love ever . . . our baby son . . . who is your baby son. You will always be in our prayers. With grateful hearts, K & S Adoptive parents."*

Dani smiles at us, tears pouring down her face, "I've read it over a zillion times before dat letter disintegrated."

We all gush happy tears. There is not a dry eye in the room . . . except for Sterling, who looks totally confused.

Drew who spots Dani.

"Dani! I got a new car to give you," he bolts over to tear-flowing Dani, "Why are you crying? It's a good one."

We laugh.

Rashida throws her hands up in the air, clanking her bracelets jubilantly. Carrie Rae shakes her head back and forth, praising God under her breath. Caroline sits properly, except for her gaping jaw and wide-eyed amazement.

Kyle throws me a matching shirt lettered with the words "Drew's Mom" on the front. He walks over, hugging me as my tears drip. Standing behind me, he rubs my shoulders gently. I lift my hand, touching his hand on my shoulder, then I give Dani the small gift bag.

"Open this one first," I say.

Dani reaches into the gift bag, reading the shirt. She bites her lip, looking upward, and turns the shirt to show the rest. Clapping, snorting, and hoots follow.

"Put it on. Put in on," chant the girls in unison.

While the girls drumroll with their hands on their legs, Dani pulls the shirt on over her shirt. She reads out loud, "Drew's Mom."

Dani covers her face with her hands. Finally, the world stops being so cruel to her.

Years of injustice and abuse pour out of her shaking body. The girls pile in for a group hug, repeating to Dani they love her deeper than the hurt she's been through.

Dani beams. She's part of the family.

Oblivious to the revelation, Drew squeezes his way to Dani, insisting she look at his car. He grabs her face, turning it towards his new car. He shows her how the doors and trunk open. Drew tells her he got her one just like his.

So much for the surprise of Drew's gift to Dani!

Suddenly he stops.

His eyes focus on Dani's new shirt. He turns to me, cocking his head to look at the extra shirt I just slipped on over my top. Both t-shirts spell out "Drew's Mom." Crunching his eyebrows together, he asks inquisitively, "I got two moms?" He pulls his face back.

"Yes, you do, Drew. You're double blessed," Kyle says.

I meet eyes with Dani, "We're double blessed."

"I got the same emotions of giving birth," Dani says, holding her belly.

"It's a labor of love for us both, Dani." Our eyes meet as our connection grows stronger.

Kyle walks over in front of Dani. "May I hug you, Dani?"

I beam with pride at the man I married. Dani stands and hugs Kyle. Kyle wraps his arms around her shoulders. Dani could use more healthy expressions of love from men. I'm impressed with my manly man, whose sensitive side brings more tears to the entire room.

Dani envelopes in this fitting hug from a male.

Tears pour down her face.

She shakes uncontrollably, sobbing.

After a moment, Kyle reaches a hand out to me, signaling to join the embrace.

I huddle in, wrapping arms around the sacred hug. Turning toward me, Dani sighs and breathes a deep breath. Taking her face in my hands, I kiss her forehead in gratitude. It's 21 years of praying answered.

The search ends for Drew's birth mom.

We hold on to our son's birth mom, bonding. Years of separation come together. I inhale deeply.

The sniffling girls circle close for another group hug.

Kyle releases and walks over to Sterling, who still stands bewildered. Kyle puts his arm over Sterling's shoulder saying, "Let's leave these girls to their book club. I noticed you have a four-car garage. Can we take a look?"

Drew jumps up hearing the words "four-car garage."

"Actually, my man cave accommodates eight cars. Come on Drew, allow me to be your tour guide."

The two men walk out with Drew bouncing along, clutching his new toy car.

Drew abruptly turns, running back to me, handing me his precious car to guard. He lifts the other gift bag on the floor, handing it to Dani.

"I picked this out for you. You're gonna love it. It's just like my new car."

Everyone giggles as Dani pulls out the toy car, hugging it, twisting left and right. Drew bounces back over to the guys waiting for the tour. I hope Kyle grabs the opportunity to talk with Sterling about deeper things in life than automobiles. I say a short, silent prayer for God to open a door, not a garage door, but the door into Sterling's heart.

We turn to Dani, rocking the toy car like a newborn baby. She sets it on her lap, stretching her arms wide for a third group hug.

"I love yous all."

After our big embrace, the gals breathe in deep.

I realize we aren't even doing our book study and our time is up for the club meeting. I stretch my head from side to side, saying,

"Let's try to answer some questions before the boys get back. Question one. Where do you find strength when you feel weak?"

"Right here in the *Bowl of Berries Book Club*," beams Dani.

We nod in silent agreement.

"I find strength memorizing Bible verses to keep me climbing," says Carrie Rae. She explains the verses at the end of Habakkuk. These scriptures inspire her when many things go wrong in life. She chooses to rejoice, finding strength regardless.

Carrie Rae quotes Habakkuk verbatim,

"Though the fig tree does not bud and there are no grapes on the vines, though the olive crop fails and the fields produce no food, though there are no sheep in the pen and no cattle in the stalls, yet I will rejoice in the LORD, I will be joyful in God my Savior. The Sovereign LORD is my strength; he makes my feet like the feet of a deer, he enables me to tread on the heights, (Habakkuk 3:17-19)."

"Those are some of my favorite verses. Didn't we share these in the vault? We need to keep climbing like the deer in that verse. Let's be joyful in the Savior again, Carrie Rae. And I am going to give you a chance to rejoice in the LORD with your singing ministry this weekend. The retreat planners invited you to sing while I sign the words," I say.

Carrie Rae opens her mouth to object, but I keep talking, "We can practice together and prepare. I'll be right beside you. All the girls already signed up for the retreat. They will be in the front row to cheer you on. Since I'm the keynote speaker for the weekend, I am speaking about Queen Esther. She did things when deathly afraid. What do you say, Carrie Rae?"

"Come on," Dani says.

"For such a time as this," Carrie Rae says.

"We'll be right there smiling in the front row," Caroline says.

"You don't have to sing. You can just come. We pitched in to pay your way. I will bring both CD tracks. I can sign drama by myself to the music on the CD. If you decide you want to, we'll use the performance track with no vocals, and you will sing while I sign. Maybe you will climb your mountain like the feet of a deer in the Habakkuk verse." I wink at her and smile.

I am convincing . . . or am I pushy and bossy . . . again?

It's getting late. What takes Kyle, Sterling, and Drew so long in the garage? Will the man cave enthrall Kyle like the fancy-pants toilet impress us girls?

CHAPTER 28

*Bear with each other and forgive one another
if any of you has a grievance against someone.
Forgive as the Lord forgave you.*
Colossians 3:13 NIV

Sterling bursts back in the house from his garage tour with the boys. He collapses at Caroline's feet repeating, "I'm sorry. I'm so sorry. I am so sorry!"

Kneeling in front of her, his arms wrap around her legs. This is definitely not the same man who walked with proper posture into the man cave with Kyle and Drew.

What happened in the garage?

He weeps in front of us girls, showing a disregard for propriety. We girls lean back in silent shock, eyes wide open. Caroline strokes her husband's hair. We sit speechless.

Nobody else moves.

"Honey, I was horrible to you. I judged you, treating you despicably," Sterling says, shaking his head.

I glance at Rashida, nodding her head with attitude in agreement. Sliding my foot over, I discreetly nudge her to stop her. This discussion should be private, but here we are.

I hold my breath. The tension thickens.

Kyle motions for the rest of us to move to the kitchen.

The group tiptoes out, but I fixate on the drama, shuffling backward in slow motion. Kyle tugs at my shirt, nudging me toward the other room. I inch closer to the kitchen, keeping eyes transfixed on the couple.

Are you kidding me? I prayed for this. Refusing to miss the scene, I cling to the doorway, peeping my head around to hear. I shoo Kyle's nudge with my flapping hand, never taking my eyes off the drama.

Finally, Kyle shrugs his shoulders, giving up. He and Drew head to the food.

The girls huddle on my backside, eavesdropping.

"Oh, Sterling, I am the one brutally wrong. I deserve the silent treatment and worse. If only I could go back in time. I don't know how you can ever forgive me . . . for . . . for what I did." Caroline leans over her kneeling husband, weeping with ragged breath.

"I am guilty, too. We both have our part. I pressured you to move up the ranks at the bank. I concern myself with appearances. You've changed since you've met these girls. You are kind when I've been incredulously mean to you. I do not deserve you."

"Can you forgive me, Sterling? I mean, deep in your depths, can you ever honestly forgive me for what I did? I . . . I . . . killed our baby!"

"I can. And here's why," says Sterling, glancing over at the doorway. I snap my head back in the kitchen, pause, then creep my eyes back around the corner.

"I told Kyle out in the garage. I told him everything . . . everything. The abortion, your confession, my silent treatment and judgement. I spilled my guts."

The rest of the girls slide their heads around the corner, listening intently.

He rubs his face, running his hands through his hair. "The thing I could not figure out was your joy, your peace, your kindness toward me when I slammed you out of my life. You glow. I could not explain it."

He turns back in our direction. We plaster ourselves back around the corner wall. I shush the girls with my finger to my lips and peek again.

"Kyle explained to me how you found peace in Christ. He explained people live separated from Christ. That was you, Caroline, until you put your faith in Christ. I knew there was something special going on inside you. You joined the God side. You've gained something in the middle of our hardest marriage issue. I wanted that peace in our storm. You had it. I did not."

"Are you telling me you want to put your faith in Jesus?" Caroline asks.

"I just did. It was like God opened my mind to my ugliness against you and against God. Kyle whipped out his phone and showed me Bible verse after verse, spelling out how I am a sinner needing a Savior. Those verses pierced me. By the time Kyle got to asking me if I wanted my faith in Jesus Christ, I knew I needed this. We have the finest things the world offers, but I was missing the priceless."

He jumps to his feet, "I am a Christian—a born-again BELIEVER. Oh, what will the members of the yacht club think of me now?! Who cares?!" He grabs Caroline by her shoulders, lifting her to stand toe to toe. "I forgive you. Will you forgive me for my judgement and cruel silence for weeks?"

Caroline blubbers, nodding and looking up into his eyes.

"I've missed you. I've missed talking to you. Oh, I've missed US," she sobs, burying her face against his chest. They cling to each other.

Rashida motions for us girls to slither away. We follow, slipping up to the kitchen counter, leaving the lovebirds in their embrace in the living room.

With all this prepared food still in the kitchen, we decide to stay longer and stuff ourselves. Standing at the counter, we pop the delectable morsels in our mouths. We all wear beaming smiles.

Forgiveness changes everything.

God changes everything.

Rashida leans over the counter, whispering in the loudest quiet voice ever, "Now I have some E-P-I-C, EPIC news. It could be amazing, but no guarantees."

The rest of us lean in. Even Kyle is in our close-up circle over the counter.

CHAPTER 29

In all thy ways acknowledge him,
and he shall direct thy paths.
Proverbs 3:6 KJV

"I have a nephew living in Chicago. His girlfriend is pregnant. They are freshmen in college and want their child adopted into a Christian home with two parents. They asked if I knew of any exemplary parents wanting to adopt who could provide well for their baby," whispers Rashida.

My thoughts fly. First, how can an atheist support an adoption to a Christian home? Rashida must be softening to spiritual things. Second, Rashida's nephew is probably black. Is she thinking of Sterling and Caroline Forbes-Radshaw, of the yacht club and white high society community? Will they be open to adopting a dark-skinned child? Kyle and I are too old to start over with an infant.

Who's she thinking about for this baby?

"I think Caroline and Sterling would be an ideal couple who could provide well for the baby," Rashida says as she looks at me. "Can you enlighten us on raising a bi-racial child in a predominately white community? My nephew's girlfriend is white. Raising my girls had moments where we had to hold our heads high and persevere, facing prejudice for our blackness. It happens occasionally, but it's mostly good. How is it for you and Kyle in an interracial home?"

"Hmm. Well, Sherry's dad made an adjustment. He nearly had a heart attack finding out Drew was bi-racial," Kyle says with a laugh,

"But Grandpa and Drew became best buddies. Grandpa was old-school. At first, he worried about what others might think. Actually, Drew is the main reason Grandpa came to know Christ. Drew always prayed for Grandpa. Grandpa and Drew were the closest of all the relatives before he passed away."

I say, "I had constant opportunities to share with kids how God creates our skin tones. I've used kindness answering questions about if I'm babysitting or who's kid this is. When I taught school, I injected my opinion on the KKK when occasionally kids talked about their family's involvement. I educate with gentleness. I don't respond in anger."

I tell about the time someone wrote "negro lover" on my chalkboard before class. Only they used an insulting word I don't repeat. As the students entered and sat down, a shy student jumped up, erasing the derogatory term. The class looked for my response. I simply thanked the student who erased it for trying to protect me from seeing those hurtful words. We talked about my interracial family positively. Some people are taught to hate. They can be prejudicial based on race.

We prefer to love all people and not judge by skin color.

I explain a few individuals from the older generation commented rudely about our interracial family. "We rarely have issues based on Drew's dark skin tone. I know Caucasian parents who adopted dark skin children and snap back at questions they don't like. I choose to respond kindly, explaining how God placed Drew in our home. We don't let the prejudiced judgement get under our skin."

Jesus is darker skinned than me, and he's my Savior.

I interject most of our issues with prejudice come from Drew's disabilities. "Drew appears typical in physical characteristics. But with his autism, he processes things differently. Others don't understand his meltdowns, his inability to adjust to changes, and his violent outbursts. Some think we should spank him more. They don't understand you cannot punish autism out of a child."

Children on the autism spectrum process uniquely.

I'm on a roll, saying, "And don't get me started with Fetal Alcohol Effects. The mother's alcohol intake causes permanent damage to her baby. The damaged brain does not go naturally over from action to consequences. We have many action-consequences charts on our walls. With 80 percent of FAE children growing to have a criminal record, most parents who adopted FAE kids are exhausted."

Oops. Getting off the subject, I talked too much. I need to be more cognizant of the time I spend talking in a group. I dominate. *Sheesh.* Okay, back to being a better listener.

"Tell about the time you and Drew went to school in the winter, and he forgot something important," says Kyle, snickering.

"Oh yeah, after a snowstorm one school morning, we were running late. Drew was in first grade. I carried a bunch of bags, hurrying him to the car. I reminded him clearly not to forget anything in our rush. We aren't going back for anything. When I started driving, Drew said he forgot something."

Everyone listens to my story except Drew, who focuses on his new car.

"I told myself this was reality discipline time. I said if he forgot something, then he would do without it at school. It's a teachable moment. Drew agreed. He said he didn't like shoes."

I laugh out loud, giggling through the rest of the story.

With much drama, I tell them, "I whipped my head around, looking at his bare feet with snow sticking to them. I yelled, 'Did you not feel . . . *my teeth clench* . . . the snow . . . *breathing intensely through my teeth* . . . between your toes . . . *slobbering now* . . . when you walked through the two feet of snow on the way to the car?!' And Drew answered simply, 'I don't know.'"

Listening to the story, Drew smiles with his entire face. He loves hearing me repeat this part of the story. Drew says, "I remember my shoes now. I check my chart."

Kyle says, "Remember the time when Drew dug your toenail clippings out of the trash for school's show-and-tell?"

We laugh.

"Drew said they were so big they were special. Or how about the time Drew was four years old and crawled under the public restroom stall into another man's stall? He stood in front of this stranger sitting on the toilet and pronounced, 'Hey Dad, there's a dude reading a newspaper in here.'"

Everyone giggles.

Gasping for air, Kyle adds, "Oh yeah, and the worst time ever was another public restroom issue with Sherry. You tell it, Honey."

"Well, I was in a tight public restroom stall with Drew. He was two at the time and squirmy. Standing while buckling my pants, I look down, gasping in horror with my mouth open and eyes popping out of my sockets. Drew slurped up the condensation on the front of the toilet bowl with one long upward lick. He was thirsty evidently."

We burst into moaning, shaking heads, crunching up our faces, and uncontrolled laughing. Ugh. I slap my forehead, rolling my eyes heavenward, remembering that one.

"Oh, I have one more fitting the theme. I came home from shopping to find Kyle and Drew in the playroom. Drew was carrying cups of water from his play kitchen set to Kyle sitting in a recliner watching the football game. Drew smiled, proud of each delivery. I watched Kyle drink the water in the little play cup, asking where Drew got it. Kyle pointed at the play kitchenette. I wondered where a two-year-old would find a reachable water source to refill the play sink. Sure enough, walking in our restroom, the toilet had water splashes all around."

Everyone hoots, pokes, and teases Kyle.

"I walked back in, asking how Kyle liked the water. He said it was good. I informed him it should not be good because he's drinking . . . TOILET WATER! Kyle jumped out of his recliner, rushed to the sink, and started rinsing off his tongue frantically. That's parenting." I smile at Kyle and Drew. *Giggle.*

Robust laughter fills the air. Dani and I both hug Drew in our matching "Drew's Mom" shirts.

"Hey, we best get photos of us moms in our shirts to honor the moment of me finding my son who I knew before I knew he be my son. Ain't that something? It's a puzzle solved," Dani says.

Dani, Drew, and I pose for cell phone photos in a bunch of poses with faces beaming and matching shirts.

Rashida leans over, asking me under her breath how I feel about sharing my motherhood with another woman. Not whispering, I tell her it takes the village of Villa to raise my Drew. I am fine with sharing motherliness.

Dani blesses Drew, and Drew blesses Dani.

It's all good.

"So, back to my question. Do you think Sterling and Caroline will be open to adopting a biracial child with dark skin?" asks Rashida Jackson. "And will the Villa community be a fine place for an interracial family to raise a child?"

CHAPTER 30

Children are a gift from the LORD. . .
Psalm 127:3 NLT

"Sherry and I agree Villa benefits interracial families. Most people in Villa accept our family and love on Drew. A few folks don't understand or agree, but they are few and far between. The village of Villa is an ideal place for an interracial family because the people look out for each other. We have challenges with Drew over in the income-based housing, but it's nothing to do with his race. It's a few people with drug problems trying to take advantage of his disability. There are mostly great renters there, but a few troubled residents prey on the gullibility of Drew. It's not everyone. It's an isolated issue. The manager of the building helps amazingly with Drew," Kyle says.

"Hey everyone, I want to show you Drew's new home and place of employment. I got the keys yesterday," Dani says.

We all clap.

"Congratulations again, homeowner!" I say.

"We're so happy for you, Dani," Carrie Rae says.

"This works out wonderfully! Wow!" says Rashida.

Dani explains to Drew about his new carwash job opportunity and housing arrangement. Kyle smiles, shaking his head. Drew bounces up and down, holding his model car as Carrie Rae sings a silly song about working at the carwash. The rest of us join in the singing, increasing in volume.

"What's all the commotion out here?" Sterling asks, strolling into the kitchen, holding Caroline's hand.

We explain how Drew seems happy about living and working at the carwash with Dani. We burst into singing as a choir again. Even Sterling joins the locomotion dance lining around the kitchen counter, singing to the catchy carwash lyrics.

Sterling dances reserved with controlled finger snaps. Caroline full-out freestyles with swinging arms. A weight the size of Texas lifted off her shoulders, and she cuts loose. Rashida dances with her rhythmic, smooth soul while rattling her bracelets. Drew holds his car in the air, bouncing with the occasional slobber flying out of his open mouth. Carrie Rae belts out the song, spinning happily. Dani picks up her car gift, zooming it in the air around our spontaneous dance club. Kyle grabs my hands as we partner dance the swing with delight.

Everything is just right.

As the singing winds down, Rashida says she has a question for Sterling and Caroline. I don't know how they will respond to her and this adoption possibility. All eyes focus on the Forbes-Radshaw couple.

The sudden silence deafens.

"Would you be open to adopting a bi-racial baby? The baby is due in one month," Rashida says, raising one eyebrow.

Caroline and Sterling smile broadly, giving each other an astonished expression. In unison, they both reply with an emphatic, "YES!"

"You will not believe this! We just prayed together in the living room. We thanked God for restoring our relationship." Sterling squeezes Caroline's hand, pulling her closer. "And we asked God to guide us with adopting again. We want to give it another try even after 12 failed adoptions. We just gave God our baby dreams. Could God be answering our prayers this fast?"

Ping.

Looking at her phone, Rashida says, "Are you kidding me? No way! I just got a text from my nephew to call him back. Are you both sure about this?"

Sterling smiles at Caroline as their eyes meet. "Yes," they both answer at the same time.

"We are more determined than ever. But we are prepared for them to change their minds. Go ahead and call him back in the living room. We'll wait here," Sterling says.

We wait in anticipation. I hold my stomach and shake my head. The anticipation causes the rest of us to munch mindlessly like during an intense movie. No one speaks. If this infant lands in this home, he or she will hit the jackpot for adoptive parents.

After a time, Rashida wades back in the kitchen. I cannot read her expression. Perhaps it's reservation, but she hesitates. Did the birth parents change their mind again on poor Caroline and Sterling? Not again!

"My nephew's girlfriend is in labor in Chicago . . . and they want Sterling and Caroline to be the adoptive parents."

"Whoopie!" I shout, waving my hands in the air.

"Alright!" says Carrie Rae.

"Congrats, you two!" bellows Dani, boxing the sky.

The cheering, back patting, dancing, and hugging continue. I notice Rashida has more to say. Uh. She's quiet.

"Okay . . . there's a major caveat. My nephew's girlfriend confessed a secret she feared telling. An acquaintance at college raped her. The rapist holds a high-society name on campus. She did not think anyone would believe her side of the story because he's a frat rat bigwig. They are not sure who the dad is, but she finally told her boyfriend."

"They can do a paternity test finding out who's the baby's father. We have lawyers. This could get complicated, but we want to stay in the adoption process. Right, Caroline?"

Their eyes meet. They turn to face Rashida and answer simultaneously.

"Definitely!"

"Well, my nephew is black and his girlfriend is white. The rapist is white, so we probably won't need a test. When the baby comes out, it will be clear who the dad is. My nephew's anger settled down, but wants his girlfriend to press charges. This could get messy if the baby comes out white. By the way, the baby is a boy."

"We're all in," Sterling says, gazing at Caroline, who nods in agreement.

"Oh boy, when Cash comes home . . . and we keep praying he be alive . . . he'll be shocked dat I gots me a shared son and maybe Caroline will, too."

I wonder about the possible legal battle. This might get as messy as a two-year-old eating spaghetti with his hands. The thought of Caroline with a toddler covered head-to-toe in spaghetti makes me giggle.

This perfect palace may go through post-baby adjustments.

Caroline mentions the chapter in this week's assignment called, *We Do Hard Things*. She memorized the Bible verse featured in the reading. She says, "I love this truth, 'Let us not become weary in doing good, for at the proper time we will reap a harvest if we do not give up.' Gal. 6:9 NIV.' This is another hard thing we do. We won't quit."

Caroline reads the Bible veraciously. And she keeps up with our book study. Her memorizing and love of God's Word inspires me.

If Caroline and Sterling adopt this baby boy, it could bring a legal hot mess into their picture-perfect life. Oh, wait. Their seamless life isn't perfect. It fell apart, but God sewed it back together. They just face another major snarl.

Who is the baby's father?

This reminds me of the tapestry illustration I use during my speaking events. I share, "Our lives resemble a tapestry. God's perspective looms from the topside of the needlepoint. It's a beautiful image. The rest of us here on earth see the bottom side with all the knots, dangling threads, and blurred imagery. In heaven, we will understand fully how God intertwines the threads of our lives for his glorious purposes. We will see our masterpiece life from the top view."

"What a gnarly mess the bottom of tapestries can be!" Rashida says.

Before we leave, we huddle up, praying God's will for this baby. Then we pray for Sterling and Caroline's empty arms to be filled. Is this right, or are we telling God what to do? We need to trust God, praying for his will with this whole baby quandary.

Life knots up.

The situations with this adoption and with Cash's predicament gnarl. For all this, I am so thankful we have Jesus. We must stay close to God for discernment. I look forward to my Bible reading time for clarity. What do non-Christians do without the Bible for strength and discernment?

Will God untie these knots soon?

Laura Loveberry

CHAPTER 31

See that no one pays back evil for evil,
but always try to do good to each other and to all people.
1 Thessalonians 5:15 NLT

Sitting at home, I reflect on Dani, all alone. She lost her baby, and Cash remains missing. Who knows if he's even alive? Caroline gains a baby, and Dani lost hers. Even with my life-coaching training, my support of Dani seems inadequate when she calls. Her tragedy deepens. With all Dani's been through, she needs Jesus to warrior through her inner battles.

She called me previously, and we talked about Caroline's conversion to Jesus. Dani agrees Caroline's a changed person and her transformation resonates. Caroline reads the Bible voraciously. She walks in peace over perfectionism. When I ask Dani if she wants God in her life like Caroline, Dani says she's not there yet.

I sigh without making a sound.

People say I'm pushy, so I attempt to back off. God does the saving. I am merely a vessel, sharing God's truths. Kyle reminds me often not to pound the Bible over people's heads. Who, me? Yeah. This explains my nickname, Bible Thumper.

After Sterling's dramatic turnaround, Dani called again, asking me about that night. She marveled at how Sterling found Jesus in his garage with Kyle, and it led him to forgive Caroline. It displayed the power of forgiveness clearly to Dani.

Dani asked me about how she could ever forgive evil men doing dreadful things to her to meet their selfish needs. We talked at length. I winced often, listening and cringing. It's hard to hear her childhood details. I shuddered, grimacing and making ugly faces she could not see on the phone. I never imagined someone could endure such horrendous torture.

She needs more than my feeble words can offer.

Dani needs Jesus.

Again, I asked Dani if she wanted to commit her life by faith to Jesus, who sees and cares. She replied, "I ain't sure Jesus cares for me like he does for you. Did God see me when I be a kid? I be working through my baby inside died. I'm not quite dar yet with the faith in Jesus. But I is getting closer. I sees it helps others."

She did not cry.

She spoke stone-cold, matter-of-factly.

I blinked back tears as my heart shattered in pieces for her.

I reminded her that God can help her understand all this mess. "I ran from God for years before I, by faith, believed in Jesus, who died for me so I could have a new life. My life got harder after I became a believer, but God gave me strength for the journey."

Dani's life couldn't get much harder.

After reflecting on these phone calls and Dani's situation, I pray to God to give me opportunities to help her. I remember a testimony I heard years ago. It's a true story. Sharing it could help Dani.

Ring.

It's Dani's number showing on my cellphone screen. I blink.

"That's fast, God."

"Okay. Lord, I will obey you. If you open the door, I'll open my mouth. The Holy Spirit's job opens her heart, right? I'll work on not being my usual, pushy self," I pray quickly.

Ring.

Let God work, Sherry. Be patient. I puff my cheeks, blowing out air, reaching for the phone on the second ring.

"Hey Dani, how's the other Drew's mom doing today?"

Dani gets right to it, saying, "Sherry, I am going on a trip. But I be working through my anger issues again. I ain't got nowhere to puts my rage at my dad. I blame him for all da wrong stuff he done to me. Now I lost Cash's baby because my dad done do me bad and all dat."

I hear her breathing hard.

"What's I supposed to do wit all dis bitterness?" she asks. "I be in my prison of bitterness when I thinks too long."

"I was just praying to God about you when you called. Do you want me to tell you about a friend of mine who found a way to forgive her father?"

"It won't hurt to listen, but I ain't thinking I can forgive it."

I cannot imagine either, but I tell the details of a testimony I heard years back.

"This woman had a father who abused her and her sisters when they were kids. He pulverized her mom when he was drinking. A mean drunk describes him. Eventually, the unrelenting, cruel father died of alcoholism. Wounds scarred the daughter, who grew to be a resentful woman. Underneath bitterness tore up her soul."

I ask Dani if I should continue.

"Yes, I be listening. I get it."

"One night alone in a dark room, the adult daughter set a chair up to represent her cruel dad, sitting in the chair listening. The dad passed away years earlier, but continued to haunt her memories. In the darkness, the angry daughter shouted out loud to the empty chair about all the ways her dad crushed her. She sobbed as the nightmare of memories rolled. Shouting at the chair with tears and snot dripping, she relived each harsh moment over the years of abuse."

Dani sighs on the other end.

"In her imagination, she pictured her own dad quivering in the chair as a little boy with black eyes and bruises. She realized her grandpa beat her dad when her dad was young. A cycle of violence and drunkenness repeated in the next generation."

I ask if she was still listening. Dani responds for me to keep talking.

"The daughter wanted to break the cycle. Her grandpa broke her dad. Somehow, the sobbing woman in the dark room with the chair envisioned her abusive dad as a young, abused boy himself. She cried out in the darkness. God gave her compassion for her dad, an abused, shaking child."

Dani sniffles, "She ain't heard no apology."

"Although she never heard his apology, she forgave him."

I hear more sniveling.

"Falling in front of the empty chair, she found the compassion to forgive her alcoholic father. She forgave her dad for every act of violence toward her, her sisters, and their mom. She remained collapsed on the floor, exhausted and drained. Bitterness lifted off her heart and into the abyss of nightfall. She let the years of pain and brokenness pour out in tears as she wept on the cold flooring."

I hear blubbering from Dani.

"That evening, she shuffled into the darkened room as a half-broken, abused and bitter woman. Liberated from her prison of resentment and unforgiveness, she emerged into a bright new morning. She gained empathy for her dad as an abused child. She lives in the light of forgiveness ever since. Today, she walks in freedom. She set her heart free by letting forgiveness flow. She broke free by forgiving."

Dani remains on the line in silence except for the sniveling.

I continue sharing another illustration. Because God loves Dani, God sent his own son, Jesus. I give details.

"God's son suffered unjustly. They ridiculed, mocked, beat with whips, scorned, laughed at, and stripped Jesus of his clothes on the cross. He was innocent, yet unjustly treated . . .."

"What? He be naked on da cross? I sees him with like baggy underwear."

"That's the artists' renditions. The soldiers humiliated Jesus. He suffered naked. They stripped off his clothing. God's own son died in pain while naked on the cross."

Dani sniffling more.

Does she relate to that humiliation with the injustice perpetrated against her? She tells me she feels shame. I cannot fathom her life memories. I wince.

"God sent a reliever. God sacrificed his son, Jesus, for you to be made clean and new. He loves you that much, Dani. God knew we would suffer in this world. He gave us a comforter to help us through our hardest seasons down here. Jesus knows your hurts, humiliation, and harsh life. You've experienced the most horrendous life of anyone I've ever known. For this mess on earth, we have Jesus to heal us. Do you want the strength and soul support God offers through his son, Jesus?"

There is a long, silent pause. I wait.

Laura Loveberry

CHAPTER 32

Envy thou not the oppressor,
and choose none of his ways.
Proverbs 3: 31 KJV

"Sherry, I'm almost be there, but not quite. I know I needs Jesus. Jesus suffered like me. My black eyes, my nakedness, my shame, my pain. I gotta thinks more 'bout all this. I might be ready someday."

Tears flow on my end of the phone.

I cannot imagine her journey.

She tells me the other reason she called is to tell me she is going to fly to Atlanta. Her grandma, on her mom's side, called to say she will pay her ticket to come visit. Dani's grandpa is on his hospice bed in the living room. He's asking to see Dani before he dies.

Dani tells me this grandpa touched her inappropriately, too.

Ugh. I roll my eyes, breathing out a sigh.

How many different father figures broke Dani's spirit? Why did she face so much hardship, Lord? I need to take a shower after Dani's phone calls. I want to wash away all the yuck.

That muck runs deep for poor Dani.

How does she do her life without God? I do not hear these types of raw conversations in my other Bible studies and small groups at church. Her issues run deep into the vastness of despair. Her poverty and hopelessness overwhelm my mind.

She talks about her grandpa with no emotion. He hugged her wrongly. She says something like, "You know how guys be bumping our chest accidentally."

I straight up tell Dani that hugs should not feel uncomfortable. If embraces are uncomfortable, they are unhealthy. I inform her that guys should not bump women's chests. My husband told me a man is aware of a woman's chest. He never "accidentally" bumps a woman there ever. Inappropriate motives lead to such behavior.

"Your grandpa's behavior reeks. Your grandfather's behavior was perverse, although not to the extent of your father's. It's not how a grandpa should be with his granddaughter."

She's blunt as she pours out her details. At least on the phone, I conceal my facial shock over the life she lived.

She wants to talk about changing to another AA-type meeting group. Often, she seeks my counsel concerning this. She quit drinking since her pregnancy. Even though she lost the baby, she wants to stop drinking altogether. She says she wants to break the cycle of her family of alcoholics.

She tells me the AA meetings confirm she is a recovering alcoholic. She heard about another church-sponsored program for recovering alcoholics. It's more Bible-based and references Jesus specifically. I encourage her to attend. She's trying their meetings out when she gets back. Dani's going to call me when she returns.

We end the call by praying for wisdom and courage.

When we hang up, a weight grows heavier in my heart.

It occurs after each time Dani calls. Desiring to fix everything, I am a control freak. I get pushy. I interrupt her, trying to convince her or force her into a decision. Do I need to listen better to Dani and back off with my opinion? Yep.

I breathe out a long, continuous sigh.

God, I need YOUR divine discernment. I rest my hand on my aching heart, puffing the air out of my mouth again. I'm going to read through the Psalms to heal my ache, seeking wisdom on how to move forward with Dani.

Dani handles suffering better than most without God.

I know God can work all this evil, turning it around somehow for good to help others escape the perils Dani faced.

I talk to God, "God, are you calling Dani for your purposes? Will she ever be able to see you, the Holy Father, as an understanding, loving father figure? Lord, Dani needs a father's lap to crawl up onto and receive love in a wholesome way. She longs for healthy love. Please be with her in Atlanta on this emotional trip. Amen."

****

"You will not believe it," says Dani, standing at my door a few days later. She bubbles over with joy, talking rapidly, flapping her hands with expression.

"Oh Sherry, I did it. I forgave my grandpa." She bounces and beams.

"What? Start at the beginning. Tell me everything." I motion her in, and we sit face to face in the living room. Sitting on the edge of her seat, she talks faster than I can keep up.

For the next hour, Dani shares about her trip.

Evidently, her grandpa and grandma started attending a Baptist church. I squeal. Praise. Hospice and church members rolled in and out the whole time she was there. Dani never had an alone time with her gramps. It confounded her. She wanted private time with her grandpa to let him know she forgave him for his improprieties. She didn't say it like that, but that's the gist.

His inappropriateness did not compare to her sex-trafficking dad and his visitors, but Dani wanted to settle things with her granddad. There was never a time, and she regretted this on the ride back to the airport.

Her flight cancelled due to fog.

She tells me she danced in a mini-circle at the airport, demonstrating hopping dance moves. She continues. Dani thought God gave her an extra day with her grandpa to talk things out. She wanted the unforgiveness issue off her chest. Her dad was dead and gone, but her grandpa is alive.

They gave her a bonus day to address forgiveness.

Returning from the airport for the bonus day, she talked to him right in front of her grandma. Dani asked her grandpa if there was anything she needed to ask to be forgiven for. Her grandfather said there was nothing Dani did to him to forgive.

Wisely, she said to her grandpa, "If there is anything you have done to hurt me, I want you to know I forgive you."

She leans back, laughing and slapping her thighs.

"I did it. I done released my angst with him!" She smiles at me, peering out from the corner of her eyes. "I think maybe I can do dat chair trick with my dead dad next."

She winks. She's just blunt and to the point.

She can't wait to forgive her deceased dad for the years of abuse.

She says her cousin from Atlanta came in right afterward she forgave her gramps.

"My cousin be drunk as a skunk. Crawling right in his hospice bed, she cried and mumbled that she didn't want him to die. She was closer than I be with him." Narrowing her eyes, she says, "We called dat a proper hug."

She throws her head back, laughing even harder.

"Wow. That was some kind of greeting," I say.

"Yeah, well, when it be time for me to go again, I ask my gramps if he be wanting a 'proper' hug like my cousin gave. He sure enough did." She laughs, "I done crawl in his hospice bed and cuddle with him for a 'proper' hug. And it be the first time I feels comfortable hugging him. He done hug me back without all dat bad junk."

"You received a healthy hug you wanted all along."

My smile remains on my face.

"Dat's it. Miss Sherry, I felt all good inside. I think I will forgive my dad with an empty chair in my house tonight. I could not wait to tell ya. Tonight, I'm gonna be free of my bitterness. I just know it."

"Are you putting faith in Jesus tonight, too?" Um . . . I think I am being too assertive again. Oops. Is this me being too forceful?

"One thing at a time, Miss Sherry. You be asking me that a lot. You pushing me. I ain't there yet. I gonna start with this forgive-my-dad thing when it's dark tonight and I be alone in my bedroom with my empty chair."

I lean back, laughing and throwing up my hands with my palms facing her in jazz fingers, "Alright, alright. I'll just pray for you and let God do his work."

I wink, grinning as we both lean in for a hug. We hold on tight. I'm proud of her for working through her bitterness and unforgiveness.

Dani's teachable.

It feels like God gave me a daughter to love. I always wanted a daughter, and this one comes with rough edges. She keeps my prayer life in order. Children do that.

Will Dani be able to forgive years and years of the worst kind of abuse? As Dani would say, "Is she ready for faith in dis Jesus?"

CHAPTER 33

For if you remain silent at this time,
relief and deliverance will arise for the Jews
from another place . . . And who knows whether you have not
attained royalty for such a time as this?"
Esther 4:14a, c NASB

We roll up to the Deer Lake Christian Retreat Center. Dani jumps out and dances around, viewing the quaint cabins and beautiful wooded setting overlooking the lake. Rashida clatters her bracelets, stepping out of the car in her bold and bright African garb. We unload our bags as Carrie Rae remains quiet behind her hair. She's sweating over her singing later tonight, no doubt.

Carrie Rae practiced her vocals for two weeks with me signing alongside. She and I met at Caroline's house to pray over the retreat beforehand. I sensed the Holy Spirit moving, gathering to pray. We fasted, praying like Esther did. Where two or three gather in Jesus' name, God confirms he is in our midst.

It's true.

We prepared for this mission field. We thrill to greet the ladies we prayed over for weeks. Excitement floats in the air along with the Holy Spirit's presence in anticipation of the weekend of sister time.

Caroline remains at home, bonding with her newborn, but the rest of our *Bowl of Berries Book Club* settles into our log cabin. We laugh, discussing if Miss Fancy Pants Caroline could handle the primitive setting. Rashida imitates Caroline, pacing around asking,

"Where's the bidet? Where's the boudoir jacuzzi? Where's my butler?" We collapse on the bunks in giggles.

We miss Caroline.

Huddling around the cell phone, we call her. We hear her baby cooing as she answers questions from our nonstop gabbing. Caroline tells us she will pray all weekend for the Spirit of God to move mountains in the ladies' lives.

Oh, the enthusiasm of a new Christian! Caroline gives the suggestion to pray over the seats in the auditorium before the ladies arrive for tonight's meeting. Why didn't I think of that?

"I'm on it! And please pray I don't choke again," Carrie Rae says.

Immediately, Caroline pours out a prayer for Carrie Rae to sing her best.

It's like she's with us.

Carrie Rae and I grab our Bibles, skedaddling to the event hall early. After sound checks, Carrie Rae and I pray out loud with our hands held out over the rows of seating. We meander between lines of empty chairs, praying for the Lord's presence to touch the lives of the women about to fill the seats.

Later, the energy rises as the auditorium fills with chatty, excited ladies. Carrie Rae and I open with our *Sisters in Christ* song. I sign to lyrics as Carrie Rae belts it out despite her butterflies. She nails it flawlessly. My signing beside her helps Carrie Rae to not panic. Plus, the announcer introduces us by our first names only, by my last-second request.

I give my Esther message, *Queen of Quite-a-Lot*, pointing out we can choose to obey God's calling, or God will use someone else to do his will. I challenge the audience to live as Esther with an acronym for TIARA. *Trials Happen, If Moments Come, Adjust to Unexpected, Roll with God, and Adventure View Life* are my talking points to live for God for such a time as this. I give an old-fashioned altar call at the end. I speak my clearest message, and Carrie Rae sings flawlessly. Our session is faultless.

I expect many will respond to the altar call.

No one comes forward.

Awkward.

Everything seems so perfect. What's up?

I remind myself it is God who does the saving. I am merely a vessel. With no one responding, I plant a smile, holding a strong outward appearance. Inwardly, I moan. The event went polished and planned, and yet, . . . no response.

In the cabin at night, sprawling on our bunks, I confess my disappointment that no one walked forward. Carrie Rae cocks her head sideways, admitting it confuses her, too.

"Over this event, we prayed. We fasted. We practiced, and I did not choke. You spoke with engagement. I don't get it," Carrie Rae comments.

Rashida, the atheist, surprises me.

Rashida praises my talk and our song. Then she suggests someone might hide a sin needing confessing. That's how her husband would pray each night. He asked the Lord to search his heart, exposing any area of sin or fault.

"Not that I do this, but this personified my husband's way before someone gunned him down," Rashida says.

This prompts a conversation on confessing our faults and areas of weakness. Each person takes a turn confessing their sins and areas needing improvement. My face cringes under the veil of darkness. As Rashida points out, I can be bossy and controlling. She hits it correctly, right on the head, but it stings nevertheless.

Truth hurts.

Everyone else confided their own faults, but the group seems to agree my domineering needed calmed down. I did not admit my faults. The group described my failings. My face turns shades of red. Beads of sweat form as I cross my arms defiantly. Good thing the lights are off.

Is this righteous anger . . . or poked pride?

Does my anger reflect the righteousness of God? Nope. The book of James holds me accountable. "Know this, my beloved brothers: let every person be quick to hear, slow to speak, slow to anger; for the anger of man does not produce the righteousness of God," (James 1:19-20 ESV).

I pray silently while a tear rolls into my ear. My head spins as I justify and defend my faults to myself under my blanket. I joke with fake lightheartedness about my bossy-pants ways, but inside I wallow in defensive justification. Taking off my favorite strawberry earrings from Kyle reminds me I can be bossy and controlling with him, too. Sheesh. The Holy Spirit convicts me I need a genuine change, but I wrestle with it spiritually under my blanket.

These accusations slap me in the face.

I am supposed to speak first thing after breakfast, and my anxiety rises. Am I to surrender my overbearing ways? God equips me with a boldness, but does my pride prevent me from searching my heart to see if there is a wicked way in me personally? Do I need a double dose of humility? Are these sisters speaking truths?

The spiritual battle rages.

I toss and turn all night. The girls sleep sound, oblivious to my inward conflict. Every time I peek at my phone clock, I sigh. Sleepless minutes toss and turn to hours. When I get up, catching my face in the mirror, my eyes widen. Who's the old lady looking back? It's me. My bags, wrinkles, and messy hair reveal my sleepless night.

I am off my game this morning.

"God, please take over for the rest of this retreat. I can't sum up enough willpower. Oh, God, please help this day be in YOUR power. Yesterday, we performed everything perfectly, reaping no results. Search me, God, and reveal my innermost sin."

I talk to God all morning, getting ready and praying over the event hall. I stop fasting. Perhaps my motivation to lose weight stifles it. Earnestly, I ask God to search the deepest crevices of my heart, burrowing deep. I don't want to be a control freak, bossy pants, or my-way-or-highway kind of leader. I really don't.

I want God's way, truth, and life living in me.

As the ladies pour into the event hall, Carrie Rae sings and I sign the opening number. Carrie Rae forgets her lines. She doesn't overreact in panic, but her hands shake. Watching me sign, she clues in, continuing . . . without dashing off the stage. That's progress, but it doesn't help with the music cutting in and out near the end. Oh, brother.

How uncomfortable to witness.

I present my *Winning Team* testimony of how I came to know Christ. I forget sections, talk scattered, and stumble. We experience technical issues and loud microphone feedback. I explain what it is to believe in Jesus, sharing the Good News that Jesus died for our sins.

The ongoing technical issues distract from the opportunity for audience members to connect with Jesus or recommit with God.

As I near the conclusion of my chopped-up message, my heart beats faster and my palms sweat. I battle in my mind about changing the end of the message. What? I skirmish with God's Spirit unbeknownst to the audience. God prompts me to confess publicly my own sins. Really?!

I am prideful, controlling, and self-centered.

Oh God, you don't want me to confess this . . . right now . . . do you? I am the speaker. Can't I keep this between you and me . . . privately? Why is a public confession necessary?

I pull the mic off the stand and walk to the front edge of the stage. Pausing for a long stretch of awkward silence, I peer into the eyes of the audience members. The ladies squirm. Whispers murmur.

My inward battle with the Holy Spirit rages.

Falling to my knees, I pour out my failures to the ladies.

"I planned to give an altar call as your speaker . . . um . . . but the truth is . . . I need a come-to-Jesus moment . . . myself."

Necks stretch to see. Jaws drop. Eyebrows lift.

"I am selfish . . . self-centered . . . and so full of self . . . ."

An older woman places her hands on her heart. Her lips move. Is she praying?

"I am a self-focused sinner . . . and worse . . . ."

Confessing my deep sins, snot running down my nose, I reveal my offenses against God.

"I battle with control, pride, and doing things in my human power. Often, I rely on myself and not on the Lord. I lack trust. I am driven to achieve, not resting in godly peace."

I acknowledge my guilt of judging people with my overactive and overthinking brain.

More women lay their hands over their heart, silently moving their mouths. I sense their prayers.

"I notice and judge hygiene—it's wrong. I say nothing out loud, but it's hurtful if people knew my innermost thoughts. Noting who carries a Louis Vuitton purse, I critique. Inwardly, I judge their outer attire, ranking their social status. I am aware of financial standing like an overthinking detective. I need a spiritual makeover."

Gasps pepper the audience.

I notice tilting heads and furrowing brows. Some shake their heads.

"Everything is all about me, Me, ME."

A few women raise their hands upward. Do they deal with the same issue?

"Selfish and self-absorbed describe my motives. I am the materialism queen."

"Me, too," says another woman, nodding her head.

"I over think. I over stink. I am over the brink," I confess.

Tears stream down my cheeks. My *Bowl of Berries Book Club* sisters pull out Kleenex, blinking and wiping their eyes.

"My being "extra" repels people. My domination of conversation runs rampant. I value my opinion above others, cutting them off in discussions. This devalues people. My avoidance of odd personalities runs amuck. And I don't know how to whisper. I'm out-of-the-box and too EXTRA!"

A giggle or two pop up in the audience, amongst more watery eyes.

I am on a roll.

"I talk too loudly. Laugh too loudly. Toot too loudly. And yes, I am uncouth. And I just vomited my sins out for all to hear."

Raising my hands in surrender to God, I breathe in Jesus and exhale my sins. I cry out, pleading for God's forgiveness and repenting of it all.

I collapse. I prostrate, fully stretched out.

Soft sniffles flood the air . . . along with my loud sobbing gasps.

Feeling a hand on my slumped shoulder triggers more sobbing. Then I hear the angelic voice I know so well, softly singing acapella.

It's Carrie Rae, singing a spontaneous chorus of *I Love You, Jesus.*

She grabs the mic, confessing her lack of trusting God with her singing ministry. As I lay sprawled with eyes shut, I hear stumbling feet coming forward. Lots of footsteps gather.

Sniffling softly, many prayers cry out publicly to God. Women walk forward, confessing their unforgiveness, their prejudices, and their personal sins. Carrie Rae hums the chorus.

The stage becomes an altar.

The altar becomes holy.

The Holy Spirit floods the atmosphere.

The atmosphere is where we die to self and surrender.

Our surrender becomes a sacrifice.

We sacrifice ourselves to God, not staged, on this altar.

As the Holy Spirit moves amongst us, ladies experience God's forgiveness, confessing their wrongs. Tears flow. Kleenex boxes get passed around. Women cry out, earnestly asking God to forgive their once-hidden sin. Another woman rushes to the crowded stage, repeating her need for Jesus. Ladies wrap arms around one another, praying out loud, confessing sins, and calling to Jesus.

As more women gather forward, Carrie Rae crescendos, singing melodiously the chorus, *"I love you, Jesus. You're always with us. Oh Lord. And I lift my hands, to you, oh Lord . . ."*

Friends huddle, praying in clusters of two and three. Some sing along with the chorus, raising hands high. Others hold hands over their heart, praising Jesus repeatedly. Lines of ladies wrap arms over shoulders, swaying to the singing praises.

Our retreat ladies and I needed freedom. The biblical Queen Esther, the subject of my first message, asked for fasting to free her people. We assume this includes praying. Her Jewish people needed set free from slaughter. God intervened.

Previously, I ask our *Bowl of Berries Book Club* for fasting and praying, too. God intervenes for us like God did in biblical days for Esther.

God's Holy Spirit floats down, moving among us.

Did Rashida recommit to God for such a time as this? Did Dani become a princess, a daughter of the King of kings tonight? What about Cash? God, where is Cash? Queen Esther's Bible story weaves with situations impossible to overcome, but an unexpected turn made a way. Will an unforeseen Esther-like twist save the day for our present-day *Cash-is-King* hostage?

CHAPTER 34

And let us consider how we may spur one another on
toward love and good deeds, not giving up meeting together…
Hebrews 10:24-25a NIV

Arriving at Dani's new home, anticipation floods my mind. I greet the book club girls, receiving hugs and joyous smiles. It's been a while. Everyone arrived before me except Rashida.

Caroline cradles sweet baby Will, short for Wilmington. The name Will represents God's will for their family. The joy of mom and baby brings heartwarming delight. We need to fill Caroline in on our last weekend retreat. She missed it, and I don't want to leave her out of the epic revival we experienced. We will tell her all about it.

Of course, she and Sterling just welcomed a newborn baby into their home. She had an important reason to miss the ladies' retreat weekend. She needed bonding time with her sweet boy. It's all good.

We hear the details of Sterling and Caroline's unexpected adoption. Rashida had explained to Caroline that the baby's father was definitely her nephew. The newborn's knuckles and ear tips are dark and the rest of his skin will eventually turn darker to match. Who knew?

The baby's father is not the white rapist.

We discuss with Dani her carwash plans and readiness for their grand opening for this upcoming weekend. Dani's hair frazzles and bags darken her eyes, but she flashes her tooth-gapping smile. She worked nonstop to prepare for the big day.

Dani winks at me, telling us she's got good news to share later about an empty chair. Everyone cocks their heads, looking confused about the empty-chair comment. I wink, knowingly. Dani glows, beaming with joy. I recognize a woman free of bitterness and resentment, despite her exhaustion.

I'm guessing she forgave her dad.

Yes. Dani forgave her deceased dad . . . in the dark . . . with an empty chair. Her heartbreaking memories don't hold her captive anymore. I read it in the countenance on her face. She radiates with the outward peace of inward freedom. I rub my hands together in excitement to hear the details of her own forgiveness breakthrough.

Thank you, Jesus.

Dani's hard edges soften because of her willingness to file them down. Mentoring Dani brings results because she does the arduous work of moving toward progress. She advances faster than anyone I mentored as a personal coach.

I hope we leave time for our life-coach questions in our book.

The gals delve into side discussions and coo over sweet baby Wilmington. Several conversations dance around the circle simultaneously. I need to keep us focused on the book, so I keep my promise to Kyle for a peaceful, relaxing evening later.

Kyle says our life is too fast-paced.

We've both helped with the carwash repairs and Dani's house renovations. Carrie Rae and I practiced our songs together for two weeks to build her confidence. My life-coaching on the phone filled several nights this workweek. Every night it's something. I need to be cognizant of prioritizing our marriage.

A quiet evening, after our book club, will be the relax Kyle and I need.

Dani's hosting differs a tad bit from Caroline's lavish spread. I grin. The kitchen overflows with cleaning supplies getting ready for the grand opening. Dani offers strawberries still in the cardboard container and a stack of chocolate bars on the cluttered counter. Leaving phones on the kitchen counter, the girls settle in the living room.

There's a good exhaustion in this room.

Dani's been working her tail off. It shows substantial

improvement. Staying busy keeps her mind off Cash's absence. Her diligence shows in her dragging feet and eye bags.

Dani plops on the couch.

"I can't move one more step tonight," Dani says.

But she keeps a content smile. Caroline's face shows sleep deprivation, too, with a similar satisfied smile. Lack of sleep comes with newborns. Wrapping her arms around the sleeping baby Will, Caroline rocks, glowing with a tired joy. I feel drained, but I eke out a smile. Despite our fatigue, being together brings a sense of peacefulness.

But where is Rashida?

We don't like to meet as the *Bowl of Berries Book Club* without all members. This reminds me to fill Caroline in on our ladies' retreat she missed.

"Hey, Carrie Rae, how about telling Caroline how you belted out your song so beautifully last weekend?" I say, smiling ear to ear with pride.

"Sherry got me to sing because her speaking message convicted me to do things when I feel afraid . . . just like Queen Esther. Esther was young like me, and she risked her life. Sherry reminded the ladies in the audience, if we don't obey God and do HIS purposes, then God will use somebody else. I was determined to use the gift of singing God gave me. I want to be used by God for HIS purposes for such a time as this," Carrie Rae says.

She winks at me with a smile, adding, "And we don't want Sherry singing off key."

She covers her ears, wincing her face jokingly. I laugh, tossing a pillow at her.

"Hey, I sang with my hands in sign language right beside you. We were a duet. But you're right, nobody needs to hear my singing voice. By the way, you sang beautifully, setting up the message with a powerful force."

Carrie Rae says, "Caroline, you would have loved the authentic sharing. Sherry spoke about Esther the first night. It went perfectly, but no one responded to her altar call. Then the next morning, Sherry shared her personal testimony of finding Jesus. Everything went wrong that could go wrong."

Dani nodded her head in agreement.

"But at the end, Sherry confessed her personal areas of sin and fell on her face before God and everyone. The next thing you know, the ladies rushed to the front like there was some kind of emergency call. So many Christians confessed sins and repented. Many became followers of Jesus for the first time."

"It be like a concert mosh pit," Dani says.

"It was a revival," says Carrie Rae, and she turns to me asking me to share how the Spirit continued to move at the third session.

"After the emotional revival, with so many confessing sins, I decided to be as authentic as possible. I shared how God doesn't promise us ease. God said we will have struggles, but we can take heart because God gives us strength to overcome."

"Alleluia," pipes in Caroline.

"I shared about our bedbug infestation, costing us thousands to eradicate and other struggles with raising Drew. I felt like Job from the Bible with all my trials."

Caroline scratches her neck.

I assure Caroline, "We got rid of the bedbugs, but my anxiety issues kicked in."

I place my hands on my heart, continuing, "I felt prompted and convicted to get real about my own struggles with worry. I talked about the challenges of supporting Drew with his autism and fetal alcohol syndrome, as well as getting him ready for adulthood. Drew, trying to live independently, increases our prayer life daily."

Smiling at baby Will, I say, "I asked any mothers with special-needs or prodigal children to stand for prayer. One-by-one these weary ladies stood, fighting back tears."

Carrie Rae adds, "We prayed in clusters over each woman standing. We cried out to the Lord on their behalf."

I describe how we could feel the Spirit of God moving as we prayed over these warrior mommas who work so diligently raising their children.

Dani joins in. "Then one of those standing ladies spoke up, and she be sobbing. She cried out she be exhausted and was losing all hope. She done say this lifted her out of a pit," Dani says, "Then all different women popped up and asked for prayers for different struggles. I couldn't believe it, but some confessed their bad and wrongs of being selfish and not reaching out to others. Whoa! They be confessing sins and calling out to God again like the morning session. Da ladies be running up to the stage and bowing on the ground, praying to God to forgive dar sins. And a bunch of ladies rush up to pray over them. I ain't never seen nothing like dat weekend."

Dani wags her head back and forth, her hands in the air.

"We experienced two mini-revivals at the retreat," I say, nodding. "When we confess our sins, we break down pretentious walls, leading others to get real with God. I talked about the absence of God's name in the book of Esther, but God clearly maintains complete control. God allows hardships. He can use all things to grow us in HIS strength when we're called to HIS purposes.

Just then Rashida bursts through the door, "I got answers to my prayers!"

Waving a plastic bag with notebook papers inside, she shouts, "Your prayers work!"

CHAPTER 35

Do not let your hearts be troubled and do not be afraid.
John 16:27b NIV

We all place our pointer fingers to our lips to shush her. She hushes suddenly and tiptoes quietly to gush on baby Will. He sleeps through her outburst.

She whispers, "Sorry, I forgot we have a baby in our group."

In a softer voice, Rashida reveals she got a mysterious letter in the mail and the details make it legit. She opened the mail while eating. As she read the letter, she started choking on her dinner. She plopped in a chair to read it several more times. Rashida put the note in a plastic bag carefully with plans to take to the police station in the morning.

Caroline says, "Well, what's the letter about? The suspense is killing us."

"It's about murder . . . the murder of my husband and our sons."

We gasp in unison.

"Read it. Read it."

Clearing her voice, she reads, *"Dear Rashida Jackson, I know who killed your husband and sons 17 years ago. One killer died in a gang fight years after your family got shot. The other brother, who drove the car, sits in prison with 2 life sentences and no parole for other gang crimes.*

You are completely safe.

The 3rd brother in the car was only 10 years old when it happened.

The older boys were drinking. They babysat their younger brother that night. The 10-year-old played with a gun he done found under the seat. He pretended to shoot out the backseat window. He ain't know it be a real gun.

When the bullet shot, he was shocked. His bro took the gun and yelled. They stopped the car. Panicking, the brother jumped out and shot your husband and other son, so they won't be alive to testify against them. It was in front of the church. This oldest brother shot at the cross on top of the church as they drove away.

Ain't nobody saw them.

They cannot ever get you and your girls. You are safe. The little brother did not know it be a real gun with a real bullet. It was an accident. The 10-year-old told no one because his brothers said his mom would go to jail if he told. His brothers called their little bro a gangster growing up. But dis little bro refused to join a gang.

He ain't never hurt another soul.

The little brother still be having nightmares. He cannot forgive himself.

He is so sorry and carries his shame with him like a 100-pound weight. He thinks about it every day. His mom died a while back, and he thought to tell the cops. Nobody gonna believe his story. The po-po would slam him in jail. He does not do crime.

This be the honest truth.

The youngest brother is so sorry for all he took from you in the accidental shooting. He knows you could never forgive him. His nightmares never end. Your husband shielded your sons with his body. He died trying to protect his kids. I hope knowing this makes you feel safe again. Your husband died a hero."

We stare at each other, shaking our heads.

"I can't believe this," I say.

"How did they know your address?" Caroline asks.

"Maybe seeing your face in the paper recently stirred it all up," says Dani.

"Who do you suppose wrote this letter? Do you think it was the 10-year-old boy who grew up?" I ask.

"I asked all these same questions. When I take it to the police, they can check for fingerprints. Maybe the prints will be in the crime database," Rashida says.

She plops down in a chair, covering her face with both hands, the letter in her lap.

She opens her hands up like peek-a-boo and whispers, "My fears are floating away. Terror lifts off my shoulders. This feels like closure. Here in Villa, the twins and I are finally safe."

A noise near the backdoor startles us. We jolt back in our chairs. My eyes dart to the door. Slowly, the handle turns.

"Who's there?" Dani asks firmly, squinting her eyes.

A man in all black carrying a gun slithers inside. Is it the same guy who robbed the bank? He has the identical fake beard stuck on crooked at the same ridiculous slant.

What's happening in our safe village?!

CHAPTER 36

Such are the paths of all who go after ill-gotten gain;
it takes away the life of those who get it.
Proverbs 1:19 NIV

We scream, and the baby explodes in reactive wailing.

The gunman waves his arms, attempting to calm us down.

"Listen, ain't nobody's getting hurt here. We just gonna take our little friend Dani here down to da bank to withdraw da money."

Dani yells, "What are you doing here?!"

"We heard ya came upon a windfall. $255,000 in cold hard cash wit your *Go-Fund-Me*. It be more than our bank heist. We be collecting on our fair share of your fame."

I slowly edge toward the door. He notices me. "Hold it right there, little missy. My partner outside makes sure ain't nobody leaves or enters. Ya got that?"

I freeze, heart pounding.

"We'll tie yous all up here," he says, pulling zip ties from his black cinch bag on his back. "In da morning, Dani will stroll into the bank and close out all her accounts. She will withdraw it all."

The front door opens. Another man walks in, wearing dark jeans and a black hoody.

"How convenient," he says, scooping up our cell phones and dropping them in his black cinch sack. He smiles.

His teeth need to be brushed, and he wears a fake beard.

"The folks in this village sure are friendly. Just ask anybody about Dani. They know where you live."

The gunman in the living room says, "I'm just telling them how they gonna hang out until we be back wit $255,000 in cold hard cash," he leers at Dani.

"If any of yous try to escape, we call our fourth buddy who be guarding Cash Jones . . . and order Cash killed instantly. We read the papers. Y'all believe Cash as an innocent hero, but the town thinks he's a heel. Ha."

"Prove it. If Cash be alive and held hostage, then let us talk to him on speaker phone on your cell right now," demands Dani, planting her hands on her hips.

She pulls off an attitude, jiving her head.

The gunmen look at each other with squinty eyes.

The one in our room waving the gun at us says, "We be in charge. We call da shots."

I notice Rashida sliding her note down under the chair cushion. The gunman notices yelling, "Everyone put yo hands up."

Our hands thrust up in the air, except for Dani's.

With resolve, Dani points, shouting, "Cash is dead, or you'd be letting us hear his voice. Your plan ain't gonna work. Y'all need to give up on this heist, too. You done botched the bank heist."

I stiffen, darting my eyes over at Dani. What's up with Dani's boldness? Carrie Rae does not whimper. Surprise. Rashida's eyes glare with fire.

Dani continues, "All over da news, it be saying ya only got less than $4,000 bucks."

Dani gives a fake laugh.

"Ha. You be the laughingstock. And my bank ain't gonna give me da the money back. I done bought this place. Caroline done put da rest in . . . in . . . What ya call them . . . stockings?" Dani says.

I curl up one corner of my mouth. It's stocks, not stockings. Why is Dani insulting the guys with guns, anyway? Why get them mad?

The gunman grabs Caroline by the hair again, like he did in the bank vault. He yanks her up off the couch as she clings to her screaming baby.

We gasp.

Baby Will scrunches his face, bawling.

"She's right. I told ya we shouldn't do this. Let's split right now. This beard itches like crazy. I say we out," the kitchen gunman says, fidgeting, looking out the dark windows. "This be a messed-up night."

Baby Will screams nonstop, arching his back.

Caroline rocks, attempting to soothe him while in the grasp of the armed intruder.

The bad guy rubs his hair with the gun hand and shakes his head. Doubt and rage mix for the dumbfounded robber.

Panic kicks in as he twitches repeatedly.

The baby screams with increasing intensity.

"I ain't letting no broad steal more money than me. Especially HER. Zip tie them all."

Then he glares at Dani's defiant face.

"This be personal with this loser. We got history in Chicago, don't we? I'm gonna settle this right now.'"

"Not on my watch," Rashida yells, lunging for the gun and diving on top of the gunman.

He tumbles backwards, pulling Caroline and the shrieking baby downward.

Carrie Rae kicks the gun out of his hand. She pulls a gun out of her ankle holster that was concealed under her pant leg. Pointing at the kitchen gunmen, Carrie Rae whirls around to aim at the gunman, squished underneath Rashida.

"Run. Get help now!" Carrie Rae yells.

The girl did not freeze. She resonates like a police officer with her firm tone and decisive action. Whoa!

I bolt for the door as Dani follows instinctively.

Egad! There IS a third gunman out here.

We dash toward the light of the fast-food restaurant down the way with the gangster pursuing. Tripping over random low spots, I sprint to the lit-up parking lot, yelling to call 911. The customer pulling into the drive doesn't see or hear us.

We slither behind a semi. It's about to pull out.

Aligning our feet behind semi tires, I peer underneath the semi rig to spot the gunman sprinting while whipping his head side by side. He's on the hunt. He fails to find us with his shifting search.

My chest rises and falls, panting and catching my breath.

"Follow me."

I slip under the semi, grab the metal bracing underneath the rig, and pull my feet up. I squeeze my flip-flop feet up under a metal strap. Dani does the same. We hide side-by-side, clutching the undercarriage of the semi.

Grasping tight, we hold our bodies up as the semitrailer rolls out. I inhale the exhaust, burning my lungs as we turn our heads toward the pursuing gunman. He squints his eyes right at us.

Egad!

He spots us.

He dashes to lurch onto the back of the tractor trailer. I roll my eyes when I hear his body thud on the back bumper. Why pursue so fiercely? The semi rolls down the road, unbeknownst to its three uninvited passengers.

We jostle underneath, gripping tight and gritting our teeth.

The rig speeds up, then turns down the side street toward the industrial park.

The railroad tracks ahead will rattle us off.

My hair whips around my face as we make eye contact. The driver pumps the brakes, slowing before the tracks. Good. Our grip lessens. We better drop off now, taking our chances with the gunman on the back.

I yell to Dani to drop on the count of three.

We lower our bodies down.

"Don't let the tires squish you."

She's got on her jeans and boots, so she'll fare better than me in my flip-flops and flimsy leggings. Here goes nothing but road rash.

"One. Two. THREE!"

CHAPTER 37

Fear and trembling have beset me:
horror has overwhelmed me.
I said, "Oh, that I had wings like a dove!
I would fly away and find rest.
Psalm 55:6 NIV

My flip-flops go flying off my feet. My hair whips in my face as we thud down. I tense and jerk as the road peels our skin off our backs like melting butter gliding on a cheese grater. As we slide down the road on our backsides, the rear tires whiz by our faces.

That's too close.

Our eyes wince from the jarring and road scraping. Action flicks are fake news. Those actors aren't fazed by the jolting of dropping three feet and sliding 15 miles per hour on their backs. It's like getting hit on the backside by a home-run hitter's bat on a third strike full swing.

We . . . must . . . fight . . . through the pain . . . and the jarring . . . or we die.

My head spins.

I determine to get up. I glance back at the gunman. The pursuer remains hellbent on getting to us. This must be a vendetta against Dani? Why doesn't he flee town? Their heist plans unravel.

We crawl to our feet, scuttling out of the road.

There's not a car in sight either direction, but the dimming taillights of the semi.

Go figure.

Where can we get help? In the dark, I squint, spotting the gunman jumping off the back of the semi. He wipes out, too.

We hear sirens in the distance. YES! Surely this attacker will back off now.

Nope.

He's like the Terminator. He keeps charging with his gun in hand.

"Hurry up," I motion to Dani, who follows me at top speed toward the mill.

We run to the office doors. Locked. I pound on the door. There's no time. What? Two figures come out of the shadows, rushing towards us from the vicinity of Dani's house.

Are those good guys or bad guys? What's wrong with these attackers? The sirens close in on us. Why don't they flee from the cops? Their plan foiled completely.

The sirens scream louder and louder. We sprint again. Ouch. These parking lot stones crunch my bare feet like Legos on Drew's floor.

Guns in hand, they impede toward us. The semi-ride-along dude stumbles closer, too. We're trapped on all sides. We dash toward the silos.

Think. Think. THINK. My heart pounds through my chest.

The only way out . . . up. Dani jumps up to grab the ladder secured to the cement silo. She whispers for me to follow. Why whisper? I catch my breath.

Heights petrify me.

"Help! Help!" I yell, scaling up the ladder on the side of the mill tower.

I gasp for air. These cement monstrosities loom over Villa. I always wondered about the view, but never wanted to climb . . . barefoot . . . in the dark of night . . . with psycho gunmen in hot pursuit.

Why do they keep chasing us? Hearing my panting, I wonder what their beef is to stay in pursuit. The police will arrive any second. Our pursuers are completely irrational boneheads. Flee from the cops, dudes. What's wrong with you?

We got psychos chasing us.

Oh wait. I remember to yell "fire" if you're about to be raped. Then bystanders will take action.

"FIRE! FIRE!" I shout as loudly as possible, breathing deep gasps of air while ascending.

"Just keep climbing. Are they following us?"

We grab rung after rung as Dani and I scale the ladder up the outside of the monolith. My breathing grows louder as the wind whips my hair.

"I'm afraid of heights. I can't look down."

My bare feet throb with each rung upward. Why did I lose my flip-flops? Why? Why didn't I wear tennis shoes? I puff out a huge huff.

"Keep climbing. I know these dudes. They be gangsters. . . . *pant* . . . They tried to get Cash and me in on a robbery in Chicago. . . . *breathe* . . . We refused. I humiliated them in front of their gang. It's an honor thing. They will never let it go. We moved from Chicago to be rid of them."

We scale upward rapidly, shouting to be heard.

"Did you tell the cops this?"

"I didn't know it be them who done the bank robbery . . . until tonight. They be bad dudes . . . *pant* . . . and dumb as a box of rocks. It's personal. He won't stop 'til I'm dead . . . *gasp* . . . I'm sure he killed Cash."

"FIRE! FIRE!"

Sweat drips off my face as I shout loud enough to wake the neighborhood. My hand slips . . . *gasp* . . .. How much farther? I grip the next rung. "What's the plan at the top?"

"Just keep climbing. I'm sorry I gots yous all into dis. Yous had nice calm lives before yous met me."

My arms feel like lead, but I keep climbing hand-over-hand.

I refuse to look down. Should I stop and kick the chasing varmint off the ladder? No. He's got a gun. He'll shoot me . . . *pant* . . ..

My bare feet pound in pain.

My arms ache and feel heavy like weights.

I grab rung after rung . . . *deep breath* . . .. How many more?

We resemble Rocky Balboa running up the steps in Philadelphia . . . only I won't raise my hands over my head at the top in celebration.

We might run up to meet our . . . downfall.

"Maybe at the top we can throw stuff down and knock him off."

I watched *Home Alone*. There's always something nearby to throw. But that's a movie . . . *breathe* . . .. We've got to think of a plan for the top . . . *breathe* . . .. They bolt everything down for high winds up there.

We have no escape strategy . . . *deep breath* . . ..

Those sirens stop right under us. Why don't they shoot the bad guys? Red and blue lights flash on the side of the cement mill towers.

"Dani, climbing was NOT our best option . . . *gasping more air* . . .. Maybe we should have taken our chances on the ground?"

"Nope. We'd be shot and splattered dead."

"We might splatter on the ground . . . if we FALL."

I need to gut out the pain for a chance to live . . . *breathe deep* . . .. Is this how Moses felt holding up his arms in the battle to encourage his troops in Biblical days? Aaron and Hur supported Moses' tired arms. Moses got help.

I need help. I'm freaking out.

"Remember, I am afraid of heights."

"What did you speak about at your retreat? Do it afraid . . . *breathe* . . . Here's yo chance to live what ya be preaching, Miss Sherry Strawberry."

"Thank you, Miss Holy Spirit Junior. By the way, if we don't make it, I'm glad to know you . . . *huff , , , puff* . . . I'll be with Jesus, so don't cry for me. Tell Kyle, Drew, and the crew . . . *wheeze* . . . I love them. How much farther? By the way, are you ready to put your faith in Jesus Christ NOW?"

"Yous be high pressure witnessing to me again, Sherry? I think I am ready. I give Jesus my life right now. I hope God gets me out of dis mess."

"So do you Believe Jesus died for your sins . . . *breathe* . . . and rose so you can be forgiven . . . *deep breath* . . . and if we fall, we fall into Jesus' arms?"

"I believe in Jesus. I give him my life this instant. Amen."

"Amen. You put your faith in Jesus. You're like the thief on the cross."

We struggle, scaling the ladder.

"Who you calling thief? The thieves be below us . . . in hot pursuit."

I don't have time to explain that the thief on the cross got saved.

"How much farther?"

I stop momentarily to take a deep breath, summoning strength I don't have. Help me, Jesus!

"I'm here. Come on, don't stop. Keep climbing . . . *pant* . . .. Don't look down. Come on. Come on!" yells Dani.

She wills me up, with her hands waving to keep ascending. Exhausted, I roll up the last rung, plopping for a millisecond before crawling to my wobbly feet.

Dani rushes over, jiggling the door handle to the little room up on the roof. Who locks the door up here? Why? Dani grabs my arm, and we hide behind the small building in the middle of the top of the tower.

We hear each step the gunman clunks on the ladder rungs.

Dani signals me with her pointer finger to her lip to hush me. The sirens of police cars wail, speeding in our direction. We hear cars skid to a stop below us. Did I hear Kyle call up in a frantic voice? If he finds out it's us up here, he'll break the police barriers and bust these bad guys' heads.

Pinch.

I'm not dreaming.

We're living a nightmare.

I slap my hands to the side of my head like the *Home Alone* movie star. We frantically jerk around, looking for anything to throw or defend ourselves. Nada. Nothing.

Think. Think. THINK! I got nothing.

Leaning against the back side of the little room on top of the towering cement cylinders, I whisper between gasps of breaths, "Our best hope is talking sense to them . . . *gasp* . . . or shoving them over the edge. What do you think, Dani?"

No answer from Dani.

"Oh God, please help us like you helped Queen Esther and Mordecai . . . *pant* . . . who were about to go to the gallows! I'm losing hope here, LORD!"

I squeeze Dani's hand, wondering what's our escape plan. We're up ten-stories tall . . . outside. The wind tousles my hair. More sirens blast, rushing closer.

Will we survive this?

I feel like Esther waiting for the King to set his hand on the royal scepter. Will we live through this ordeal? I am not looking down . . . *pant, pant* . . .. These are the gallows. Who's going to face the fate of evil Haman in the Queen Esther narrative? Will it be us . . . or the gunmen?

Bang. Ping.

We shriek. A bullet whizzes. Why shoot when the police spotlight points at you? What kind of desperate criminals are you?

"Can't you just give yourself up? Raise your hands and let's all get out of here alive." I yell, voice quivering.

No answer. We hear a creepy laugh.

"I know that laugh," Dani whispers intensely.

We hear steps clopping on the rooftop as the gunman approaches. Is Kyle down there watching? So much for our relaxing evening. My heart pounds out of my chest. I hear it beat . . . *pant, pant* . . .. I clutch my turning stomach. I'm about to throw up.

I ready myself to run.

Who makes it off this tower . . . alive?

Bang!

CHAPTER 38

My heart is in anguish within me;
the terrors of death have fallen on me.
Psalm 55:4 NIV

Bang! Bang!
The gangster shoots again, slithering around the corner.
We peel off the wall, evading around the backside.
Dani shoves me ahead of her to run the 30-foot-long plank to the other silo. Screams echo below. It's a long way down. I dare not glance down.
The spotlights follow us. Dani follows. Our hands guide along the rails as we rush to the other side. Sheesh. The walkway is open-air and narrow between silos.
We make it halfway across.
"Give yourself up. You're surrounded," belts out an authoritative voice from a bullhorn below.
I hear a shot and whip back around. Dani faces her attacker, holding her arm. Dani's hit.
"Yous got what you want. Leave Sherry alone. She's got nothing wit you," Dani barks.
"Freeze right there, or I'll shoot," shouts a female voice.
It's Carrie Rae. She's the third one pursuing the pursuer. Where did she muster such bravery?
The gunman lurches at Dani, grabbing her shoulders, leaning her over the guardrail.
"You'll die just like Cash. I shot him and tossed him over a

211

bridge," he tells her, mushing his nose against her face as she struggles.

He did it. He confessed to killing Cash. Cash was innocent. Will this crazed criminal do the unthinkable to Dani?

He will.

He shovels her over the railing, yelling something about nobody dishonoring him. My knees give way as I bend in the fetal position. I wait to hear Dani splat. Screams from the crowd forming below pierce my ears. I don't look down.

I melt in terror.

Dani's gone.

Bang!

Carrie Rae shoots the gunman. He grabs his side, lurching for me.

I roll back on my shoulders, kicking forcefully. I hear his gun clunk out of his hand.

Good!

He clutches my legs, twisting me out over the edge.

Not good!

He hangs off the edge as I kick fiercely.

My peripheral vision distorts. I block out all sounds, hearing only my breathing. All else blurs. The gunman wraps around my leg, dangling. He writhes, squirming and hanging off of me. His fingers press deep into my leg . . . ten stories high with gusting wind.

Pure terror.

My elbow wraps around the guardrail post. I clutch my hand on the other side. My triangular locked elbow holds me strong as I grip both hands tight. Who knew that my bent elbow and my interlocked arms can bear this bulky weight? We both now dangle over the edge. He clasps my leg underneath me.

Screams below pierce the night.

"KYLE! I LOVE YOU!" I shout my last words. This is it.

Carrie Rae rushes to secure my grasp of my hand with her one hand. Her gun hand points toward the other gunman.

"Go back down, or I'll shoot," she yells at the other gunman on the silo. She fires a shot. She hits his hand and his gun goes flying. What a shot!

My grip holds on my other hand, but the robber's grasp on my leg slips as my leggings slide down. Are you kidding me? My underwear stays. Praise. Who thinks about this when dangling in danger? I do.

His fingers slink down. I kick my legs. The gunman drops with my leggings in his grasp. Flailing his arms, he plummets to his demise. The screeching and screams tell me a large crowd gathers below. I don't look down.

I sway, attempting to rock my legs back up.

My chest heaves. My arm muscles twitch, losing the grip on one hand. Swaying in the breeze, I dangle by a single arm with a slowly sliding grip.

My hair whips into my eyes.

I writhe, clenching with my last ounce of strength.

This is the end.

My head thrashes in panic. Veins bulge in my neck and arms. The spotlights blind my vision. I cannot . . . keep my grip . . . or pull up my legs.

I am slipping . . . downward . . . toward the screeching voices.

Laura Loveberry

CHAPTER 39

I will praise you as long as I live,
and in your name, I will lift up my hands.
Psalm 63:4 NIV

Carrie Rae slaps her hand over mine, cementing my failing grip. She reaches down, pulling my legs up. In the split second I lost my grip, Carrie Rae rescues me. She clings to me, gasping deeply.

With veins popping and sweat dripping, she pulls me on top of the walkway.

We heap in a pile, but we are safe.

Between gasps of air, she tells me the cops climbed the ladder. They apprehend the other gunman.

"It's over," Carrie Rae expresses.

But my fingers cling, locked to the rail again. Now, I cannot release my hand. I cannot move.

"KYLE! KYLE!"

I know I am safe, but I cannot move. I freeze with shock and cannot free my grip. I am secure on the plank, but my mind won't let me let go.

"KYLE, WHERE ARE YOU?"

"You got this. Let's just crawl along the plank. You don't need to stand. Let's just crawl." Carrie Rae's voice soothes me.

I inhale deeply and exhale. Keeping my arm hooked, I bring my knees underneath me.

"Did that guy pull my pants off?"

"I'm afraid so."

"I do still have on my underwear, right?"

"Yes. They appear to be your heart-shaped strawberry granny panties," she snickers.

I giggle.

We both laugh, releasing a level of stress.

Carrie Rae coaxes me to release my iron grip on the rail and crawl. She crawls backward, persuading me, face to face, as I crawl forward. Don't look down. Don't look down. Keep crawling back to the silo.

I hear a soothing, familiar voice. It's got to be Kyle!

I look over Carrie Rae's shoulder and see Kyle standing on the silo. That's my knight in shining armor.

Kyle's jaw clenches with eyes of a tiger. His arms reach to rescue me.

I crawl faster.

Kyle clutches me, lifting me to my feet. He wraps me in protective arms.

I melt into his manly embrace.

We hear roars and cheering. I think the entire town gathers below. Holding onto Kyle, I peer down for the first time. Whooping and hollering continue. It is the entire community, the firetrucks, the police cars, the celebrating village people.

Then I realize I'm in my underwear. At least it's not my skimpy briefs. This morning, out of clean laundry, I put on the only pair left . . . a gag gift . . . granny panties. Who knew I needed more coverage today?

"Honey, I'm in my heart-shaped strawberry underwear," I whisper.

I giggle. Kyle chuckles. Carrie Rae squeals with laughter. The policemen, who arrived up the indoor steps, shake their heads and suppress grins.

Raising my eyebrows, stark reality returns. I puff out my air.

"Kyle, I can't believe Dani died."

"About that . . . well . . . let's go down. Would you prefer the outside ladder or the inside stairs?"

"Inside stairs," I say weakly.

"Good choice," says Carrie Rae.

Kyle takes off his shirt with the collar keeping on his t-shirt and hands his polo shirt to me. I slip my feet through the neck of his shirt, creating my makeshift skirt. Once I tuck in the sleeves, button the neck hole at my waist, it looks like a red skirt. My hair is askew. Only one strawberry earring remains. It's gnarled in my hair.

We're somewhat ready.

We walk through the previously locked door and down the inside steps, commenting about how boring the trip down compares to the trip up. With lips flapping and arms flailing, I talk a mile per minute, telling Kyle how we hitched a ride under a semi-truck. I yack all the way down.

Exiting the bottom door, my eye catches the police officers shoving a handcuffed dude in black in the back of a patrol car and pulling out. He looked an awful lot like the guy I kicked off my leg. Baffling.

The crowd erupts, cheering his departure and our coming down to ground level.

In the commotion, our friends, family, and the rest of the *Bowl of Berries Book Club* greet us.

All of them.

Rashida Jackson, Caroline Forbes-Radshaw, baby Wilmington, Sterling Forbes-Radshaw, Drew Strawberry, and . . . and . . . DANI JONES!

What?

I rub my eyes. How? I squint to be sure. I don't believe what I behold! My eyes double in size. My mouth opens to scream, but no sound comes out.

CHAPTER 40

. . . with singing lips my mouth will praise you.
Psalm 63:5b NIV

Dani grins widely with an arm wrapped in white gauze. We stretch our arms, running hard into a bouncing wrap-around embrace. We wince when our raw backs feel the pressure, but who cares?!

Dani is . . . ALIVE!

"What? . . . . How can . . . you fell from . . . like ten-stories tall . . . I saw you FALL over the rail," I stammer.

My mind jangles.

A huge circle gathers around our reunion. Dani swoops her arm toward the firetrucks.

"Villa's finest spread out dar net wit firemen and police gripping it tight," Dani says, looking over at them in admiration.

"I knew I be dead waiting to fall into Jesus' arms like you be saying. Then, what the heck?! I did thud hard and knock da wind out. But next thing I knows . . . I be flying back up in the night sky . . . and down . . . and up . . . and down . . . then I thought those firefighters be God's angels. They be all around me. They done saved me on dat drop with the catch net. I ain't believe it myself, but I be alive."

The surrounding crowd cheers and claps.

Dani reaches over, grabbing the policeman's bullhorn, asking how to use it. With her mouth to the mega horn, she announces to the cheering crowd, "Dis firemen and police be great catchers. Let's hear it for da life net! Let's hear it for da rescuers!"

The crowd's response deafens with cheers, hoots, and hollering! I signal Carrie Rae to follow me as we ask to climb on top of the firetruck. We straddle the hoses.

My back, bloodied with road rash, bleeds through my filthy shirt. My red skirt looks clean, but it's actually Kyle's shirt off his back, and I'm barefoot. The red skirt matches the red blood on my back and the red firetruck. So, there's that. Who thinks of matching like me? No sane person.

Carrie Rae looks pretty good. Her hair's a bit tousled by the high winds up at the silos.

We are Carrie Rae and Sherry Kay . . . and it's time for a concert of praise on top of the firetruck. Carrie Rae and I stand, feet spread, atop of the red cab of the truck.

I belt into the megaphone. "I thank God for Rashida jumping on the gunman to protect us. *Cheers.* I thank God for Carrie Rae, whipping out her gun, chasing down the bad guys and scaling those silos to do it." *More cheers.*

I point up dramatically to the top of the towering silos.

"I thank God for Dani never giving up the escape. And let's all thank our fine firefighters and police officers for taking action to catch Dani and save her life!" *Cheer explosion.*

The street crowd erupts like a crazy dance party at New York's Times Square. Only this time, the countdown ball didn't drop. No. Dani Jones dropped from ten stories high, bounced around, and she lives to talk about it.

Reporter cameras flash.

I look over to see my Drew in his glory, sitting below in the front seat of the other firetruck. He flashes a grin the size of those silos.

Police spotlights shine, dancing around on the cement towers like disco ball lights. Kyle beams his broadest smile. The crowd grows in numbers with all the commotion.

"Carrie Rae Hucklenuckle . . . yes, it's Hucklenuckle . . . *clapping* . . . will now sing her new song she wrote . . . while trapped in the bank vault. It's called . . . *Praise Chorus* . . . Sing along. It's catchy," I announce from behind the mega horn.

Looking at the firemen lined up, I shout, "And you guys did GREAT to catch Dani!"

Cheers rise from the crowd as I hand Carrie Rae the bullhorn. I yell in her ear, "After tonight, nothing's too scary for you. Do it again. You're not afraid. Sing, giiiiirl!"

Carrie Rae belts out, *"I will praise You as long as I live. In your name, I lift up my hands. I will praise You as long as I live. In your name, I lift up my hands."*

I do the signing with dramatic motions, encouraging the crowd to lift their hands and sing along.

By this time, most of the village gathers around the firetruck. Many dance and sing exuberantly. Some raise their hands, singing along. We celebrate under the starry night, alongside the towering silos.

I gaze around at all the bobbing heads, bouncing smiles, and belting voices.

What an epic night to praise our strong and mighty God!

Carrie Rae continues. *"Whatever I go through, whatever I do, oo, oo, with singing lips, I'll glorify You. I will praise You, as long as I live. In your name, I lift up my hands . . .."*

She sings through the chorus again and again.

Nobody wants the night to end. I pinch myself. Something so unbelievable happened tonight.

In my overflowing joy, I gaze down on our group. I thank God for Rashida and her twin girls singing beside her. Tonight, Rashida found the peace she sought in a revealing letter from a stranger. Oh, and she squashed the gunman momentarily, giving us time to escape. Her bitterness fades as closure sets in.

Looking over at Sterling with his arm around Caroline, I smile broader. She coos down at the baby that fills her once empty arms. It's years of waiting like a long labor of love for their special gift. But their most precious present is their peace in knowing Jesus. Oh, how truly rich their lives grow now. She surrendered her secret and embraces Sterling and God's forgiveness. Baby Wilmington sleeps soundly, with the boisterous praise singing all around.

And look at Dani over there, dancing wildly.

The gauze of her Band-Aid comes loose, whipping around as she flails her arms. She dances erratically. Attending the Christian version of AA meetings brings Dani's drinking problem under control. Mentoring her brings reward to my life-coaching soul. I smile, watching her dance freely. She's a pliable work in progress. Her tortured past no longer binds her.

She's free indeed.

She's got high-suspense bedtime stories to tell her "kids." Her "children" are the future clients at her new home and at the Dani and Drew Carwash and Car Repair Shop. Drew's got two moms now. One mom can brag of major movie-stunt skills jumping off towers. The other mother can't hardly crawl across a bridge plank between two silos without quivering and wetting herself. *Ha. Ha.*

Hey, I didn't pee myself up there. Huh?

I glance back at Carrie Rae, singing boldly as I dramatically sign her lyrics for the crowd. We make a great team. I can't wait to tell Carrie Rae the news of the record label. They want to sponsor us both for a speaking and concert tour across the United States. They plan to schedule an event at the Cherokee Reservation where Carrie Rae first got saved . . . and end the tour in Hawaii.

Kyle negotiated the Hawaiian island's last leg of the tour. In Hawaii, they will pay for all the members of our Bowl of Berries Book Club and family for a two-week stay. Carrie Rae won't need her arm twisted to sign that contract. We'll suffer for Jesus there. I smile.

Aloha, Hawaii. Here we come.

Carrie Rae will welcome my signing beside her as she sings with her God-given talent. Eventually, she'll sing on her own. For now, we are officially Carrie Rae and Sherry Kay when she signs the contract. Teaming up will be fun!

Carrie Rae saved the day.

She whipped out her ankle gun, saving our lives at Dani's house and on the top of those silos. I glance up at the ten stories of cement with blue and red police lights pulsating on the sides. Valiant describes Carrie Rae.

Even with my back a stinging mess, I beam a blessed smile from on top of this firetruck's impromptu stage.

Carrie belts out one last verse. *"My soul thirsts for You, in a dry and weary land. Because your love is better than life. I will praise You as long as I live. In your name, I lift up my hands."*

Officers turn off the red and blue lights. Mill personnel secure the lock on the steel box to prevent climbing the ladder from the ground level. Somebody may get a scolding for leaving it open, but I'll deliver a bowl of strawberries to the mill for providing our escape.

The night dies down and people disperse.

The *Bowl of Berries Book Club* circles up. We usually go arm behind backs, but Dani and I still wear our bloodied shirts sticking to our backs. *Wince.* We hold hands instead. As our eyes meet, we exchange grins. Our bond grows unbreakable, unshakeable, and unflappable.

We gaze around the circle, smiling and shaking our heads.

CHAPTER 41

. . . but that you be perfectly united in mind and thought.
1 Cor 1:10b NIV

God meets us right where we are.

The LORD mixed our misfit group together like a variety pack of berries. Our lives intertwine like vines with deep-rooted secrets, shocking plot twists, and adventures to prune us beyond our ability to bear. God dips it all in chocolate. Our love grows like a red strawberry.

When it's dipped in chocolate, we taste and see the LORD is good.

We've cultivated fruitful lives, digging deep into the darkest seasons of our past. Faith grew us. We stumbled into the garden of our souls as five complete strangers . . . and we walk out, flourishing as five sisters grafted into family.

Okay, we ran out at gunpoint, actually. But we unlocked the vault of our souls. We discovered soulmates who sparkle like precious jewels. Our bond—priceless.

"If only Cash were here," says Dani, looking up. "God rest his soul."

"I got proof he died a hero. Cash certainly sacrificed his life for Caroline's life," I say.

"Amen," Caroline says, looking out of the circle and back at her husband holding baby Will.

"I heard a confession proving Cash's innocence," I say.

"We knew it all along!"

"Ya got dat right. And I be a BIG miracle to be standing here. I done got shot . . . fell off those towers . . . and here I is wit out a scratch," Dani says with her gauze dangling down. "Well, a little scratch."

"I don't know how Dani and I will ever get our bloodied shirts off," I say with a grimace as the medic walks up.

"Girls, I hate to end the party, but these two need to go to the hospital to be checked out and cleaned up. My boss gave me orders," says the medic in uniform.

Several police officers approach our sacred circle for our individual statements.

We know the drill.

Before we break the circle of handholding, I remind the girls, "Hey, we're halfway done with our last chapter in *Invite Delight*. Let's bring our Bibles and study the book of John at my house next week, too."

All eyes shift over to our lone atheist.

Rashida breaks into her bold smile. "I'm good with that."

I raise my eyes upward, breathing deep. This is a night of MIGHTY miracles.

We move our circle inward with our hands piled up in the center like a timeout team huddle. Smirking, Carrie Rae comments on the possibility of Miss Sherry being frontpage news with a photo of her dangling off the railing . . . in her heart-shaped berry underwear. "The Headlines will be *'Mrs. Michigan Kicks Butt . . . Wearing Strawberry Granny Panties.'*"

This draws a huge laugh and a horrid picture in my mind. I forehead slap myself. Hey, why didn't I pee on the villain before I did my dropkick? I'm slipping. *Giggle.*

"The subtitle will be, *'Fearless Hucklenuckle Saves the Day. Who's Laughing Now?'*" I reply. We girls giggle. Carrie Rae smiles, unashamed of her name, brimming with Cherokee pride. She never froze tonight. Faced with fear, she responded heroically. She does not hide behind her hair.

Her confidence beams forth as the strength of the LORD shines through Carrie Rae Hucklenuckle.

"What about this caption? *'Rashida Jackson Jumps on Gunman.*

Squishes Him so Girls Escape,'" jokes Rashida. "I slowed the dude down with the weight of these bad-boy buns."

She slaps her derriere, jives her head, raising her brows. Her hands move like conducting a gospel choir. Her artsy, colorful bangles and bracelets clank on her swooping arms.

We giggle.

"Well, it should read, *'Cash Jones Dies a Hero,'"* Caroline says in a teary voice. "What would be my fate if it hadn't been for Cash Jones?"

I see her look to heaven, whispering, "I am . . . because you were, Cash. I'll try to live a worthy life."

My eyes brim instantly.

"Wait, da photo on the frontpage should be my furious swan dive off da silo. The caption be, *'Dani Dives into a New Adventure. Dani and Drew's Carwash and Auto Repair,'"* Dani states with her tooth-gapping smile.

High-fives and laughter bring back the celebratory mood.

The end of this day tastes like the last bite of a chocolate-covered strawberry. It's not the strawberry Cash sucked all the chocolate off and put back in the bowl. Nope. It's like the plumpest, ripe strawberry with warm, sweet chocolate oozing off the berry, flowing down my fingers.

It's a lip-smacking, finger-licking, oh-taste-and-see-the-LORD-is-GREAT kind of night.

Looking around at each beaming teammate in our timeout huddle, I take the lead with our hands piled up in the center. Lifting my face upward, I thank God for smiling sister soulmates. I express gratitude for our spiritual growth since locked in the vault. I slap my hand on top of the stack of hands in our sacred circle and lead the cheer, "To 'sistahood!'"

We throw our arms and our cares up to the LORD who answers prayers. With our hands raised to heaven, our *Bowl of Berry Book Club* shouts in unison, "S I S T A H O O D!"

FUNERAL EPILOGUE
PART ONE

Blessed are those who mourn, for they shall be comforted.
Matt. 5:4 NIV

It's hard to believe more than a month has passed since Dani Jones got tossed off the ten-story silo and survived, thanks to a rescue net. Praise God. The confession by Cash's murderer closed the case. Though search and rescue teams never found Cash's body, we will memorialize him today.

Cash regains his hero status in the eyes of the village, the state, and the entire nation.

Hordes of onlookers, grievers, and Cash fans line the streets on the route to his funeral. From the curb to the sidewalk, it looks more like a parade crowd than a funeral procession. The Villa Bible Church can't accommodate the crowds, so the venue changed to the Villa High School gymnasium.

The word spread to roll up a one-dollar bill, tie it with a green ribbon, and pin it to your shirt. Everyone wears one in honor of our village hero, Cash Jones. The trees lining the streets of Villa wrap in green ribbons. Once again, the ribbon tails wave to us in a fitting salute as the winds pick up on this sunny day.

Today, we celebrate the life of Cash Jones.

From my car window, I giggle, seeing the teens with rolled-up sleeves and flexing biceps, showing their "Cash is King" temporary tattoos. Their other arm outstretches toward us with a fist. Yeah, the knuckles display C-A-S-H, handwritten with permanent markers. The viral video of Cash fist pumping his "Cash is King" tattoo hits over a million views. It's famous. Teens copycat his look to honor Cash at his memorial.

Wouldn't Cash eat up all this fame like a chocolate-covered strawberry? If only he lived to see it all.

Caroline gave each of us "sisters" a pair of strawberry earrings to wear today to honor our berry-munching hero, Cash Jones.

We arrive at the packed gym and slip into our reserved seats in front. There remains a small aisle leading up to a stage set up under the raised basketball hoop. An abundance of flower bouquets, tied in green ribbons, line the backstage wall. Four front steps lead up to the microphone stand.

We reserved the front row chairs for the *Bowl of Berries Book Club*, for Reverend Clyde and his wife Gerrie of Villa Bible Church, and for a few distant relatives of Dani. Cash has no living relations. The church parishioners become Dani's true family. A small table, donning a black tablecloth, stands near the lone microphone on the stage. The display table holds a vase full of strawberries, dipped in chocolate, and skewered with long wooden sticks, designed to look like a bouquet of red roses.

There is one huge strawberry on a stick without chocolate.

We know it symbolizes the strawberry Cash sucked the chocolate off while in the vault. I giggle. I lean over, pointing out the plain strawberry with a whisper to Dani.

She snickers.

Dani spreads the comment down the line of book club gals in the front row. We giggle. Yuck! We hold our hands over our mouths to squash our giggle eruption at this funeral.

Beside the vase of strawberries on sticks, stands a life-size photo of Cash kissing his "Cash is King" bicep. His fist juts at the camera with his right hand. C-A-S-H letters spell out across his knuckles. It's the vault photo we all agreed represents Cash best . . . and it's bigger than life.

What a character!

A copy of the *Invite Delight* book and of the *Holy Bible* set on the table. The display represents our heroic Cash Jones and the *Bowl of Berries Book Club* whose lives Cash saved.

Carrie Rae plans to perform a song she wrote. She remembers attempting to sing a song at her parent's funeral and failing. She prays she can pull this off for Cash's honor. Hucklenuckle's confidence in singing grows stronger.

I think she'll sing through her song gloriously to honor our fearless Cash. We plan to all sing together the *Praise Chorus* song as the funeral ends and lead the audience in celebrating the life of Cash Jones.

We have stacks of Bibles in the back to offer as gifts at the end.

The murmurs hush as Pastor Clyde steps up to the microphone. He welcomes everyone, and introduces our first speaker, Caroline Forbes-Radshaw. I turn around and smile at Kyle, Drew, Sterling and the twins, who sit directly behind us. We sisters take a deep breath, grasp hands, and listen to Caroline while praying intently for her.

Caroline clears her throat, standing with perfect posture. She shares how she owes her very life to Cash, who stepped in front of a loaded gun pointed at her. Cash stepped in as a hostage. In a quivering voice, she explains how this would be her funeral, if it was not for the heroics of Cash Jones.

Caroline places her hand over her heart.

"I am alive . . . *sniffle* . . . because Cash risked his life to save me. The bank-robbing kidnapper confessed to killing Cash . . . *sniffle* . . . by throwing him off a bridge. Cash died, so I could . . . ."

Unexpectedly, Caroline stops talking, her eyes widen as if she saw a ghost. Her legs wobble . . . and down she falls, collapsing onto the stage floor with a thud.

The crowd gasps.

Rushing up the stage steps, Dani scoops up Caroline's limp body. Dani turns, facing the audience. Her eyes focus on the back of the gymnasium and pop open the same as Caroline's did. Dani's face contorts while her arms go limp, falling to her sides in bewilderment. Poor Caroline, not yet conscious, flops to the floor, thudding loudly down the stage steps.

Thud.

Thud.

Thud.

Instantly, the rest of us book-club girls rush to Caroline's aid.

Dani's face, frozen and oblivious to Caroline, drains to white as she stares with bulging eyes at the back of the gymnasium.

Dani is in shock.

One by one, we follow her gaze. Our mouths drop open.

FUNERAL EPILOGUE
PART TWO

He gives power to the faint,
and to him who has no might he increases strength.
Isaiah 40:29 ESV

A lone figure limps slowly up the aisleway. All eyes in the gym turn toward the bearded man walking.

It's a dead man walking!

Cash Jones?

He's alive?!

Rashida yells, slapping a hand on her hip, "You got some explaining to do, Cash."

The audience gasps in unison, gawking.

Cash staggers up the aisle.

His left leg drags. Cash's long, straggling hair swishes into his face as he lurches with each step. His face appears ragged.

"I got shot in the back."

The crowd gasps in bewilderment.

He falters another step. "And I got shot in the leg, . . ."

He wobbles forward, eyes focusing on Dani, remaining on the top of the stage in a frozen state of confusion.

". . . then the bank robber mushed his face into mine yelling about vengeance and . . . hurled me off a bridge."

Another loud breath from the audience erupts. Murmuring whispers spread, then fade to silence.

"I splatted after they tossed me over and crashed into da river below the bridge with a force knocking me out. The current contorted my body. I thrashed around, not knowing what direction be up. My lungs nearly burst. I could not hold my breath no more."

Whispers trickle through the crowd, staring in bewilderment.

"I remember gasping for air, but swallowing water instead. In the dark river, I kicked frantically, but I be sinking. I prayed to God, if he gets me out of dis, I would give him my life." Cash hobbles another step forward.

Silence holds the room, leaning in to hear Cash.

Many in the crowd grab cell phones and start videoing.

He speaks loudly, "It be dark, and I faded off. I woke up confused, cold, and in pain on the side of da river bank. My face mushed in mud. The bridge—no longer in sight. I ain't know where the heck I was. I be shaking, crawling to shore. My bullet wounds be covered in black leeches. I picked off each one. My leg be messed up."

With the audience enraptured, Cash continues, "I tore my shirt and wrapped my side and leg wounds. I done made a splint with two sticks and staggered along with a tree branch for a crutch. I dragged myself through an apple orchard into an abandoned barn. There was a rusty old car inside. I crawled into the dusty backseat, sleeping for days in and out of consciousness."

The audience leans forward, mesmerized by every word.

"My fever be burning me up. I prayed to God to break my sweaty temperature. I promised God that I'd give him my life if he healed me. When I looked at the bullet wound, it be red on da edge and moldy inside."

Cash inhales a deep breath. "I knew I be a goner with gangrene. I saw an old western movie scene where the dude laid on maggots to eat out the infection. Who knows if I be hallucinating or what, but I found an old hollow log crawling with maggots, and I laid on it. Pretty sure I passed out again."

The audience moaned in unison.

"I ain't got any idea of how long I laid there. But I remember thrashing, shaking, trembling, sweating. I knew I be dead. I prayed to God again. If he'd just let me see my girl Dani one more time, I'd give God my life."

Women in the audience let out an endearing, "Aaawww."

Cash nods his head, winks, and goes on talking. By this time, he is more than halfway up the aisle.

"Who knows if it happened, or I dreamed it? I ate apples and pears for days. I drank river water from an old bucket. One night, I snuck up to the farmhouse, peaking in da window at the news station. That's when I discovered the police had me as a suspect. I didn't know what to think. I went back to da abandoned barn to rethink my options."

Cash inhales deeply, lifting his chest.

Then he exhales and lowers his shoulders.

"So, I prayed to Jesus. 'I give you my life. I believe! Now, can you give me a sign if I should let Dani know I be alive?' Later, I snuck back up to the farmhouse. I peered through the window. And it be announcing my funeral tomorrow on da news. I just knew I needed to let Dani know I be living."

He staggers to the front.

"So, this morning, I hitched rides to make it back into Villa. And here I am, standing in front of the love of my life. You done give me the determination to stay alive."

The women in the crowd sigh in unison at the romance.

Cash, by this time, drags himself up the stairs and stands face to face with speechless Dani.

Cash grabs her face in both hands, asking, "Dani Jones, nothing can stop me from asking you to marry me. Not getting shot. Not thrown off a bridge. Not floating down a river. Nope. Not even moldy gangrene can stop me from getting back to you. Will you marr . . .."

Just then, Rashida karate chops the back of his good leg, and Cash bends instantly down on one knee. He gives Rashida the familiar stink-eye look.

"Hey, ya gotta get down on one knee to ask," Rashida says. She cups her hand near his ear, whispering loud enough for me to hear. "And I know you sent me the 10-year-old's confession apology letter. I forgive you entirely, my dear friend. You are free and clear with me. It was an accident. You were just a kid. Carry on with your proposal."

She smiles, winking at Cash with a peaceful expression. Any remaining trace of bitterness wipes off Rashida's radiant face.

Cash puffs a sigh of relief, grins ear to ear, and gazes back up toward his girlfriend's eyes.

On one knee he says, "As I was saying, will you, Dani Jones, marry me and be my lawfully married bride?"

His hands hold her hips. He has no ring.

"We'll tattoo our rings." He winks at her and continues gazing into her eyes.

As she smiles back with her new pearly whites, he notices the gaps in her teeth are gone. Her smile melts him. He loves whatever smile she gives him, before her dental work and after.

He awaits her answer.

FUNERAL EPILOGUE
PART THREE

KING OF KINGS AND LORD OF LORDS
Revelation 19:16 b NIV

Dani bounces up and down, nodding repeatedly.

"Yes, I'll marry you, Cash Jones. You are my hero."

Cash rises, grabs her face again. He kisses her forehead, her nose, and ends with planting a kiss on her mouth. The microphone picks up everything being said, even the sound of his smooching.

The gymnasium erupts in stomping and cheering. The two lovebirds appear oblivious to all the eyes staring as they embrace amidst the deafening cheers of celebration.

I say, "Hey, why don't ya get married right now?! We have the place, the people, the pastor. Yeah, we even have the flowers."

They both look at me, turning to each other, laugh, and say, "Why not? Let's do it!"

I ask the Pastor to officiate.

"Are they evenly yoked?" Pastor Clyde asks me, with eyebrows raised.

"What? We be cracked eggs who fell off walls. What cha asking about scrambled egg yolks?" Dani asks.

"He wants to know if you are both believers in Jesus Christ." I say, giggling.

"Yeah, I put my faith in Jesus before I got thrown off the mill,"

Dani says.

"I gave Jesus my life after I got thrown off the bridge," Cash says.

They are arm in arm and Dani's grip won't let go.

"I require sessions of marriage counseling," the Pastor replies.

Gerrie, Pastor Clyde's exuberant wife, jumps up shouting, "Honey, we eloped without marriage counseling. Our marriage lasted 50 years and more to come. Can we make an exception for these two destined to be together? Let's marry these lovebirds and celebrate their lives right now!"

The crowd cheers, starting a drumroll of slapping their hands to the legs, feet pounding.

Addressing the audience, Pastor says in the microphone, "Okay, we heard from my queen. We're rolling a wedding here in fifteen minutes. Talk amongst yourselves. If you need to go, leave now. Otherwise, remain in your seats. The wedding will start when Carrie Rae opens with her song in a few minutes." They can get the marriage license this afternoon.

The cheers and foot-stomping excitement explode.

The energy level in the gymnasium matches the intensity of the state finals.

We go from glum to glory. Nobody saw it coming.

We become part of an epic event. It feels like clenching a championship in overtime with a full-court press and a last second three-point shot swishing through at the buzzer. Only it's not a game. It's bigger than life! It feels like how Lazarus' friends must have felt when seeing Lazarus walk right out of that grave. Today, we witnessed a reported dead man walking . . . alive again!

Pinch.

Cash Jones lives and will walk down the wedding aisle!

The event planner in me kicks in. I huddle up our group.

"The *Bowl of Berries Book Club* can be the attendants, if that works for you, Dani?" I ask.

Dani nods big in agreement. I curl my finger toward Kyle, signaling him to join the discussion.

"Dani, do ya want to wear my Mrs. Michigan gown? My formal white dress is just two blocks away. It's in my closet. It's short in the front and long and flowy in the back. Likely, it could fit. Do you want any other bridesmaids besides us? Is this too fast? Are you in . . . ."

"I am down with it all. You know you be my bridesmaids. This is the BEST EVER with my besties here and my Cash back from the grave. It feels like I be dreaming."

"Okay, Kyle, can you snatch the dress out of my closet and meet us outside of the girl's bathroom in, like, two minutes? The gown is in the back of my closet in a white garment bag."

"On it," Kyle says, darting for the exit.

He turns back, shouting, "Ask Drew to walk his birth mom down the aisle, maybe?"

Cash crunches his eyebrows together in utter confusion.

"It's a long story," Dani says to Cash, who shrugs a "whatever."

Dani turns to Drew. "Want to walk me down the wedding aisle, son?"

Nodding his head, Drew says, "Sure. I'll walk anywhere with Dani. I get to walk with Dani. I get to walk with Dani . . . ."

We huddle up quickly, discussing keeping the songs originally planned for the funeral and adding a wedding march. After planning the fastest proposal-to-wedding-in-the-history-of-the-world, we girls high five, jumping up and down. The funeral dinner will make a wonderful wedding reception. This pulls together at warp speed. I look up to spot Kyle in the back with my white garment bag, breathing hard breaths from hurrying.

"Kyle's back with the gown. Come on. Let's do this," I say.

We hustle to the back and slide Dani into the gown in the girl's locker room. It's a perfect fit. We pause for a quick moment and tear up.

Whipping out my purse, I frantically apply blush, lipstick, and mascara on Dani while Carrie Rae thanks God, praying over us. We beam smiles, snap cell phone photos, and shake our heads, realizing Dani will marry Cash in a few moments. The wedding party dresses in formal black with our strawberry earrings. Dani's glowing in brilliant white, matching her radiant smile.

We leap from sadness to gladness.

Starting the ceremony, we hear Carrie Rae singing gloriously the ballad, *Flow Over Me*. It spells out Cash's journey to faith in God after deep despair. We shake our heads in wonder as God pulls all the details together right down to the lyrics of this song planned for a funeral.

Carrie sings, *"It's two o'clock in the morning, and I am not asleep. I'm floating down a river of hopelessness and defeat. But there's a hand that can reach me, and pull me from this rapid flood. Because I am a child of God, bought with HIS lifesaving blood.*

The song crescendos. *"Wonderful Counselor, Everlasting Help in Trouble, My Savior, Shelter in the Storm, Prince of Peace, God Almighty, God of All Comfort, God who Saves Me, The Great I AM, Great Mighty and Awesome God!"*

The lyrics run true to Cash's life journey, and the emotions in the gymnasium overflow with applause. The buzz and excitement in the crowd builds just as the lyrics grow in momentum to give glory to God Almighty, the Great I Am, for all he does for us.

Rashida signals the cue for the wedding march song, freshly downloaded. One by one, we glide up the aisle, dressed in black dresses, carrying our strawberry rose-shaped "flowers" on the skewer. Kyle loaned Cash his sport coat and pinned the plain strawberry to the lapel.

That will probably stain it, but who cares?

This day could not be more monumental.

Dani beams at Cash with her pearly whites, floating up the aisle in layers of sheer white with sparkling jewels. A perfect fit. Drew only steps on her dress once. They giggle and proceed.

Cash never takes his eyes off his bride as tears pour down his manly face, splattering on his sport coat.

Pastor Clyde goes from funeral to wedding seamlessly, welcoming all the guests back. He explains the gospel, using Cash's example of faithfulness to Dani. He gives the audience the opportunity to find unconditional love in Christ. Wrapping it up, he celebrates the bride and groom's true love journey.

Rashida, our onetime atheist, asks to share, "Greater love has no one than this, that a person lays down his life for his friends." She talks about her murdered husband and about Cash offering to be a hostage while risking his life. She boldly proclaims, "Jesus gave his life for all."

Caroline rushes over, tears flowing as she hugs both Dani and Cash. Rashida joins with a wrap-around embrace. Carrie Rae and I slip into the group hug, weeping while swaying.

I consider adding to the message, but press my lips shut. It's not about me.

It's a day like no other.

We don't want to let go. We rock back and forth in our circle embrace. Cash blubbers—a mess of emotions and gratitude. He lifts Dani high above the circle of friends and slides her back down his body, embracing her while locking lips passionately.

Pastor Clyde asks, as their lips remain locked, "Do you solemnly swear to love Dani, cherish her, provide for, and protect her, for better or worse, for richer or poorer, in sickness and in health, as long as you both shall live, so help me God?"

"Heck, yeah! I mean, I do." Cash mumbles, still latching lips on Dani.

"Do you, Dani, promise to love, honor, have and to hold from this day forward, for better, for worse, for richer, for poorer, in sickness and in health, to love and to cherish, till death do you part, according to God's holy ordinances and pledge to be faithful?"

"I do!" Dani mutters, because Cash holds her close. His lips mush into hers.

"I pronounce you man and wife . . . and you can . . . *er* . . . carry on . . . *um* . . . continue . . . you can keep kissing your bride!" The crowd cheers. The lip lock does not break. "Ladies and gentleman, I pronounce . . . latched together in this eternally long . . . nonstop . . . everlasting kiss . . . Mr. and Mrs. Cash and Dani Jones!"

Cash dips Dani dramatically. Their unending, passionate kiss remains zip locked.

The gymnasium erupts louder than any barn burner, triple overtime athletic event!

After the record-breaking longest smooch, Cash unlocks lips, grabs the microphone. "Ladies and dudes, Dani be my hot momma bride. Yowser!"

Exaggerating in excess, he pokes her with his finger, pulling his hand back, animating she's too hot to touch. Flapping his hand erratically, he pretends her hotness scorched his finger tip. He blows the fake burn with dramatic overacting.

"You are hot, hot, hot!" He taps her shoulder, jerking back his hand, flapping to cool it again.

Dani loves it.

We collapse, laughing at the red-hot antics.

The crowd hoots and hollers.

Oh, how I cherish this sizzling wedding only God could arrange.

Right on cue, the background music starts in with the *Praise Chorus* song and Carrie Rae Hucklenuckle belts out the verses. We girls sing out joyfully to the Lord while our hands raise up to the heavens. The most of the spectators join in the singing. Instead of a solemn funeral, we witness undying love at the liveliest of weddings.

God still raises people up from the grave today!

Rashida rocks in freedom out of her tomb of bitterness. Caroline dances in elation, no longer buried in guilt . . . and a new mom. Carrie Rae shakes off what holds her down, singing boldly and self-assured with her Hucklenuckle name. I die to myself, striving to be less bossy, humbler, trusting God's holy ways above my human fretting. Dani forgave her dad's ugliest of offenses as she rises to new heights of pure beauty and joy on her wedding day. Cash kicked his way up to the surface . . . and out of his grave.

God does immeasurably more than we asked or imagined.

Dani and Cash Jones hold each other close as music, hand raising, freestyle dancing and singing abound on all sides of the gym. Media cameras record the astonishing turn of events. Folks shuffled in for a formal funeral. Now, feet bopping, they celebrate the unexpected life in jubilation. Cash got saved. It's breaking news! No grave. Mr. and Mrs. Jones reunite in the life they crave.

I lift my hands, signing to the lyrics, *"Whatever I go through, whatever I do, oo, oo, with singing lips, I'll glorify YOU. I will praise you as long as I live. In YOUR name, I lift up my hands . . . ."*

The music fades to a close. Flowing jubilant tears, I look around the stage, shaking my head, undone by the day's events. Popping the chocolate strawberry flower in my mouth, I taste and see that the Lord is greater than I can fathom.

We link arms, beaming in solidarity as the crowd settles.

Holding his new bride's hand, Cash limps back to the microphone, saying, "I got something else to say to yous all."

Uh oh! What will Cash say next? No one knows. My eyebrows raise, anticipating. Kyle slips in beside me, squeezing my hand. I glance over, smiling as we both breathe in, waiting for Cash's next line.

"Thanks yous all for coming, even if yous thought it be my funeral. This wedding be better, huh?!"

The crowd explodes in applause, rumbling their feet on the bleachers. He smiles at his new bride, beaming back at him. News reporters scoot closer to the stage, snapping photos.

"I . . . I . . . can't believe dat God . . . answered my prayers . . . fo my smokin' hot wife," he says, nearly breaking down. Dani squeezes him tightly with her head tilted upward, eyes blinking with tears. He pauses, brimming with watery eyes.

"Dani be . . . my queen . . . and . . . I . . . I . . . be her . . ." Cash pauses. I know what he is about to say. He leans his head back, looking heavenward, stopping his sentence midstream. One arm pulls his new bride closer and his other hand pinches back his manly tears.

I freeze, holding my inhale as Cash takes off his sports jacket, tossing it down. What is he doing? He pushes up his sleeve, exposing his famous tattoo.

It's altered!

He crossed off the word "Cash."

What?!

I squint at the crudely carved lettering above it. Focusing my eyes, I read the added word knifed into Cash's arm. It's spelled correctly. It's cut permanently into his skin. It's a major mindset shift.

My eyes pop.

He carved the name "J-E-S-U-S" deep into his arm.

Smiling ear to ear, Cash bulges his biceps, flexing his newly engraved "JESUS is King" tattoo.

Cameras focus, clicking in rapid succession as the media mob captures the moment. Lights flash continuously. Turning his head toward the sisterhood, Cash winks, flashing his gregarious smile.

Returning his wink, I nod my head, mouthing, "Praise the Lord." Placing her hand on her heart, Caroline burst into grateful tears. Swaying, Carrie Rae closes her eyes, lifting her hands up to the Lord. Rashida rattles her bracelets, dancing in a circle. Dani squeezes Cash tighter.

Cash repeats, "Dani . . . be . . . my queen. But . . . but . . ." He fist pounds the area of his renovated-tattoo and thrusts his index finger upward announcing, ". . . JESUS be da real King. New life he done bring! We all need King Jesus."

Fist pumping the air, Cash shouts repeatedly, "Jesus . . . is . . . King!" The gymnasium lights up! Many in the bleachers join in pounding their feet, chanting, "JESUS IS KING! *Stomp.* JESUS IS KING! *Stomp.* JESUS IS KING! *Stomp . . . .*"

I exhale a sigh of relief, witnessing Cash's transformation, glorifying God.

Leaning my head gently onto Kyle's chest, he wraps his arms around me. The roaring celebration for Jesus ignites around the gymnasium as the "JESUS IS KING" proclamation spreads like wildfire.

Melting in gratitude, I whisper, "Thank you, Jesus. You make the impossible possible. Only the King of kings could orchestrate this . . . BEST . . . DAY . . . EVER . . . in the history of the *Bowl of Berries Book Club.*"

THE END and the Beginning . . .

"Now to him who is able
to do immeasurably more than all we ask or imagine,
according to his power that is at work within us,
to him be glory in the church
and in Christ Jesus throughout all generations,
for ever and ever!
Amen."

Ephesians 3:20 NIV

READER OPPORTUNITY

Very truly I tell you . . .
John 3:5b NIV

What would happen if you unlocked the vault of your soul?

Readers note the following disclaimer: If you read this next segment, it's at your own risk. Continued reading could alter your life forever. You proceed at your choice. This could change your destiny. Be aware that reading this next section could have a life-altering impact. The decision weighs on you to keep reading . . . or not.

If you scan this sentence, and you are a born-again believer in Jesus Christ, will you stop for a moment to pray? Pray for the seeker readers who do not know Jesus personally. Please, pray these readers make a life-transforming decision when they contemplate the next few paragraphs. Pray for non-believing readers to convert to faith in Jesus Christ.

Pause.

Thank you for praying.

If you long to know Jesus in an authentic relationship, as demonstrated by the fictional characters in this novel, you can get real with God right now. Read the following non-fiction paragraphs. For seekers holding this book, today can be your life-altering day.

Fellow readers prayed over you. The novel you just read is fictional, but this section is nonfiction and interactive. The Bible verses referenced in this novel hold the truth that can set you free from your sin and from death.

"For God so loved the world, that He gave His only Son, that everyone who believes in him will not perish, but have eternal life." (John 3:16 NASB). That verse explains Jesus loves you and died for your sin, so you can live in heaven. *". . . for all have sinned*

and fall short of the glory of God," (Romans 3:23 NASB). We all are sinners. We break God's moral law. But God offers a free gift. *"For by grace you have been saved through faith; and this is not of yourselves, it is the gift of God; not a result of works, so that no one may boast."* (Ephesians 2:8-9 NASB). We cannot earn or be good enough for heaven. We, by faith, believe. *". . . Though your sins are as scarlet, they shall become as white as snow . . ."* (Isaiah 1:18b NASB). Jesus can wash away our sins and make us new and clean.

I invite you to talk to God. Believe God sent Jesus to die for our sins so you and I can find forgiveness. Repeating words of a prayer don't save, but BELIEVING in Jesus does. Believe Jesus rose from the dead so you can have heaven with Jesus. You can put faith in Jesus based on the Word of God, the Bible.

Perhaps you want guidance for your communication with God that you believe. You may use your own words or possibly this guide to believing, *"Dear God, I am a sinner. Thank you for sending Jesus to earth to die on the cross for my sins. Thank you, that Jesus rose from the grave, so I can have a new life in heaven when I die. My faith is in Christ today and forever. I turn from my sins. I believe in Jesus! Thank you for loving me and accepting me into the family of God by faith in Jesus Christ. By this faith, I am a follower of Jesus, a born-again Christian. In Jesus' name, I pray. Amen."*

It's about believing in Jesus Christ. If you trusted sincerely by faith in Christ just now, welcome to the family of God. I encourage you to find a Bible-teaching church, to talk to God daily, and to read the Bible every day for guidance on your newfound faith. These are ways we grow in the Lord.

Pray. Read. Grow. Share.

You can spread your faith to others by sharing how you came to know Jesus in a real way. It's called your testimony, your God-story. Share Bible verses. Give others a Holy Bible.

God's Word never goes void.

Perhaps you will pass along another *Bowl of Berries Book Club* book as a gift to a seeker friend. Or better yet, give them a Bible. It may lead to a dialog on spiritual matters and an opportunity to share your newfound faith in Christ. People crave purpose and peace in life. Ask them if they desire to put their faith in Jesus. Sharing your faith rocks as one way to love God and love people.

Together, we readers can spread the Good News that . . . JESUS is KING! New life HE brings! *

---

* *If you want to know more about becoming a Christian, Focus on the Family counseling department is a ministry counseling service available at 1-855-771-HELP (4357). FOTF phone number is NOT an emergency crisis line. Laura Loveberry does not have a direct affiliation with FOTF.*

Laura Loveberry

DISCUSSION & LIFE COACHING QUESTIONS

CHAPTER 1 - 6

1. How do you respond to crisis situations?
2. In a group of strangers, how do you approach conversation? Do you sit back or do you initiate the engagement? And why?
3. If you meet a stranger, how do you describe yourself in one paragraph?
4. What is your plan if held hostage? Would you be calm or panicky?
5. Explain your comfortability level in a diverse group.
6. Do you know anyone in the "Big House?"
7. What are your thoughts on the prison system?
8. Are you familiar with prison ministries, and describe your involvement, if any?
9. Do you like your name? Why or why not?
10. Describe how you introduce yourself in one paragraph.
11. Describe a gift you possess and share how you use it.
12. Describe your personality by a type or style of shoe. (e.g., moccasins, stilettos, army boots, colorful-beaded sandals, blingy flip-flops . . .)
13. If you were to write a farewell letter, what would you say?
14. If someone trapped you in a vault today, with no way out, describe any regrets you would have. (Is there something significant you should do before you die?)
15. How would you handle the possibility of death coming around the corner?

CHAPTER 7 - 10

1. Do you know someone with Cash's bold and uncouth personality? How do you respond to audacious characters?
2. Describe your level of hygiene. Are you casual like Cash or extreme like Caroline?
3. Describe your handwriting. What does your handwriting style say about you?
4. If you were to write a farewell letter, who would you send it to and why?

5. How would you react to a second day of confinement?

6. Share a time when you laughed at an inappropriate situation and could not stop.

7. Rashida experienced a horrid injustice. Describe an injustice in your life and your response.

8. When someone opens up and shares private hardship, how do you respond?

9. Are you a fixer, listener, adviser, sympathizer, and or dodger?

10. Do you attend church as a family? Why or why not?

11. Caroline shared her inward battle. Do you have a secret battle? If so, where could you find relief? (Keep in mind, discussions in this book club can be intimate. If you reveal your personal ache, confirm everyone agrees to confidentiality.)

12. When reading about Caroline Forbes-Radshaw, readers assume initially her life is perfect. What first impression do you give to other people?

13. King David, known as a man after God's own heart, wrote many inspiring Psalms; yet the Psalmist was a flawed person. How do you carry onward in light of your mistakes?

14. Caroline turned to Jesus, grabbed forgiveness, and embraced her new life in Christ. Have you met anyone in your sphere who transformed radically for the better? Describe their positive changes.

15. Rashida is uncomfortable with the direction of the conversation. Can you describe a time when you received push-back for addressing an important issue?

CHAPTER 11 - 15

1. One of Invite Delight discussion questions revolved around screen time. Describe the amount of screen time you average per day. Should you improve the balance of your time and, if so, how?

2. The characters discussed Bible reading. Describe your Bible reading habits or your reading habits. Do your reading habits improve your wellbeing or harm your mental state?

3. Cash describes his girlfriend's past life; it's horrific. Do you know anyone who survived a horrendous childhood, and if so, how have you encouraged them to move forward?

4. The group attempted the *48-hour Kindness Challenge*. Could you go 48 hours only talking with kind words to everyone and only using positive body language and tone? Explain.
5. The *Bowl of Berries Book Club* is bonding. Describe a club or group you have been involved with where you felt a sisterhood.
6. Cash got caught in a lie with chocolate smeared on his face. As a child, did someone catch you lying? And if so, what happened?
7. The characters discussed bitterness as a poison you give to yourself. What are your thoughts on bitterness?
8. There are givers and takers in life. What category would you fall under and why?
9. Carrie Rae lost her parents and kept a positive outlook. Rashida lost her husband and boys and projects anger and bitterness. Which one of these characters best describes your response to tragedy?
10. If grief ever overwhelmed your heart, how would you want others to help you heal?
11. Cash stepped in to save Caroline from being a hostage. Describe a time when you stepped up to help another or a time when someone stepped in to help you out of trouble.
12. Rashida threw a bag of feces at the gunman. Have you ever felt the need to do something, but it may not have been the best choice, and if so, describe the moment?
13. The characters prayed popcorn prayers in the vault. What are your prayer habits and routines? (e.g., take-turn-group praying, church praying, dinner time praying, nighttime praying, all-throughout-the-day praying . . .)?
14. Rashida called Cash a weasel, but later, Cash became their hero. Share an instance where someone who was flawed stepped forward unexpectedly to do the brave thing.
15. Sherry and Carrie Rae wrote a song about sisters-in-Christ. Describe someone in your life who is like a sister to you. Describe a deep friend with whom you can share everything. If you don't have a friend like this, have you ever tried being a friend like this to another?

CHAPTER 16 - 20

1. Describe a time when you are emotionally and physically

depleted. How did you restore to well-being?

2. When the swat team burst inside the vault, the girls were not sure if they were the good guys or the bad guys. Describe a time someone startled you in terror, but it turned out fine?

3. Have you ever taken an ambulance ride, and if so, describe the circumstances?

4. Kyle is a loyal husband. Do you have someone in your life loyal to you, and are you a loyal friend to another? Tell us how the relationship grew strong.

5. Sherry is concerned for Cash. Describe a time you were concerned for someone, but the situation was out of your control, and you just had to wait and pray.

6. Describe a time you bonded with a group or person and were so thrilled to reunite again.

7. Dani is from a different social and economic background than the group. Tell me about your association with people from different backgrounds than you.

8. What are your thoughts about cursing?

9. The fictional community wrapped around supporting Cash's rescue. Describe a time when you rallied to support a good cause.

10. Sherry missed her book launch meeting, but sales are flying with promotion now. Describe a time when your plans failed for a project, but it came together unexpectedly.

11. Sherry gifted the book club with her book. Describe your favorite book, and/or share your favorite book to gift to others for inspiration.

12. Carrie Rae regrets she did not intervene with her weapon. She froze. Describe a time you froze when you could have stepped up. What would you have done differently next time?

13. Hucklenuckle gets embarrassed when people laugh at her name. How do you like your name, and if you could pick a new name, what would it be?

14. Dani suffered sexual abuse as a child. Have you survived abuse at some level, and if so, how do you move forward?

15. Adoption stories hold emotion. If adoption impacted your family or extended family, share the journey. Would you ever consider adoption or foster care? Why or why not?

CHAPTER 21 - 25

1. Regrettably, Carrie Rae flopped at her concert debut. Describe a time you wanted to run away because of pressures. Did you panic or push through?
2. Describe a time you did something scary.
3. Sherry had an allergic reaction to bedbug bites. Have you ever experienced welts from bedbugs, chiggers, poison ivy, fleas, nervous hives, bees, wasps, or spiders? Share your story.
4. Do you have a fear or phobia?
5. Carrie Rae's friends support her. Describe a time when you received much-needed friend support. How did you feel?
6. The girls shared embarrassing tales. Share a funny story you survived and laugh at today.
7. Dani experienced a miscarriage. Can you relate to this hard season in life, and if so, how can you minister to others in similar situations?
8. Carrie Rae wrote a song commemorating the sad day. What is your go-to song when you feel melancholy?
9. How does music minister to you in tragedy?
10. Have you ever felt helpless to help in a hospital situation? Describe it.
11. Sterling gave Caroline the silent treatment. What are your thoughts over the "silent treatment," and do you have a different solution for progress in a disagreement?
12. Caroline and Sterling live in luxury. How satisfied are you with your dwelling, your neighbors, your location?
13. Caroline hosted with an abundant food scape. Describe your favorite dish to bring to parties.
14. Have you ever felt out of place in high-societal surroundings? Why or why not?
15. Dani is working through her barrenness. How can you minister to someone who is barren?

CHAPTER 26 - 31

1. We all heard of WWJD, "What would Jesus do?" The question in the book was, "What would Judas do?" What is the point of asking "What would Judas do?"

2. Dani's friends helped her make wise choices with her funds. What would you do with a gift of $250,000 dollars?

3. Dani and Caroline came up with a solution to help Drew live productively with his disability. How can people help families with disabilities?

4. Sherry embraced her adopted son's birth mom without feeling threatened. What are your thoughts on birth mom and adoptive mom meeting with the adopted child?

5. The Habakkuk 3:17-19 Bible verse encourages readers to climb mountains with God's strength though they face troubles. What major mountains have you climbed like the feet of a deer?

6. What do you think of Sterling's apology?

7. Caroline was kind to her husband through his silent treatment. How do you relate to this? Have you ever showed kindness toward someone who was mean to you?

8. Kyle shared Bible verses and lead Sterling to accept the Lord. Have you ever guided another person to understand and make big positive changes in their lives? If you did, share the details.

9. Rashida had concerns about racial tension if a white couple adopted her dark-skinned nephew's son in a town predominately Caucasian. What are your thoughts on interracial families, and would it be difficult for a minority to be accepted in your community?

10. The characters shared humorous stories about raising children. What is the funniest child-raising incident you ever heard?

11. Sherry listened and mentored Dani on the telephone. Do you call and encourage others, and if so, are you a good listener? Do you offer spiritual advice? Are you more direct or subtle in your approach?

12. Dani's bitterness is understandable. How do you handle bitterness when it creeps into your heart?

13. What do you think about the empty-chair forgiving? How would you benefit from forgiving someone who has since passed away?

14. Dani describes Sherry as pushy with her faith. How do you feel around people who assert their faith? Are you one who can be aggressive with opinions on faith? If so, how is that working?

15. Do you have friends with childhood scars? How do you support

them?

CHAPTER 32 - 41

1. Describe your best experience at a camp or weekend retreat.
2. The characters planned and executed the first retreat session well, but no response. Describe a similar time this happened in your life.
3. Describe when your feelings got slashed during a group discussion.
4. If you experienced the Holy Spirit impacting a room with power, share it.
5. What are your thoughts on the emotional experience of this second session at the retreat?
6. Sherry mentors Dani with success, as Dani improves herself eagerly. Who has been a helpful mentor in your life?
7. Who do you look to for guidance?
8. Dani's exhausted from cleaning for the grand opening and Caroline develops sleep deprivation with her infant. Describe a time you experienced sleep deficiency or fatigue for a worthy cause.
9. The girls experienced a deep connection at a women's retreat. Can you recall a time when a retreat or group gathering affected your life?
10. Rashida received a mystery letter giving her closure. What was the most impactful letter you ever received?
11. This time, Carrie Rae does not pause in panic; rather, she leaps into action. Are you a person who freezes in fear or jumps to action in terror situations?
12. Have you ever failed in response previously and responded better next time? If so, explain.
13. Have you ever experienced a chase scene like this? If so, please elaborate.
14. Describe your attitude towards reading suspense and chase scenes.
15. Would you be able to physically outrun or evade in a pursuit scene? Explain.
16. Heights petrify Sherry. Talk about you and heights.
17. The firemen caught Dani in a rescue net. Have you ever saved

someone's life, and if so, how? Have you ever come close to death, and if so, share your near-death experience?

18. Carrie Rae learns to sing in public while pushing through her fears. What is something you push down your fears to do?
19. The gals joked about news headlines. Have news reporters ever wrote about you? And if so, share your story.
20. In the end, the book club culminates in sisterhood. Name a time when you felt the most bonded as a group.

EPILOGUE

1. Whose was the largest, or most emotional, funeral you attended?
2. The gals giggled at the funeral after spotting the strawberry with no chocolate. Share a time you laughed at an inappropriate time.
3. What is your most shocking and unexpected moment?
4. Describe the most unique proposal you ever heard. If married, what was your wedding proposal like?
5. If you could have one more day with someone who died, who would it be? What would you say?

READER'S OPPORTUNITY

1. What are your thoughts on the *Reader's Opportunity* inclusion in this novel?
2. Is your faith in Jesus Christ? Are you a Jesus believer? Why or why not?
3. Do you know people who walk by faith? Tell us about them.
4. Do you share with others your journey of faith? Why or why not?
5. How important is it to attend a Bible-teaching church, read a Bible daily, and pray?

APPENDIX

Readers can call
Focus on the Family's Counseling Department at
1-855-771-HELP (4357)

FOTF grants permission to be noted in the appendix.
FOTF phone # is not a suicide or crisis emergency line.

Laura Loveberry is not affiliated with FOTF.

Dr. Laura Loveberry
SPEAKER   AUTHOR   LIFE COACH

Dr. Laura Loveberry captivates audiences nationwide with her dynamic speaking. Laura encourages and equips women at conferences and retreats with witty books and lively speaking. Her doctorate in ministry gleans from her uplifting books: *Invite Delight, Goodbye Chaos Hello Calm,* and *Bowl of Berries Book Club.* Laura motivates health and fitness with her *Fit for a Queen* book and *Walk the Talk* workout DVDs. She serves as a life coach to readers. Loveberry reaches thousands with her *Life is the Berries* articles in *Simply Hers, Everything Men,* and *Simply Senior* magazines. Connect with Laura for your speaking event by visiting www.LauraLoveberry.com.

Laugh with Laura school assemblies promote literacy and learning. As a former art teacher, Laura delights in drawing hundreds of caricatures at schools, festivals, and receptions. Children laugh and learn with her art books: *Paint Splat Hero, Cartoon It, Caricature It,* and *Splatter Paint Hero.* For school and community events, contact Laura at www.SplatterPaintHero.com.

As former *Mrs. Michigan America,* Loveberry now crowns herself "Glamma" to three grandkids just a golf cart ride away. Laura and hubster Mark Loveberry feel "BERRY" blessed living in a quaint Michigan village.

You can connect with Laura at:

www.LauraLoveberry.com
www.splatterpainthero.com
loveberrylk@gmail.com

Laura Loveberry

Dr. Loveberry ignites audiences as an inspirational speaker at women's conferences, retreats, and outreach events.

For booking information:
www.lauraloveberry.com
loveberrylk@gmail.com

Laura Loveberry

Women's Inspirational Books:
Bowl of Berries Book Club
A Sweet Sisterhood Novel

Invite Delight
Insights to Sweeten the Soul

Goodbye Chaos Hello Calm
Insights to Soothe the Soul

Fit for a Queen
Health & Weight-loss Book

Workout DVDS:
Walk the Talk Workout DVD
Easy, Breezy Walking with Weights

Wholehearted Living Workout DVD
Advanced Aerobics with Weights

Music CD:
Silent Witness Break Free CD
Regina Holroyd Vocalist/Songwriter, Loveberry Lyrical Songwriter

Bowl of Berries Book Club Songs CD
Repackaged *Silent Witness* Songs

School-based Art Education Books for Children:

Splatter Paint Hero Special Edition
Children Laugh & Learn the Color Wheel (Hardcover)

Splatter Paint Hero Activity Book
Children Color the Story & Draw Step by Step

Paint Splat Hero
Children Laugh & Learn Color Theory

Cartoon It
Fun Story & Step-by-Step Caricature Drawing Course

Christmas Tree Farm
(Only available at the Loveberry Tree Farm)

Faith-based Caricature Drawing Book:

Caricature It
Step-by-Step Caricature Course for All Ages

Special Thanks

Per my request, Rosalie Currier edited the opening chapter. Her pen splashed the pages redder than a bowl of berries. I dove into learning the craft of writing based on corrections from Red Sea Rosalie. She agreed to "look over" my entire novel, making suggestions. Talk about a sea of red! Rosalie simplified, restored, and empowered my novel. Her overflowing corrections blessed me like earning a literary degree. She gave of herself, not expecting anything in return. She is a giver. Rosalie agreed to do a content edit for both my nonfiction books, too. She aligns with the evangelical purpose behind the pen. Currier, a respected journalist, grew into a close friend. If you make it through this novel, it's because of Rosalie. She guided me through writing my first novel, for you, the reader, to make it to the celebrated end. Topping off the editing was Comma, Comma, Comma Queen, Michelle Patrick. She sniped out the missing commas with diligence. Lisa Wood added grammar support. I love my proofreading team. This book does not happen without them. We walked through the Red Sea of suggestions.

Getting feedback from Mary Kyle, Abby Loveberry, and Jodie Johnson was helpful for my rough-draft novel. My mom, Wilma Kyle, and my aunt, Valta Doyle, listened to my editing issues, giving constructive recommendations. My bestie, Regina Holroyd, listened to entire chapters by phone, giving sound advice. Another BFF, Debbie Donihue, offered insightful cover design suggestions. My Sweet Sisterhood Bible Study Group of Sue Irwin, Bev Siefkin, Barb Robb, Lore Botham, Sue Pfaff, Sandy Bartlett, Kathy West, Carol McHolme, Donna Drovdahl, Bobbette Miller, Julia Littley, Renee Hardy, and Chelsea Bell blessed my socks off with their prayer power! I am grateful for their spiritual support. Patrick and Lisa Cook offered excellent book design, tech support, and branding. Maranatha Christian Writers Conference aided every step with Eddie Jones kicking in a cartoon suggestion. My Loveberry Ministries prayer team of Kathy West and Diane Morningstar bless beyond words. And my Quincy community rocks with the village support. You're my "Villa." What a wonderful place to live and generate writing ideas from friendly folks like Rev. Clyde and Gerrie Mills.

The administration at *Kingdom University International* supported me throughout my 600+ page doctoral disquisition. It utilized my three books. This women's novel and my two nonfiction books are outcomes of the degree process. Whew! Dr. Thurston Willoughby, Dr. Deb Willoughby, and Dr. Linda Tarver inspired me. Dr. Richard Wendorf, my cousin and fellow *KUI* graduate, encouraged me to pursue my doctorate degree and to finish my novel with an evangelical purpose.

I would be remiss if I neglected to thank my amazing hubster, Mark Loveberry. He helped with funding, advice, editing and motivation. Mark Loveberry inspires me nonstop, giving support for each step of our journey following Jesus. Every morning he holds my hand, prays over me, and kisses my forehead. Every. Single. Morning. Mark remains my knight in shining armor.

My gratitude overflows, acknowledging the contribution of these fine people.

We navigated the Red Sea. Jesus gave me purpose, passion, and the power to prevail. Thank you, God.

Ministry support matters.

Laura's Library

School Based:

Splatter Paint Hero Special Edition – Kids laugh while reading Arty's antics and learning the color wheel. This full-color hardcover includes bonus cartooning lessons.

Splatter Paint Hero Activity Book – Young readers love coloring the story, drawing step by step, and enjoying art activities in this compact paperback version.

Paint Splat Hero – It's a silly story teaching color theory. Kids love this full-color paperback.

Cartoon It – This delightful paperback shares Arty's overcoming story of learning to draw funny faces. A bonus caricature drawing course is included.

Faith Based:

Caricature It – Faith-based caricature course for ALL AGES.

Laura's Women's Library

A Sweet Sisterhood Novel

In **Bowl of Berries Book Club,** who could imagine a variety of women trapped in a vault with a tattooed dude? No one. But a book club sprouts out of a botched bank robbery, a bowl of berries, and a brand-new book. Their bond grows. As their lives intertwine, will their deep-rooted secrets, shocking twists, and crazy adventures prune them? Will they cultivate fruitful lives after digging deep into their past? What would you find unlocking the vault of your soul? Five complete strangers are about to find out.

Insights to Soothe the Soul

Goodbye Chaos Hello Calm is a welcoming read of standalone chapters with refreshing encouragement. Open the door to hope and humor. Hug hello to happiness even in the hard. Discover peace under pressure. This delightful giftbook packs with insights for fruitful living.

Insights to Sweeten the Soul

Invite Delight offers hope, humor, and heartfelt encouragement. Find tips to transform. Savor insights to craft the life you crave. Laugh with Laura. Sista, say hello to happy in the hard. These aha standalone chapters challenge us to better ourselves. It's a perfect pick-me-up gift for friends.

INVITE DELIGHT

Insights to Sweeten the Soul

LAURA LOVEBERRY

GOODBYE CHAOS

HELLO CALM

Insights to Soothe the Soul

LAURA LOVEBERRY

BOWL OF BERRIES BOOK CLUB
A Sweet Sisterhood Novel

Who would think a jewelry artist, a bank vice-president,
a poverty-stricken alcoholic,
a self-conscious singer, and an inspirational speaker
would end up in a book club together?

I certainly wouldn't. Never in a million years. Who would ever plant this variety of women together along with a tattooed dude? No one. But an unexpected book club sprouts out of a botched bank robbery, a bowl of berries, and a brand-new book. Who knew? Their bond grows deeper than anyone expected. As their lives intertwine, will their deep-rooted secrets, shocking twists, and crazy adventures prune them beyond what they can bear? Will they cultivate fruitful lives after digging deep into the darkest season of their past? What would you find if you unlocked the vault of your soul?

Five complete strangers are about to find out.

Will the unexpected, but possible, happen?

Readers will laugh out loud, love the women, and
learn to lean into the LIGHT in the hard seasons.

Booklovers will taste and see the sweetness of LIFE…
and enjoy the read ….
like a strawberry dipped in chocolate!

Dr. Laura Loveberry

Dr. Laura Loveberry, national retreat & conference speaker, ignites audiences and writes witty books inspiring women to overcome. At school & community events, she draws 100s of caricatures, offering her art books for children.

www.LauraLoveberry.com

LIFE COACHING QUESTIONS ARE A BONUS FOR BOOK CLUBS.